SHADOW WALKER

ANYA J COSGROVE

Shadow Walker

Cover designer: Fiona Jayde Media

Shadow Walker/Anya J Cosgrove

ISBN 978-1-9993901-1-2

Created with Vellum

"True friends are always together in spirit."
- L.M Montgomery, Anne of Green Gables

1

CRUSH

Alana

The stink of cheap alcohol and immaturity saturated the air of the huge condo-turned-dorm. Each room buzzed with college students, most of them complete strangers. Nothing extraordinary in sight, yet.

Monsters prefer to sneak up on you, much like an over-populated birthday party.

My best friend Kelly wanted to boost my social life, and I couldn't fault her for being the champion of lost causes, but I hated surprises. *And* crowds.

A sheepish grimace on her red-painted lips, she handed me a beer and leaned beside me against the living room wall. "I didn't know so many people would show up. I invited your man, though. He said he'd come."

I tucked my long curls behind my ears and groaned. "Stop calling him that. We're not even going out."

"That will change tonight if I can help it," she said, bouncing her eyebrows up and down.

Kelly loved to tease me about my crush, Thom Walker. Thom and I had met in art class, and he had a great sense of humor, not to mention he was major eye-candy.

Wednesdays and Fridays had become my favorite days of the week since the start of the semester. We'd grabbed coffee after class a few times, but I couldn't tell if those outings were dates or not. He had a knack for sending mixed messages, and my current theory was that he had a girlfriend.

"Lana." Kelly elbowed me and angled her head towards the entrance.

Thom stood in the doorway in all his six-foot-three muscular glory, and I gulped.

Nervous fingers played with the hem of lace on my mid-thigh. Kelly had talked me into a short, black dress. I peeked down at my naked legs and feared her extravagant fashion sense had betrayed me. How short is too short?

This dress was walking the line.

Clothes and boys were usually the last things on my mind, and I blamed Thom for my newfound girlishness. Despite my heated cheeks, I put on a carefree smile and made my way to him.

"Happy birthday." He leaned in and pecked me on the cheek before reaching into his coat. "Here. Sorry, I didn't have time to wrap it."

He handed me a DVD. *The Fifth Element.* It was his favorite movie, and I'd mentioned I'd never seen it.

I beamed. A kiss and a gift? Had to mean he was interested. "Thanks."

"I brought someone. I hope it's okay."

A gigantic neon-light spelling *girlfriend* ignited in my head.

To my extreme relief, another guy appeared behind him. A tall, leathered-jacketed, imposing guy. Wearing black from head to toe, complete with the blackest hair I'd ever seen, he was about the same height as Thom but loomed over us anyway like a thundercloud.

Thom unlaced and pried off his muddy shoes. "Alana, this is my brother Liam."

"Nice to meet you," I said, extending my hand.

Hands tucked in his jean's pockets, Liam gave me a curt nod and barely spared me a glance. Had I made such a bad impression in so little time? This damn dress... too short indeed. I gripped the hem of lace again, discreetly inched it down my thighs, and bit my lips. "Come in. Want a drink?"

Thom pointed at my bottle. "Beers are fine."

"I'll go get some. The kitchen is a war zone. You can put your coats here." I waved to the jackets piled on the ottoman and jostled my way to the refrigerator.

Kelly followed me. The crowd made way for her, a graceful eel in a sea of clumsy fishes. "Who's tall, dark, and handsome?"

I grabbed two beers in the refrigerator. "Thom's brother."

"Introduce me." The sharp interest in her voice spelled trouble.

"I don't know, Kelly, he looks sort of..." I hesitated as I removed the caps from the two bottles, searching for the right word.

"Hot?" She grinned.

"Weird."

"Weird how?"

There was something off with him. I couldn't explain it, but the back of my neck had been tingling since he walked in. "He hasn't said a word yet, and he wouldn't shake my hand."

"He just arrived. I'll whisk him away, so you can be alone with Thom," she said with confidence. Between her perfect glowing skin, long sexy hair and Latina charm, Kelly Moreno rarely got turned down by boys.

I shook my head. "You don't have to."

"Good grief, girl. Will you make the first move already? It's not the 1950s anymore." She pinched my arm and pushed me back to the living room.

The boys were waiting by the ottoman. Liam glared at the crowd, and Thom scratched the back of his neck as they spoke animatedly, their voices swallowed by the ambient noise. They stopped arguing as we drew near.

I handed both brothers a beer and got two small "thanks" in return.

Kelly smiled at Thom and turned to Liam. "Hi, I'm Kelly, Lana's best friend."

Liam nodded in acknowledgment.

I shot my best friend a sideways glance. *Told you he was weird.*

"So, Liam, are you a student too?" She asked, eager to spruce up a conversation.

Tall, dark and stoic took a gulp of his drink and shook his head.

"Liam's between jobs," Thom said.

Undeterred, Kelly fluffed her hair. "What field are you in?"

Liam finally graced her with an answer. "Security."

"Why did you quit?"

"I didn't."

"His contract expired," Thom added.

After a few more monosyllabic answers worsened by Thom's insistence on answering in his brother's place, Kelly gave up and jumped at the opportunity to meet new arrivals.

Liam retreated to the back of the room, and both Thom and I failed at pretending he wasn't there.

For close to two hours, Thom's brother leaned against the wall in the corner, silent as he typed on his phone. He didn't mingle with anyone, and a disapproving scowl discouraged any girl from approaching him. Dracula as a chaperone came to mind.

It was strange and definitely not the night I had hoped for. Whenever I'd managed to make Thom laugh, he'd shot his brother a furtive glance and sobered up like he was doing something wrong. The more I tried to act as if everything was normal, the more annoyed I got that Thom allowed this ridiculous awkwardness to continue. Didn't Liam have anything better to do than ruin our evening?

Students popped in and out of the apartment, and every time someone bumped or brushed past us, Thom's shoulders rose a little.

"Hey, are you okay?" I asked with a smile, trying to diffuse the tension running rampant between us.

"Yeah, why?" His jaw clenched, and he might as well have said no.

"I don't know. You're jumpy. What's going on?"

He was about to answer when Liam appeared behind him, both their jackets propped over his arm. "Thom, it's 12:01." The words had a solemn echo as if Thom's carriage had turned into a pumpkin at midnight.

Thom winced. "I have to go."

This non-date had been a complete bust. Kelly was right. If I wanted our relationship to progress, I had to take the matter into my own hands. "We could watch that movie you bought me on Wednesday after class?"

Thom ran a hand through his ashy blond hair and stared at the floor. "I'm going out of town this week, but I'll text you. We can watch it some other time."

A non-committal response and not very encouraging. Was he brushing me off?

His lips formed a thin line. "Sorry."

I opened my mouth to ask where he was going—maybe the answer might shed light on this bizarre night, and on whether he was giving me the cold shoulder—but Liam elbowed Thom and tapped his watch.

How rude! This guy was lucky that I was out of my element and surrounded by strangers. Otherwise, I would have given him a piece of my mind. Why didn't Thom tell him to relax? Who cared if it was twelve o' something? Did he expect the bogeyman to walk through the door?

Thom cleared his throat and gave his brother a pointed glare. "I'll be right behind you."

Liam walked out without saying goodbye. *Good riddance.*

Thom let out a stiff sigh. "Ignore him. He's upset with me and left his manners at home. I thought the party would distract him… I was wrong."

"Don't worry. I hear siblings are a handful." As an only child, I didn't have those problems.

"Happy birthday again." He hugged me goodbye, and we lingered in the warm embrace, his toned body flush against mine. "Bye."

"Bye." My guts squeezed in longing, and I hoped the strange vibe had nothing to do with me and everything to do with his standoffish can't-say-hi-or-bye brother.

As the door closed behind Thom, Kelly joined me. "No luck, huh?"

"None." Big fat zero luck on the birthday kiss I'd daydreamed about all week.

"I think he likes you." She draped an arm around my shoulders.

My optimism about this crush had withered significantly, and my mind was almost ready to file Thom in the never-going-to-happen drawer. "We'll see. He turned me down for a movie night." I fished for my jacket. "Thanks for the party though."

She pouted. "You're leaving already?"

"I'm pooped. See you Monday. Unless you want to drive to Ludlow with me and see your Mom tomorrow?" I offered, knowing she hadn't visited our hometown in a while.

"No. My mother is still harboring that horrible guitarist at her place. Say hello to your Mom for me, and we can grab lunch on Monday." She gave me a quick hug and returned to her flock of admirers.

Kelly and her mother had a rocky relationship whereas my parents would be waiting for me with gifts and my favorite cake, eager to hear all about my week.

I was lucky.

THE WALK to my apartment usually took 10 minutes, but my normal rhythm was undermined by the damn heels, and by the halfway point, my calves were burning. The black stilettos clanked on the curb with each painful step, and the strange tingles at the back of my skull came back in full force as I crossed the boulevard to reach my street.

An eerie impression that I was being watched fueled the tickling, and I craned my neck to look around. Sure enough, a man trailed a few strides behind me. I picked up the pace.

So did he.

I kicked myself for not carrying that pepper spray Dad had shoved in my suitcase when I'd moved away to college. The man's long shadow was almost on me when I beelined for my building. I hurried into the atrium and checked to see where he was headed, but he blew right past my address, a hood covering his face.

My shoulders sagged in relief. *See? Everything's fine. You're being silly.* His black-and-white checkered hoodie rang a bell, but I couldn't recall where or when I'd seen it. It bugged me, and I gnawed on my nails until I got to bed, the pressing feeling I had forgotten something important nagging my brain.

2

IN THE SHADOWS

Alana

"Wow! Thank you so much," I said as I opened my parent's gift, a brand new electronic tablet. I ran my fingers along the sleek black leather case, a big smile plastered on my face. Mom and Dad always spoiled me for my birthday.

"You're sure you don't want another piece of cake?" my mother offered.

I shook my head. "Positive." I couldn't eat another bite, my belly already full of her infamous Oreo, peanut butter and Nutella cake.

It tastes as sinful as it sounds.

Dad stood up. "Well, I'll leave you girls to gossip a bit." He kissed us both on the cheek before walking out.

I joined Mom at the sink and grabbed a towel to dry the dishes.

"You don't have to help me, honey. It's your birthday," she said with a smile.

"I don't mind."

She resumed scrubbing the pan and gave me a sideways glance. "So, who's this boy you keep mentioning?"

My cheeks burned. "Thom? He's just a friend." I hadn't meant to bring him up, but Mom had this crazy sixth sense when it came to boys. She could always tell when I liked someone. As a teenager, I'd found it atrociously annoying. Still did to be honest.

"Is he in your class?" She asked, working her Mom-magic in overdrive to coax information out of me.

I played with a strand of hair. Getting through this conversation without sounding like an infatuated fourteen-year-old would be a challenge. "Yes, but he's a bit older."

The circular motions of the brush stopped, and she raised a brow at me. "How much older?"

"Now, don't go all mama bear on me. He's only twenty-three."

Thom was twenty-four, but it never hurts to embellish things when your mother asks you about a crush. I'd just turned twenty. No longer a teenager, no one could ever again invalidate my decisions with expressions like *teenage angst*, *teenage tantrums*, or the scandalous *teenage hormones*.

"And he's nice to you?" Mom was using her gentle parenting voice. She clearly thought he was my boyfriend.

I clicked my tongue. "Mom, I told you, he's just a friend. But yeah, he's nice."

She failed to repress a soft chuckle. "Okay, okay. I'll back off."

The infatuated fourteen-year-old had won, and the twenty-year-old cringed in shame. We put away the dishes and chatted about anything but Thom until way past eight.

"I need to go. I have homework. Where's Dad?" I swiftly packed up my gift and birthday card into my bag.

Mom glimpsed into the living room. "I don't know. Maybe he went to Larry's to watch the game. He probably thought you were going to stay over."

Hockey was sacred to my dad.

"I really need to get going but give him a kiss for me. I'll see you next week."

She nodded and handed me the leftovers from dinner.

Score. "Thanks, Mom. Love you."

We hugged.

"Love you too. Be safe."

I put on my coat, grabbed my school bag and headed out into the windy suburban night. My feet dragged along the stony path to the driveway. All I had to look forward to for the rest of the night was an empty apartment and a pointless struggle against my history essay.

"Leaving so soon?"

I dropped my keys, searched for the source of the shout, and spotted my father on the roof. "Daddy! You scared me to death. What are you doing up there?" I bent down to retrieve my keychain.

"The satellite's antenna is loose. I figured I'd give it a little love," he said, his coat flapping in the wind.

I tightened the thin scarf around my neck. "Good luck!"

"Good night, honey. Be careful out there."

I blew him a kiss.

It was cold for April, and I dearly missed my gloves as I unlocked the door to my blue Yaris. I caught my reflection in the window. The birthday crown Mom had made me was still tangled in my hair. Before it flew off my head, I pried it from my loose, strawberry-blond curls and tucked it safely into my purse.

I checked my phone to see if Thom had called, and disappointment tightened my guts. The screen was silent, no missed alerts. Strange. We normally texted back and forth a few times a day. No text plus his behavior from the night before... He was brushing me off.

A gut-wrenching yell crushed me back to reality, blowing any Thom-related thoughts from my mind. I spun around in time to see my father slump down the roof. A loud cracking sound pierced the chilly air, and my heart froze.

"Dad!" I sprinted to him.

His body was sprawled on the driveway, and short rasps heaved his throat. One arm hung from its socket, twisted in a sickening way. A scream tore from my lungs, but I barely heard a whisper above the pulse at my temples. Mom stormed outside, and a choir of sobs and whimpers followed as she yelled at the 911 operator she had on the line.

"Dad?" I grabbed his hand as I knelt beside him.

Blood pooled against the asphalt, right below his skull. I reached for his head and shuddered as my fingers dug into the gooey, red liquid matted with his gray hair. A heavy boulder nested in my chest. Help wouldn't arrive in time.

As if to confirm my prognosis, his eyes lost focus, and hiccups choked me. Shocked by my impotence and uselessness, I clung to him in despair.

In an instant, the world shifted.

An alien sense scratched from inside me, my body no longer my own. These eyes belonged to my father, and his thoughts were my thoughts. I was most disturbed by the debilitating pain slicing through me, no, us. Memories appeared, and I traveled through them, lost and confused.

Five teenage boys were playing tag in a park, us among them. Huge trees blew in the sultry wind, thick with Spanish moss. Sweat dripped down our back, the humidity scorching. A female voice called for the students to go back to class.

The priest asked us to place the ring on Mom's finger. Our palm was sweaty, and we almost dropped it. Crisis averted, we met the tender gaze of the woman we loved. The white dress flowed around her perfect figure. So, beautiful, we thought.

A baby cooed in our arms, her round cheeks pink. The hint of saliva on her lips bubbled, and she laughed. How cute. "What's her name?" We asked. "Alana," a soft melodic voice answered.
We were so excited to bring this little girl home. We couldn't have one of our own, but we would cherish and care for this angel as if she was our flesh and blood.

Everything stilled like someone had pressed the *pause* button on a remote, and I blinked, falling flat on my ass in my parent's driveway.

Where had those hallucinations come from? Had I witnessed a

recess at my Dad's elementary school, his wedding, and my adoption? Nothing weird ever happened to me.

My bloodstained hands were too warm, almost hot, despite the cold, and Mom's panicked voice sounded like a sluggish drawn-out tune. The sunny yellow of her shirt forced me to squint, the color too bright for my eyes.

Even though he had been dying the minute before, Dad suddenly jumped to his feet. "I—I'm fine." Eyebrows creased in bewilderment, he straightened his coat and turned to me.

I gaped at his outstretched hand in awe.

The ambulance blazed in next to us, its red lights casting a creepy glow over the familiar houses.

Mom's gaze darted from my dad to me several times as tears flooded down her cheeks. Dad squeezed her shoulder and greeted the paramedics. "Thank you for coming. I fell from the roof, but I'm not hurt. I got lucky, I guess."

Lucky? Did he really believe that?

The blood on my hands spooked the medic closest to me. "You okay, miss?"

I rose to my feet, and nausea rippled in my stomach. "Yeah, it's my dad's blood."

The coagulated blood on Dad's head caught their attention. "Come with us, sir. You might have a concussion."

Dad hesitated. "I feel great."

"Don't be silly, Robert. We are going to the hospital, and that's that. Lana can follow with her car and drive us back. This is not a negotiation," Mom said, her hands gripping his arm.

Dad paused, assessed Mom's grave face and opened his mouth. His fingers drummed against his legs, and he gave me a peculiar look. "Okay. But hurry after us, honey." His furrowed eyebrows and shaky tone sent my mind into overdrive.

Had he witnessed the hallucinations, too? Did he have an explanation?

I nodded in agreement.

The ambulance backed out of the driveway, and sirens resonated through the night.

In a haze, I watched it disappear around the corner, my mind trying to catch up. The dark pool next to my feet both repulsed and captivated me. Too much blood for a scratch, and yet... What about the broken arm? I hadn't imagined that.

Caught in the riddle of what had just happened, I forgot my promise to hurry and stared at the accident scene for a few minutes, waiting for my iffy mind and wavering stomach to settle back into place.

A large shadow swelled against the ground.

A man came from behind. His huge hand stifled my scream as he punched me hard in the stomach. Dizzy, I staggered against my car. A windowless van screeched in, and the smell of burnt tires assaulted my nose. Two burly men descended upon me wearing creepy black tunics reminiscent of the ones in clichéd cult movies.

I fought to escape their bruising hold, but they were too strong. They tossed me into the van and held me down against the carpet. The fabric burned my knees and elbows as I thrashed in vain. A paralyzing terror gripped me, and I shivered as if icy water had been poured down my back. Where were they taking me?

All the hurdles of the road echoed in my bones as they drove away from my home. The men congratulated each other for a job well done and passed a bottle of liquor around. Acid simmered at the back of my throat.

When the vehicle stopped about ten minutes later, one man said, "Get up," but a kick resonated in my thorax before I obeyed. They wrenched me upwards and pushed me out of the van. My feet scrambled to keep me from falling as I stumbled across the curb. With my hands braced on my knees, I gasped for air.

"Go ahead. Scream," a snide voice said.

The crisp air of the night jolted me to action, and I shrieked for help, but the neighborhood was dead silent. Eyes wide, I took in the barren landscape. A fog hung thick in the air, the dark street empty but for a line of industrial dumpsters.

A cruel laughter rocked the men's bodies. "See? Nobody cares."

"What do you want?" I asked.

They snickered.

"Why are you doing this?"

"Enough questions." The driver closed in on me and punched me square in the face.

I recognized him. He was my parent's new neighbor, the owner of the little white poodle my mom always fussed about. I'd seen him walk his dog a few times. My stomach churned as I caught a glimpse of the clothes underneath the robe and recognized a familiar checkered hoodie. He was the one who'd followed me home last night. I spat at him, the blood in my mouth tainting his shirt red.

"Have fun with this one. She has character." He returned to the van while two other men grabbed my arms and dragged me forward.

A third trekked behind us, unaffected, a loose cigarette hanging from the corner of his mouth. The nasty dude on my left had a bushy, red beard, and an ugly scar deformed his eyebrow. Easy to identify out of a line-up.

Realization kicked me in the gut. Oh God. No masks on their faces. They didn't intend on letting me go.

I'd never see my parents again. I'd never finish school. I'd die among the paint-peeling dumpsters, my carcass gnawed on by rats.

My knees buckled. In front of us was a dead-end. A half-torn off metal door marked the entrance of an abandoned building, and I dug my heels into the ground as we drew closer to it. Death awaited me inside this dump.

Wicked fingers dug deep into the skin of my arms, making my hands numb. Exhaustion crept inside me, one muscle at a time. A few feet from the door, every ounce of my strength withered away.

This is it. This is how I die.

One second, they were pulling hard on my arms, and the next, I was free. My legs wobbled, but I managed to stay upright.

In a blur, my two captors rose into the air and crashed against the nearest building as if a tornado had swept them up. Their two lifeless bodies fell to the ground. The third man dropped to his knees, dead. A curved knife poked out of his chest.

A cold sense of relief gripped my heart at the unforeseen turn of events, and I searched for an explanation. The alley was empty, and I couldn't see a thing out of the ordinary besides the three corpses around me.

Was I responsible for those deaths, somehow? I blinked at the sight of the blade, convinced that, whatever had happened earlier, I hadn't done *this*. I didn't know where the hell I was, but, at least, I was alone.

My respite was too brief.

A man, also wrapped in a black cloak, appeared out of thin air. His tall silhouette sliced the fog. Perched on the ball of his feet, he looked ready to lunge, and the predatory stance curdled my blood. The edges of his body shimmered as if his molecules were too dense for the space he occupied, and I thought my heart might sprout wings and fly out of my chest when I met the man's stare.

Black pools rippled beneath his long lashes and sucked the light away from his chiseled face.

Not human.

3

CRAWLING

Liam

The industrial district, abandoned at night, is the perfect venue not to be disturbed. Nobody wanders here at this hour except unsavory individuals that are up to no good.

I solemnly swear I fit the profile.

My trusty dagger hidden in the palm of my hand, I approach the dark figure standing guard. Dressed in an embroidered black tunic, the lookout has a hood covering his face. It matches mine. He expects a demon in satanic robes; I don't want to disappoint.

I appear next to the guard, a nervous man in his mid-40s who is small and lean as I tower above him.

"She's in the back," he says, mistaking me for his employer.

I plunge the blade into his spine. The metal twists upward, severing his spinal cord.

Hot blood pours against my fingers. I sidestep and check my robes, happy to see I've avoided the worst of the gush.

Blood is a pain to wash off fabric.

A smirk festers on my lips as the guard exhales his last breath. I *love* killing. Stabbing, beheading, slitting throats, etc.

Death weaves the fabric of my soul.

With a swift pull, I free the knife from the body. The empty shell emits a dull thud as it falls to the pavement and splashes blood on my new Nikes. *Fuck!* I should have snapped his neck.

The blade reeks, and my nose wrinkles. The sentry was human. My brethren use humans for rough legwork, a practice that works to my advantage. Humans are soft and weak, whereas demons are harder to kill.

I have only moments before the chattering of the other demons becomes louder in my head as I battle to keep the Collective's whispers at bay. If I can't hold them off, I'll fail. Violence only heightens them, an annoying side effect of using my powers.

I blend with the shadows of the dimly lit alley, itching for more action, and catch up to the other three humans and the hopeless witch.

Sandwiched between two black cloaks, the girl is a lost speck of color, her long fiery hair catching the light of the moon. One side of her face is swollen. The bruise blossoming on her cheek displays a vibrant mix of red, black and blue.

To demons, witches are holy, their blood a powerful and rare commodity. Demons would have worshiped her, bled her drop by drop until nothing remained.

Used to be my job.

My elders trained me, almost like a dog, to fetch, to track, to capture and to harvest witches. I used to be their favorite pet, but now I'm free. There are no strings on me.

I smash the two men holding the girl against the wall of the adjacent building. The sound of their skulls cracking at the impact makes me perversely happy. Crimson blood splutters down the brick.

The third man grabs his gun, his eyes searching for me, but he only sees the dagger when it penetrates his still beating heart.

In shock, the girl's terror-stricken mind reels at the sudden freedom, and her face creases in question. I'm invisible to her eyes. A lustrous halo of power surrounds her, luring me in. The flawlessness of her aura is a true sign of her potent bloodline. I let the veil of shadows fall so she can see me.

Reflected in her eyes, I am nothing but a monster.

She springs to life, charging in the opposite direction. Smart. I've met this girl, not long ago, in more civilized circumstances. She used to be beautiful. Now, she looks delicious. I place myself in front of her to block her course, moving too fast for her to see. My demon exults as she collides with us, her delicate skin brushing ours.

A distraught whimper escapes her lips, and her striking, green eyes widen. Searching for an explanation, she peeks over her shoulder to where I was standing a second before. Furrowed brows betray her confusion, and her gaze jerks back to me. She draws a sharp intake of breath, her jaw slightly agape.

She doesn't recognize me. The black eyes and cloak don't help trigger her memory, and fear oozes from every pore of her fair skin as she shrinks away.

My brain is muddled. Like an alcoholic forced to stare at the purest scotch ever made, I thirst for a sip of witch's blood, my entire mouth desiccated. Sandpaper drags against my tongue, and I swallow hard.

"Please," she begs.

The Collective presses against my mind once more. I don't have the luxury to explain. I throw Alana over my shoulders and feel her shiny waves of hair crash against my back. Vain struggles rock her body, the wind muffling her sobs and cries as I run to my car.

A few steps from my goal, a blinding pain sends me stumbling, and I drop my precious cargo. The Collective's voices slip under my defenses.

"Not now," I protest through the mental link.

"We'll kill her, Liam. No. Better yet, we'll make you kill her," one rotten voice snickers.

In my mind, I see Alana's slender body lying in a puddle of blood. Witch blood is my kryptonite. What I wouldn't give for a taste... But I can't. Using witch's blood makes it easy for them to read my thoughts and manipulate me.

The roars relent, and the silence is deafening. The other demon spent a lot of energy to push into my brain for that short time, which means he's close. Too close.

Let him come, my beast boasts, starved for a challenge. My human side prompts me to hurry.

Alana fled about two hundred feet in the wrong direction during the interlude, so I rip the cloak from my body, trusting my regular clothes to spook her less, and capture her in my arms once more. She screeches at my inhuman speed.

"Alana, let me help you." I press on her shoulders, my fingers digging into her skin. "I'm Liam Walker." Recollection paints her features. Alleluia. "We need to leave. *Now.*"

Her muscles relax under my palms, and relief washes through my hazed brain as she abandons herself to my grasp.

Dazed and drunk by her closeness, I whiz to the car, settle her back on her feet, and open the passenger side door.

Adrenaline rushes through my veins when an imposing silhouette crashes down from the roof of the adjacent building to the hood of my car, smashing the front half to smithereens. Smoke rises from the engine as it whines and coughs its last breath.

The demon has arrived.

Fuck.

Four other men with military grade rifles join him and fan out on either side.

"Liam Walker, never had the pleasure, but your reputation precedes you. I'm Jim Olsen." He hops to the ground, sight riveted on Alana as he speaks.

"Never heard of you." I've never met him, but he's definitely older and more powerful, not a beginner that's still hooked on blood. Otherwise, he would have lashed out at her without thinking. "Not cool trashing my car."

His frosty glare assesses me with confidence, and it hits me: I'm going to lose.

The speed and stamina brought on by a regular fix of witch blood is significant. Sobriety weakens me. Cornered, I analyze my options.

If I fight, I'll lose. If I try to run with her in tow, the snipers will shoot, her blood spraying everywhere. I shudder at the thought.

My inner devil rejoices, offering me a tempting alternative.

No. I've spent years learning to shield my mind from them. Years of not giving in, years of not falling off the wagon, not counting the miserable months during which the withdrawal from blood ripped my soul to shreds. All this pain endured only to give up now? For what? For this one girl? She's not worth it.

I can disappear without a scratch, leave her behind, her meaningless death added to a lengthy list I never mull over. The only trouble is: she's not just another witch.

My brother cares for her.

My opponent motions for his men to wait. They are pawns and don't understand the stakes. The demon not only expects me to use her blood, he's counting on it, willing to sacrifice a queen to check a king. I slice open my palm in a swift, fluid motion. A dark red wave splashes from the cut.

I put our fate in her frail hands and close her fingers around the hilt of the blade. "Do it too."

Disbelief is written across her lovely face as she meets my gaze.

"Do it." If she doesn't, she'll die. If she does, I'll die.

Lips pressed into a determined line, she cuts herself. Heartbeats hammer at my temples, and my throat bobs in anticipation. I take one last breath as a man before giving in to the evil I used to be. There is no other way.

I seize her wrist, hard enough to bruise her, and crush our wounds together. The intoxicating essence cascades through the blood link. Its potency and savor is exquisite, and I hiss, labored breaths rocking my lungs.

The rush of power rakes through me.

The Collective pushes in. *"Good boy, Liam. Now turn her over, and your defection will be forgiven."*

"Never." My nerves pulsate in euphoria. Age, experience, strength, numbers, weapons, none of that matters anymore. A blood channel to a newborn witch is unbeatable.

I am unbeatable.

The devil in front of me sneers despite my newfound superiority. The distinct timbre of physical closeness allows me to recognize his voice among the swarm in my mind. *"Welcome back to the fold."*

I let go of Alana and launch at him, but my murderous grip only finds air, his form vanishing without warning. I howl in disappointment.

Gunshots thunder in my direction, tearing through the murky fog, and metal mosquitoes drill my skin. The bullets spurt back out and bounce off the ground with a distinctive clink. My enraged demon murders the four men as I revel in her taste.

One foot on the throat of the only man still alive, I wait for his bothersome gurgles to subside, until all I hear is the regular thump of a lonely, quickened pulse.

A sense of peace washes over me as I absorb the scene I painted.

The organic palette transformed the achromatic asphalt. The crisp whiteness of bones from mangled ribcages is sprinkled in the narrow street. Guts snake out of ripped abdomens in bluish-purple streaks, and the soft pink of torn muscles contrasts with the grayish yellow of fat that was once flesh. A flamboyant crimson shade of barely-dead blood polishes the canvas with its profuse, pungent strokes.

Death is art, and I'm a devoted artist.

A spark of life clashes against the hues of destruction. The witch is huddled on her scraped knees in the center of the carnage. She's been drained to the point of exhaustion, and, yet, I need more. My cells are vibrating in need, gasping for her. Oxygen is obsolete. I fall to my knees beside her and pull her palm closer. The red liquid seeping from the cut possesses me, and I lick it. A steely zest invades my senses. I hum.

Without a doubt, the sweetest I've ever had.

I kiss her pulse point, and she flinches. God, I want to bathe in her blood.

"Do it," the voices urge. *"Drain her and come back to us."* I picture her bound to my bedpost as I carve intricate patterns into her skin with the alluring red ink. *"Don't fight it! Come home, Liam."*

Their constant pressure only strengthens my resolve. I summon every ounce of self-control I have left and hold my breath to block her scent. My hand glides across her wrist to her upper arm, and I yank her body closer. Her heart flutters; I can't think.

With my other hand, I grab the phone in my pocket and pass it to her. "Call Thom."

"Let me go," she pleads.

"I can't." I convey repentance in my voice, a difficult task given my altered state.

The pull of the blood tugs and twists my intestines, punishing me for my restraint. Enthralled by her fragrance, different from any other, I hide my face in the crook of her neck. She tries but fails to extricate herself from my firm grip, her squirms taunting me.

THE NEXT THING I KNOW, we're not alone, and my senses flare. There's a man here with us. I crouch next to my girl, ready to protect the spoils of my battle. Ready to kill. The sight of my brother makes me pause, but I'm willing to slice him in two if it means I can keep her.

A foul, acidic stench assaults my nostrils as a tailor-made aconite bomb explodes at my feet. It's a weapon of my invention, the linchpin of the "in case of emergencies" arsenal, which Thom nicknamed humorously the "if Liam goes apeshit again" kit. Junior has better faith in me than myself. To him, it was a superfluous precaution, but I treated it as crucial.

As usual, I've been proven right.

Before I can exhale the poison, my little brother pulls out the family colt and shoots me three times in the chest. The special iron rounds we crafted together bite into my flesh, unforgiving. Oblivion comes over me like a soothing wave as Thom's expression of absolute disappointment digs deeper than the bullets ever could.

I am a devil after all.

4

YELLOW BRICK ROAD

Alana

The moment between sleep and consciousness usually goes by in a heartbeat. It takes you from the dream realm and releases you back to reality, fresh to face another day.

Or it doesn't, and you feel like shit.

I moaned, and my constricted lungs wheezed. Cramps rocked my body, my muscles throbbed, and an incapacitating ache radiated from every cell. *Damn, I hurt.*

Sticky debris pricked at my fingers as I wiped away the clusters of sleep from my eyes. Trying to find a comfortable position, I rolled on my back. Bad idea. It spasmed, and I gripped the mattress. The unfamiliar silk sheets under my palms spooked me.

Shit!

I took in my surroundings. The bedroom was huge and lavishly decorated. Cut white lilacs brightened an austere, drawered cabinet that matched the large dresser in both style and size. I felt minuscule in the center of the king-sized bed.

This humongous bedroom was a completely different universe than the one I had fainted into. My memories were fuzzy. I recalled

Thom had cradled me in his arms and set me in the front seat of his old Ford pickup truck. Trembling with exhaustion, unable to make a sound, his reassuring words had sounded like mumbles to my unfocused ears.

I didn't have the presence of mind to ask where he was taking me. Apparently, here.

But where was here? And why didn't the hospital or my home strike him as a better option?

A fresh wave of pain rushed over me as I crawled out of bed and gingerly stretched, trying to bring some flexibility back into my stiff muscles.

My entire being felt numb, or rather diluted, as if my soul had been ripped apart and fumbled back together by a preschooler with a red glue stick. I massaged my blue wrist to hush the angry bees buzzing under the skin and stared in disbelief at the deep, self-inflicted cut. What the hell had I been thinking?

Dried filth cracked as I moved to inspect myself. My long-sleeved jacket had shriveled around my forearms, my shirt clotted to my chest, and heeled muddied boots were laced to my feet. Relief sank in. Nobody had undressed me while I was unconscious. I unhooked the scarf around my neck, baffled that it hadn't choked me yet, and reached for my jean's pocket. Empty. My cell phone had been stolen during my abduction, and there was no land line in sight.

My parents must have been worried sick.

A folded set of clothes laid beside an elegant sink in the adjoined bathroom, a brand-new toothbrush and toothpaste on top.

The reflection in the mirror stuck me in place. *Is that really me?*

The tears on my cheeks had dried, leaving flaky salt trails. A mix of dried blood and gooey dirt smeared my skin, not masking the pulsating bruise on my face. The painful swelling deformed my cheekbone. My arms and chest were freckled with blemishes, and I suspected from the pain that my back was no better. My long, glossy red waves had morphed into a mess of knots and were clamped to my neck like a dead rat's tail.

Fresh tears exploded from my already sore and red eyes, and the numbness took a backseat to panic. My puffy lips cracked as I sobbed, a hint of fresh blood on my tongue.

The memories from the night before crashed back into place. The life draining from Dad's face, the hallucinations, the horrible men. The black cloaks, the eerie appearance of Thom's brother, the arrival of the other men, the cut on my hand, the blood...

It was too much.

I retched into the toilet, a thick green foul liquid, all that was left from my birthday cake. I wiped my mouth with my jacket's sleeve, hugged my legs, and leaned against the bathtub for support.

I'd been a hair's breadth away from death. It wasn't a dream, a prank, or even a mindless act of violence. These men had targeted and stalked me for God knows how long. I couldn't make sense of it all in this state, but as I cried my heart out against the cold white tiles, I was all too aware I'd almost been erased from the world.

A few minutes later, out of breath from the sobbing, I climbed back to my feet and splashed my face with ice-cold water. I had to get my shit together, or I'd spend the whole day prostrate on the floor.

I brushed my teeth hard and wished I had a tiny mop to clean my entire body as thoroughly. The filth on my clothes and the bruises on my face made me want to barf again.

The next natural step was to find Thom and call home, but I had to shower first. Nobody else should see this wreck, and I couldn't go back home looking like roadkill. Plus, I hoped a good scrub might wash away the trauma as well as the dirt. My parents would insist on going to the police station, and I needed time to gather my thoughts. Half the things I'd seen were impossible, but I was positive I hadn't bumped my head.

I stripped and cowered under the spray of water. Warmth enveloped me, a security blanket calming the storm of unanswered questions swirling in my mind.

A sharp cry flew out when soap came in contact with the nasty cut. The pressure from the jet made it pulse, and I grimaced. With the blood and mud washed away, the cut was damning evidence that I hadn't imagined the crazier parts of last night.

Despite the sizzling water running down my back, shivers went up my spine, and coldness crept into my heart.

When Liam had flattened his cut to mine, I'd heard voices. In my head. As he savagely ripped apart the armed men, the voices cheered him on. I'd closed my eyes and seen the mangled bodies through Liam's sight, and, for a horribly peaceful second, I found it beautiful.

Trembling like a leaf blown by a hurricane, I switched the water off. The shock had made me see things. The voices couldn't be real. I hadn't switched bodies with him, or my father. That was impossible.

I dried myself in a hurry and plucked the clothes that were left by the sink. A loud knock startled me, and I shot out of the bathroom, adrenaline pumping in my veins.

"Alana? It's me, Thom. Can I come in?" he asked through the door.

A nervous hiccup distorted my weak "yes", making me sound like five-year-old. I placed my wet hair behind my ears.

The door inched opened, and Thom walked in, each movement slow and steady. He kept a good distance between us. His usual smile was replaced by a somber frown as his gaze searched mine. "Stupid question, but, how are you?" An eagerness to help shone across his open face, and my heartbeat stopped running off in spikes.

"Not... so bad," I lied, trying a weak smile.

I wondered how one was supposed to act in this situation. He'd helped me, brought me to his home, and provided me with fresh clothes and toiletries. *Should I thank him for letting me crash?*

While I struggled with the etiquette of these preposterous circumstances, Thom took a tentative step closer. "Do you want to talk?"

Yes, I wanted to talk. To him? Not sure.

He was supposed to be a normal college guy.

He'd deceived me. I bet he was everything but normal. His brother had killed in front of me without batting an eyelash. Heaven knows what mayhem they muddled in. Mobsters, maybe?

I eyed him with suspicion, wondering if the whole ordeal was his fault. Maybe they thought I was his girlfriend. Maybe he owed them money. Maybe they'd slipped me something. As a drowning man clings to a buoy, my brain gripped that possibility.

It would have explained a lot.

In this lovely house with the lights on, the idea of monsters that go bump in the night seemed silly. Demons didn't exist, and paranormal phenomena were crazy and impossible.

The nagging cut begged to differ. The flesh hung agape, yet it didn't bleed. Instead, it burned, the margins alive with tingles, and it looked bigger than yesterday. Cuts weren't supposed to get bigger, nor were they supposed to sap my strength. Cuts were just cuts. You put a band-aid on them, and they healed. End of story.

Thom followed my gaze and winced. "Here, I'll help you with that." He disappeared into the bathroom for a few seconds and emerged with a first aid kit in his hands.

I sat in silence while he disinfected and wrapped my wound with gauze before putting adhesive tape around it. He moved with such ease that I figured he was accustomed to doing that sort of stuff. The mob theory sounded more and more probable.

"You're quite the nurse." My voice came out rough.

He scratched his neck. "I run into trouble more than I care to."

As I'd suspected. "What illegal scheme are you involved in? Drugs?"

With a defeated hunch of the shoulders, he said, "You think you were drugged? You weren't."

"You're lying," I tapped my foot, trying to pick a fight.

A small sigh was all I got in return.

I stabbed a finger in his direction. "Give me your phone. I want to call home."

Instead of complying, he asked, "Do you have questions, about what happened?"

How was he so calm? I loathed him for being calm, for making me question myself. Did I want to make sense of it or forget? Weird things *had* happened, but I remained in one piece, didn't I? Drugs were the only sensible explanation.

The crush I'd had on Thom belonged in the trashcan, and I vowed to sweep it there fast. Romance and prudence did not go hand-in-hand.

Thom cleared his throat. "They grabbed you because of what you did, because you're different."

Part of me understood what he meant, but most of me wanted to hide under the covers.

Different. The word echoed in my mind. How was *I* different? I'd always been the definition of normal. School during the day, average marks. I always handed my assignments on time, but never early. A part-time job as a waitress near college helped pay my rent. I visited my parents on Sundays and went out with my friends every Thursday. Saturday nights existed for laundry and movies or the occasional date. Anything *but* different.

Tired of this conversation, I decided I was done. "I want to go home." Leaving this place and never returning was my new priority, and I trekked forward towards the door.

Thom sidestepped, a deliberate attempt to block my way. Panic rose in my chest, and my throat constricted. I wasn't allowed to leave.

I was trapped. Again.

"I can't let you go. I'm sorry. They will find you if you leave. They can track your powers," he said.

Anxiety thickened in my blood.

Crazy talk! I couldn't stand crazy talk, I was a down-to-earth girl. This fell *way* beyond the requisite for crazy. An eighteen out of ten on the insane-o-meter, light-years from unwell, over the mentally unstable mark, and straight past to the loony-bin reject.

"Are you mad? I don't have any *powers*."

As soon as I heard it, I knew I was lying.

Dad, I'd healed him. It wasn't a figment of my imagination. My arms fell at my sides. I'd rationalized that the hallucinations had been a symptom of post-traumatic stress on my part. Was it? Or was it real?

I chewed the possibility, not liking the taste.

Maybe Thom was insane? Maybe this was all a joke? A cruel prank?

"This is crazy," I snickered.

He met my disbelieving stare head on. "It's the truth."

"Stop taking me for a fool."

No way magic existed. I kept hoping for a camera crew to appear and say, *Gotcha*!

No way I had powers.

Me.

I wanted—no needed—to deny it as long as possible. The sturdy foundations of my life would be blown to pieces if I so much as contemplated magic could be real, and I could feel them shift beneath me.

My mind buzzed. I felt faint and nauseous and angry. I wanted to cover my ears and scream. Turning away from Thom, I gripped the bridge of my nose to try and stop the monumental headache coming on.

"Alana, whatever you may think you saw or did yesterday, it was *all* real. You're a witch."

The urge to argue took over, and I spun back to face him. "I saw and did nothing!"

Blue eyes bore into mine. "You saw my brother."

Arms clenched on either side, my shoulders hitched at the mention of the demon with the black eyes. Had I imagined his steel grasp and his incredible speed?

Definitely not.

Eyes cast down, I stroked my arm. Bruises had appeared, each of his fingers leaving a separate purple mark. Pointless to doubt *he* was real.

"Why can't I leave and forget about this?" I grabbed my forehead, wishing to make it so by thinking it hard enough.

Thom didn't answer. Instead, he stood in silence as I paced the room.

My teeth ground together. I was torn between forgetting what happened and reliving it to find another logical explanation. Hysteria threatened to devour me, so I forced my body to stand still and turned my attention back to Thom. "If I have powers, why didn't I know about them?"

Surprise raised his brows. "You didn't have them until yesterday. People like you are rare, and they hide to survive."

The uneasiness within me skyrocketed while he spoke. My fight-or-flight instinct kicked in, and an all-consuming urge to get the hell out trampled what was left of my rational side.

I leaped forward, but Thom put himself in the way again. "Please, please, *please,* Thom, let me go," I begged on the verge of tears.

His lips formed a tight line. "I can't."

I swallowed back a sob. Crying in front of him was not an option. I wouldn't make a fool of myself, even if fear crept inside to set up shop in every crevice of my being. I wouldn't allow panic to consume me and make me weak at the knees.

And what is my go-to remedy for fear?

Anger.

Who crowned Thom boss? Wasn't he a good guy? Did I know him at all?

"Go to hell! I'm leaving!"

Would he go so far as to physically restrain me? He'd been extremely careful not to touch me so far. I tested my hunch and marched towards the door, towards my freedom. He let me pass.

I was about to cross the threshold of the room when he said, "If you go back home, you *will die."* The despair in his voice shook me. "I don't want that, so you won't find a way out of here. I will explain everything in detail when you're ready. These men won't hesitate to kill you or everyone you love if they think they have a snowball's chance in hell at getting you back. If you must hate me, I get it, but I'm trying to save you and your family."

I turned to glare at him. The moisture glistening beneath his lashes begged my heart to trust him in spite of my head.

Doubt crawled. If there was such a thing as magic, could it prevent me from leaving? If I left, would it put others in danger? Were my parents in danger now?

Rebelling further was beyond me at the moment. Magic. The word weirded me out, and my nose wrinkled.

We marinated in an awkward silence. He sounded sincere in wanting to keep me safe, but I still didn't trust him.

My dilemma must have showed because he said, "I'll give you a bit of time to think things through. It's a lot to digest." As he was walking out the door, he paused. "I'm so sorry you have to be involved in this. You have no idea."

Being sorry wasn't enough.

A series of strangled sobs grated my larynx as I tamed my wet hair with a brush I found in the vanity. When it was smoother than a baby's butt, I crouched to the floor and leaned against the edge of the bed. Anxiousness made my stomach churn, and I hugged my knees. My simple happy life was gone, evaporated like water in a desert, with no oasis in sight.

It took everything I had not to burst into tears again.

I BIT OFF HALF my fingernails and was still undecided about whether to give Thom the benefit of the doubt. I drew blood and cringed, disgusted at my lack of control over the habit.

Looking for a distraction, I pushed back the curtains on each side of the window. I was on the second floor of a brick house. The window opened to a yard that was furnished with a wicker table and chairs. A few spring flowers grew in tidy patches around the patio, where a bird feeder hung from a hook. A small chickadee flew to the line of big trees delimiting the thick forest.

A big house with no neighbors. A great location for holding someone against their will. I turned the window's handle to discover it didn't open wider than an inch.

This was a prison.

A claustrophobic ache encircled my heart, and I rushed to the door. Gasping for air, I yanked it open wide. Thom sat on the other side, sifting through a book. The sudden outburst startled him. With him guarding my door, sneaking out wasn't an option.

Annoyed, I narrowed my eyes. "If, and I say *if*, I decide to believe you," I shot him my best determined glare, "I have to stay here—where I'm safe—and not tell anyone where I am?"

The book snapped shut, and he put it aside. "That's right."

Doubling back, I left the door open behind me as an invitation, and he followed. I lured him deep into the room, ready to bolt at the earliest opportunity. When he was a few feet away from the door, I asked, "Do I have to stay here for the rest of my life?"

If he said yes, he'd better be prepared to run after me down the stairs I'd glimpsed in the hallway. I was ready to James Bond my way out of here.

"Not *at all.*"

Hope inflated my chest, and I raised my brows at him, waiting for specifics.

He combed his fingers through his hair and avoided my gaze. "It's complicated."

"Tell me."

"You have to stay until you can hide that you're different." The details would have to wait.

"I do that, and I can go?"

With a quick nod, he answered positively.

I was regaining some control. Maybe I could do this. "How?"

"Witches give off a kind of flare, like a beacon. You can learn to turn it off."

"Fine. Teach me." I said, eager to be done with it.

With a brisk shake of the head, he denied my request. "It's not that simple. It will take time."

"How much time?" How long did he expect me to play along?

The grim line of his mouth spoke volumes. "I don't know, exactly. The witches we've helped so far took anywhere from eight months to two years."

I sized up the room—my new cell. Two years sounded like ages. Would he ever allow me to go home again? To my family, to school? Was there a life after this?

Was he a lunatic making this all up to keep me captive?

How I wished I could talk to my mom and tell her everything. Ask for her advice. We talked every day. She was my moral compass, my go-to judge of character. How could I ever live without her?

The dire thought drained all my energy. Tears threatened to pour over my glassy eyes, and I bit the inside of my cheeks hard to delay a meltdown.

"I need to be alone." I dismissed Thom quickly, so he wouldn't see, sat on the comforter and gripped the edge of the mattress.

Magic. What a joke! My mind was split into two conflicting parts. The skeptic part, who rejected all this nonsense violently, and the intuitive part, who sensed truth in everything Thom had said.

I'm more of a Scully than a Mulder, and I didn't want to believe.

But I was faced with irrefutable *proof*. Mainly my stroll down my father's memories and the miraculous healing. Oh, and let's not forget the demon with the black eyes.

Either Thom spoke the truth—though not the whole truth—or I was, in fact, insane. The first option suited me better. Even if it was nuts, I could heal people, and monsters were on the hunt for me.

By the end of that first afternoon, I'd stopped wallowing in self-pity. How quickly I came to terms with the fact that supernatural beings existed still baffles me. Now, I can barely remember how simple and easy life was before I discovered the *other*world. Carrying a dagger in my boot would never have crossed my mind. What did it feel like not to be constantly looking over my shoulders? To go out at night without thinking twice? To meet strangers with my guard down?

They say ignorance is bliss. I say ignorance gets you killed. I still miss it, though.

5

LOSING MY RELIGION

Alana

The orange rays of sunset reflected in the standing mirror across the window and blinded me. The day had come and gone, and I'd been staring into space too long. I got up to re-angle the glass and frowned at my appearance.

The clothes Thom had lent me were my size, technically, but they didn't fit. The yoga pants were too short, their wide brim didn't reach my ankles, and the sneaky shirt kept inching down my breasts, a wardrobe malfunction waiting to happen. My hair was no better. I bent down and fluffed it with my fingers.

Where's a hairdryer when you need one?

The result was less than satisfactory, so I gathered my thick mane to one side and braided it. Index and thumb held the extremity while I fumbled around the bathroom for a hair tie.

A dried-out rubber band was all I could find, and I took care not to snap it in half. These suckers are tricky. My looks were the only thing I could control, and I wanted to appear level-headed and strong.

A knock lured me back to the bedroom. Thom, I guessed, and I stuck my tongue out at the closed door. The doorknob jiggled, but I'd locked him out. *Ah! Suck on that, you stupidly handsome witch kidnapper.*

Truthful or not, knight in shining armor or not, Thom was holding me captive, and I reserved the right to resent him as long as I wanted. Maybe forever.

"You must be starving," he said, his voice muffled by the thick wooden door.

I was famished but too proud to admit it. Open the door? No way! "No, I'm perfectly fine. Thank you."

"I made lasagna."

A treacherous growl squeezed my stomach at the mental image of a steaming cheese crusted lasagna. As much as I hate to yield, I love lasagna—any pasta, really—and hate Mondays. My mother used to call me her tiny grumpy Garfield.

Hunger triumphed over sulkiness, and I opened the door. Thom cracked a smile, but I served him a pout with a frosty glare on top. This was not a humorous moment or even a pleasant one. He'd better revise his attitude.

His grin faltered. "Come on. I'll show you the kitchen."

Taken aback by his answer, my crafted scowl slipped. "What? I'm not on room arrest?"

"You're on house arrest. It's slightly different," he joked.

Should I have been grateful for his attempts to break the tension or insulted?

Settling for put out, I trailed behind him. The staircase opened into the downstairs living area. The upstairs walkway led to four rooms total, two on the right and one on the left of mine.

Thom motioned to the closest one, "Liam's bedroom." The name gave me goose bumps. He pointed at the next one. "Mine."

"And the other one?" I asked as I jerked a glance behind us.

"Lilah's, but she moved out a few months ago."

Not recalling him talking about a sister, I asked, "Who's Lilah?"

His features softened. "The witch we helped before you. She has powers, too. I've asked her to come and meet you."

My gaze lingered on the door at the end of the corridor. Another witch? And she'd moved out? Interesting.

Only the old-fashioned creaky hardwood floors betrayed the actual age of the house. Everything else looked shiny and new, from the white furniture that stood in front of a 70-plus inch television, to the artsy canvases hanging on the walls. Video games littered the floor. Boys and their toys.

The kitchen had stainless steel appliances and a massive, redwood dinner table surrounded by eight matching chairs. It didn't look like it had seen a lot of dinner parties.

Not the type of furniture—not the type of house—you'd expect two guys under thirty to own. I guessed they had inherited the house from their parents. Thom had confided after class one day that his parents were dead. When I'd asked how they'd died, he'd mumbled *car accident,* and I hadn't pried further.

I sneaked a glimpse from beneath my lashes. Had he lied? Had he edited their deaths? He couldn't have said *a bunch of blood thirsty monsters murdered them.* A car accident sounded way too normal.

"Where are we?" I asked, stowing the question about his parents for later.

"We're at our *safe* house," he said, emphasizing the word safe.

"You just happen to live near Amherst?" I fished for more details, hoping to pinpoint our exact location.

Thom bit his lower lip. "We're not in Massachusetts. We're in southern Virginia."

"What?!" I was shocked we'd driven straight through the night without me being the wiser. Shouldn't I have woken up at some point? Whatever supernatural reaction had been put in motion when Liam had crushed his cut to mine had not only drained me but dazed me for hours.

I was the farthest from home I'd ever been. Born in Ludlow, Mom had met Dad in college, and they'd moved in together in her childhood home after graduation. I'd been raised there and loved it with all my heart with its heat in the summer and snow in the winter. I'd never traveled south of New York.

"Anywhere but here is too dangerous. Even the big cities would be suicide. This is not a normal house," Thom explained with a casual shrug.

The aloofness in his demeanor awakened my temper. "And I'm your prisoner."

"I'd rather you consider yourself my guest," he said sheepishly.

Words flew out, "I can't believe you expect me to stay here willingly. The paranormal stuff is hard enough to swallow."

Granted, he'd saved my life. But driving over state lines without my permission, not being able to call anyone, it was too much.

He leaned forward, serious. His obnoxiously blue eyes made me gulp. One step closer, and I'd feel his body heat, and I had to smack myself hard to back away.

The richness of his voice sent shivers down my spine as he said, "I'll make you a deal, give me two weeks, and I'll do anything I can to convince you. If afterwards you still believe you'll be fine on your own, I'll drive you home myself."

"Two weeks?" I repeated aloud, considering the offer. Sounded reasonable, so I extended my hand, "Deal."

The handshake lingered, his hot skin heaven against my cold palm.

With perfect timing, the oven beeped, and I peeked inside. A bubbling lasagna waited for us, broiled to perfection. My saliva pooled at an embarrassing speed as Thom served us each a generous portion.

"I hope you like it. It's a family recipe." He passed me the utensils.

I carved a big piece with my fork. The mix of salty cheese and tomato sauce delighted my taste buds. With each comforting bite, my body relaxed. Thom was a capable cook. It wouldn't suck completely to be stuck with him in this house, but I didn't tell him that.

My lips curved at the mental image of Thom in an apron. Did he also bake?

After his third and my second piece, we cleaned the dishes, babbling about unimportant stuff like the typical Virginia weather, and whether or not the next superhero movie would be any better than the others. I was desperate for some normalcy, even though it was fake as hell. I should have been scared to death, but to my extreme surprise, I wasn't.

When we were done with the chores, leftovers tucked in the fridge, the mood shifted.

The bright gleam in Thom's eyes dimmed. "I have to take care of something. You can watch TV if you want."

Whatever that *something* was, it wasn't good.

"Aren't you worried I'll try to escape?" Why would he risk leaving me alone?

"I'm not. We have a deal. Besides, there's a spell on this house, and, without a key, you won't find a way in or out."

Skepticism was a knee jerk reaction. "You're messing with me."

A wide grin illuminated his face. "Nope."

Was this reverse psychology? Maybe there was no spell. Maybe he underestimated me.

REVERSE PSYCHOLOGY, my ass.

After half an hour of exploration, I'd discovered two more bedrooms, one half bathroom, the door to the basement, a library, an office—with no computer to send an e-mail from—and the laundry room.

No phones. No path leading to the outside world.

I'd even checked the back of the closets for hidden panels and humiliated myself pulling on random books for a secret mechanism.

A brilliantly-made prison. How to escape without a door? Sledgehammers don't just lie around, and to hurl a chair at a window seemed premature and messy. Defeated, I sprawled out on the couch, familiarized with my new *home*.

My frustrated gaze fell on Thom's bedroom.

Could I?

Hell yeah!

I tiptoed upstairs, the theme from *Mission Impossible* trumpeting in my mind.

The treacherous wood floors whined, and I peeked downstairs to verify that Thom was nowhere in sight. A thrill ran down my spine as I turned the doorknob and entered his sanctuary.

The room's layout mirrored mine, but the decoration had a more masculine taste to it. Books, papers and clothes formed eclectic piles on the furniture and floor. I grinned. Thom was untidy. A picture of an older couple, his parents, no doubt, embracing the kid versions of Liam and him, stood on his dresser. Happiness shone on their faces.

A twinge of excitement pinched my heart when I spotted a laptop on his bed. I leaped on the mattress and opened it. It was password protected. *Damn.* Disappointed, I chewed the inside of my cheeks. He'd thought of everything.

A noise reached my ears, coming from downstairs. Time to go. My timing sucked, and I slipped out as he came up the stairs. Caught red-handed, my career as a spy hadn't lasted long.

He cracked up. "I'm impressed. It usually takes four or five days before people break into my room."

"Sorry," I said, unrepentant. If he had the right to kidnap me, I was justified in snooping.

It was only fair.

In my peripheral vision, the older sibling's room beckoned.

Thom followed my gaze. "Liam's way more uptight about his privacy than me." The gloomy warning lacing his words was unmistakable. He might as well have said, Liam is a dangerous psychopath who might kill you if you try to sneak into his room.

I was terrified of running into the devil by accident. A question burned my lips, and I tried to sound casual as I asked, "Err, is your brother *here*?"

Epic fail. I'd nailed the terrified mouse imitation instead.

Thom's face crunched up with worry. "Liam," he hesitated before continuing. "Liam's indisposed."

What did he mean by that? The mysterious undertones in every other sentence pissed me off. My thoughts flowed back to the shimmering, black demon, how his tortured voice had clashed with his violent behavior, how his hands had dug into my hair, how his lips had brushed against the pulse point of my neck.

I'd forgotten a crucial detail, the sound of three gunshots tearing the air.

"God, is he okay?" I asked wide-eyed, praying Thom didn't shoot his brother dead for me. "You shot him!"

"Liam can heal himself from a lot, bullets included. Don't worry, he's fine," he said, not only for my benefit. Who was he trying to convince?

What is he? seemed like a rude question to ask. How do you politely inquire about someone's species?

A heavy atmosphere settled as the weight of the situation thickened in my bones. One prisoner upstairs, one brother riddled with bullet holes God knows where. No wonder Thom looked beyond tired. Unable to take the tension any longer, I left Thom to his thoughts and entered *my* room.

Still unfamiliar with my new living quarters, I pawed at the wall to find the switch. A feeble bedside lamp ignited, the only source of light besides the red glow of the alarm clock.

The dark forest glowered from outside the window. An uneven wind rapped the sinuous branches of a tall oak against the glass like untrained fingers on a piano. Fog blanketed the earth, and the knitted trees reaped the light of the moon. Shadows danced along the grass, playing tricks on my mind.

I squinted at a blotchy dark spot, sure something was moving down there. *Eek!* A man was hiding behind the large pine. I blinked, trying to focus, but he'd disappeared. Had I imagined him? I stared at the tree in question for a minute longer, but I didn't see the tall, dark shape again.

To be safe, I yanked the drapes shut. I drew myself a scorching bath, hoping to burn my fears away. The water did the trick and purged the throng of questions that were thundering in my brain.

With a fluffy towel wrapped around me, I looked for a fresh set of clothes. What I found was bewildering. Pants and shirts filled the first cabinet drawer to the brim, tags visible on them, all my size. Same thing in the next one. My arrival had been planned.

Duh! How dumb was I? Why had I not realized this before?

I smacked my naive self.

At school, Thom had approached me on purpose. It was no coincidence we'd met, no coincidence I was here. The thin trust I'd started to nurture towards him evaporated. Why hadn't he said anything? Did he think I was stupid? Hoped I wouldn't connect the dots?

My hot temper begged me to rage downstairs at once, but I reined it in. Better to collect my thoughts, hatch a plan, and wait until morning to confront him. If his answer didn't satisfy me, he'd have to deal with a broken window and a broken nose.

Upon waking the next morning, I was primed for a fight. Taking the stairs two at a time, I entered the kitchen to find Thom in front of the stove. My thoughts drifted when I saw him, and my accusing questions got stuck in my throat. Dark blue jeans hugged his hips, and he was naked from the waist up. A sparse stretch of sand chest hair ran on his muscular torso. As he waited for the eggs to cook, he scratched the stubble on his chin, his light blond curls tousled.

God, he's hot.

Suddenly feeling underdressed, I considered the white lace trim of the gray night camisole I was wearing. Nipples threatened to show through the thin cotton and the pajama shorts barely came to my mid-thighs, so I was practically naked, too. Blush crept on my cheeks and chest. We looked like two lovers having breakfast after a night of passion. Not that I'd had any of *those* in a long, long while.

I gave myself a brisk, inward shake. *Stop it.*

Thom chose this moment to notice me. "Good morning. Sunny-side up, or scrambled?" He asked with a dashing smile.

Ignoring the fact that my heart skipped a beat, I gritted my teeth together and forced myself to go on with my original plan. "Did you know I was going to end up here?" I asked point-blank.

The seriousness of my voice seemed to surprise him, and he removed the frying pan from the stove. "Yes and no."

A cryptic answer, again. I gave him a dirty look that commanded he stop being enigmatic. "Which is it, Walker?"

He winced. "I knew you *might* end up here."

Busted. I crossed my arms, waiting for an explanation. *Better be a good one.*

He took a deep breath. "Certain people have the latent ability to become witches even if their ancestors are not. They are called random witches and come from human bloodlines. That potential has a limited time frame, a few weeks at most. You weren't supposed to *activate* anymore." I frowned, and he caught my unspoken question. "You had turned twenty, and nothing had happened. We were going to move on."

I digested his words. My plan to break a window switched to the back-burner, and I found myself content with his answer, at least for the time being.

As I thought back on our last meeting, the night of my birthday party, everything made more sense. The sweet goodbye kiss on the cheek had felt like an adieu. He was going to leave, never to be seen again. That's why he hadn't texted me back the next day. "You move from girl to girl until one becomes a witch, and when they do, you save them?" I summed up, and he nodded. "Why?"

How did he end up with this occupation? I didn't remember seeing *witch guardian* in the university brochure.

"Because they deserve to be saved." He didn't say it out of self-aggrandizement but in earnest.

My stupid heart swooned. "How do you know where to look?"

He shifted his gait from one foot to the other. "Liam knows."

As soon as he spoke his brother's name, the shroud of worries reappeared, and I quickly changed the subject. "So, I'm a witch?" I stated out loud, curious to see how it sounded.

The veil clouding his face lifted, and he grinned. "Yes."

"And I can heal people?" A useful power, at least.

He whistled. "Pretty cool power, very advanced too. Most witches can read thoughts or have other types of telepathic abilities, but few can influence reality and bend it to their will."

Again, a bunch of gibberish flanked his words, and I fought the urge to roll my eyes. "Why am I able to do that?"

Was it reversible?

"Some have it, most don't. It's very mysterious. And it doesn't have to be girls. Guys can be witches too, but we call them warlocks. The only thing we know for sure is that it runs in your blood."

Fed up with mystery before 9:00 a.m., I asked, "How did the bad guys know? I had just discovered my powers."

He set both plates on the table and sat down. "Good question. I thought I had taken care of that."

I'd forgotten to tell him the neighbor was involved. "One creep lived across the street from my parents. I recognized him. He must have seen me heal my dad."

"The guy with the poodle?" Thom shouted, sounding surprised and pissed.

"Yes," I said with a quick nod.

"Fuck! We checked him out. I followed the bastard for a week."

I frowned, confused.

Jaw locked, Thom said, "People like him are called seers because they see magical flares. They spy on you until you activate, and then grab you. I found your assigned seer. He masqueraded as the history teacher's assistant. They must have put two seers on you. Damn it." He punched the table. "Your extraction was a mess. Usually, everything goes smoothly. They're too busy watching a load of potentials. We choose one and stay close. Sometimes, we miss one at the other end of the continent, but the ones we find, we save."

"How do you manage to kidnap—" he looked pained, so I switched gears. "I mean *save* witches without getting into trouble?"

"Well, the demons have many seers. It takes a long time before they realize that one of them is *missing.*"

I got the picture. They killed them.

Was I okay with that? I thought about the horrible man that had kidnapped me and grimaced. *The bastard had it coming.*

"They must have known we were watching you. At least, I hope it's that. Can you imagine? Double seers on everyone?"

I really couldn't. Did he realize he was basically speaking another language? When I'd asked about them getting into trouble, I'd meant trouble with the police, not demons.

"What—" The sound of the doorbell interrupted me.

Thom leaped towards the living room. I followed in his wake and gasped when I spotted the front door near the staircase where there used to be only an empty wall.

Magic house: 1. Me: 0.

6

BLURRY

Alana

A pixie-like woman stepped into the house, her stylish raincoat dripping from the heavy downpour. A bag fell at her feet, and she used both hands to shake her umbrella outside, careful not to soak the hardwood.

Piercing baby blue eyes met my curious gaze, and a gentle smile showed a straight row of pearly-white teeth. Ringlets of radiant blond hair stopped right over her shoulders and framed her delicate features. Her cheeks were pink from the chill, and her lips were painted with a crisp, red lipstick.

She was a fashion icon and I was standing in my jammies, perfect.

"Hi, I'm Lilah." She extended her hand with grace, her melodic voice matching her beauty.

"I'm Alana." I smiled, happy to meet someone like me.

"Nice to meet you," she turned to Thom, "Hey you." Barely whispered, the simple greeting conveyed a bottomless love.

Thom enveloped her in a bone-crushing hug, her lean figure swallowed by his broad shoulders. Her pink nails gripped his back as if he was the only thing preventing her from plummeting down a deep canyon.

Eyes closed, their embrace lingered, and I shifted from one foot to the other.

"I came as soon as I got your message. How is he?" she asked, her voice muffled by Thom's shirt.

"It's bad." He looked lost, and a vulnerability I had never witnessed before shone through his pained frown.

Lilah whispered what I assumed to be words of comfort, though I couldn't quite hear her. They were in their own world, and I was intruding.

"That blood did a number on him," Thom said.

Blood?

"Let's sit and talk?" Lilah offered, looking back at me.

Grateful for the acknowledgment, I nodded, and we sat around the L-shaped couch.

Lilah got right down to business. "I guess Thom made this point crystal clear, but you can't leave the house until you learn to block their magic GPS thing-y. It will be hard—believe me, been there—but we can protect you from *them*."

Anxious, I nibbled on my fingers again. "Why me?" A selfish question, but I needed to know. Afraid of sounding too self-centered, I rephrased, "I mean—why *us*?"

She laid her hand on mine. "Because life sucks."

"When your powers activated, they turned you into a lighthouse. *They* can feel you from afar," Thom added.

Lilah tucked a blond lock behind her ear. "*They* could find you anywhere but here."

They were going slow, afraid to freak me out, but I wanted all the answers. Immediately.

"Who are *they*?" I asked.

Thom raised an eyebrow at Lilah.

She gave him a quick head nod, and he leaned towards me. "They are called Shadow Walkers, named after their penchant to warp reality. Darkness feeds them, the night their playpen."

I scoffed. "Seriously, Thom, enough with the poetic nonsense you add at every other sentence. You're totally losing me."

A soft giggle escaped Lilah's throat. "She's right. You do sound like a Film Noir narrator."

Shadow Walkers.

The name reverberated in my mind, giving me the creeps. Actual monsters existed. I wasn't hallucinating.

"Half demon, they have incredible powers, and they consider themselves better than humans. A superior race," Thom said.

Half demon? I prayed to God I'd never meet a full-blooded one. "And these Shadow Walkers..." I could barely bring myself to say the word, "they want my blood?" Lilah and Thom both nodded. "Why? Are they like vampires?"

Thom chuckled. "No, they don't eat it to live. The blood is just the vessel for your powers. In fact, it's less wasteful for them to inject it directly into their bloodstream. A drop can keep any demon alive for days without further sustenance. But Shadow Walkers use witch blood to juice up, and that's the real problem." His voice dripped with disgust, and his expression darkened. "Elders have the young ones hooked on witch blood."

"Hooked?"

"They crave it beyond reason. It makes them faster, stronger, but they lose themselves. They are easier to control in this state. The Shadow Walkers share a mental link to each other. It's called the Collective. They can share thoughts and give orders from miles away. That's how the elders use the youngsters as puppets."

Liam's haunted voice came back to mind. *I can't,* he'd said when I'd asked him to let go of me. Goosebumps went up my arm at the memory. "Liam is one of them."

Thom nodded. "He has the purest brand of blood in his system right now. Newborn blood, and a lot of it. It could take weeks for him to fully recover from such a dose. If he ever recovers."

Lilah clicked her tongue. "Don't say that."

A desperate sigh choked him. "You didn't see him, Lilah. He's completely gone."

"We'll get him back," she said, adamant. To her, there was no other option.

Thom's fists unclenched, but the crease of worry on his forehead stayed in place as he turned back to me. "Also, you must never go in the basement."

Why? Wasn't Liam tied or imprisoned down there?

"Thom and I learned to keep Liam out of our heads, but you are completely at his mercy. His powers lie in trickery and illusion. He can project an entire make-believe world around you, can make you see whatever he wants. He could trick you to open his cell or worse."

Liam being able to manipulate me into doing anything scared me to my core. He wasn't human. Could he be trusted, ever? I stopped myself from speaking the words, but I couldn't hide the grimace on my face. I didn't want to live in the same house as a demon, especially if he could hoodwink me into seeing crap that wasn't there.

Lilah stood up. "I need to see him."

"Want me to come with?" Thom asked, but she shook her head. He scratched the back of his neck. "Stay far away. If he can reach you, he *will* kill you."

She acknowledged the warning before walking away.

I bit my bottom lip. "How come you're not... like your brother?" I didn't ask whether he was because I knew he wasn't. There was no thundercloud around Thom, only sunshine.

"The demon lineage works as a supernatural genetic disorder, but it's impossible to predict who will get it. Liam was the first in five generations of Walkers to turn. Dad wasn't even invited to the extended family meetings. The demons thought our lineage too diluted.

"The human relatives benefit from the powers. They receive anything they can dream of —money, power, fame—as a trade in for the soul of their child. If you want my opinion, they're worse than the actual demons."

"I take it your parents weren't willing to cooperate?"

"My great-great-great granduncle is a demon, the last Shadow Walker to turn in the Walker bloodline, before Liam. Our parents succeeded in staying out of his way and off the entire clan's radar for decades. They weren't aware—"

A guttural roar rose from beneath our feet and quaked the house. Pictures on the wall shook and threatened to fall. Liam was not happy to see Lilah. Or too happy.

If I understood this correctly, he lusted for witch blood, and Lilah was one. It didn't have to be *my* blood, he wanted *all* witches dead. Silver linings kept crapping into my lap.

"Did you say your great-great-great granduncle *is* one?" I asked, trying to stay focused on the conversation despite the fear spiraling in my veins.

Thom passed a hand over his mouth. "Witch blood is invaluable to Shadow Walkers. It extends their life up to three or four times the normal human lifespan. James Walker is 133 years old, but he doesn't look a day over 40."

My blood was the elixir of life to an entire race of demons? Boy, was I screwed.

ON. OFF. On. Great, it worked.

I flipped the light switch off one last time after adding a lamp to *my* bedroom. The demon in my basement would not scare me. I wouldn't allow it! But I'd sleep with the lights on. Just to be safe.

I walked back to the upstairs hallway and rested my hands on the handrails. The last couple of days, this house, all the supernatural talk, it had been beyond draining. My sight traveled to the absent front door, and I wondered how magic really worked. Was the door there at all times, and I just couldn't see it, or had the actual molecules of wood and brick changed when Lilah had come in?

Lilah's door cracked open. The sudden movement startled me, and my knuckles tightened on the rail.

"Sorry, I didn't mean to frighten you. Want to chat?" she offered.

Eager to learn more about her and hear her story, I accepted her invitation.

She was fresh out of the shower, flowery robe tied around her waist. Her blond hair was still wet, and it hugged her pale and haunted features. The face-to-face with Liam hadn't gone well.

A thought dawned on me as I noticed her room was almost identical to mine. "You redecorated the house, didn't you?"

She grinned, her frown evaporating. "How did you know?"

"Wild guess. Thom can't even color coordinate his socks."

She giggled, and I did the same, her laughter infectious. *Look at us, already thick as thieves.*

"You are handling this like a champ. For days, I refused to even speak to Thom," she said as she unpacked her bag. "I thought I would have to talk to you through your closed door."

"Thom and I had become good friends back home. Plus, I almost died, and he saved me. That helped." I kept the part about having a huge crush on him to myself.

"Did he ask for two weeks to convince you?" she asked in a conspiratorial manner.

The speech had sounded rehearsed! "Yes."

"Are you convinced yet?"

"It's difficult to swallow."

"Life as you knew it is pretty much over." A straight-shooter, Lilah wasn't sugar-coating anything; I liked that.

"How did you do it? Wasn't it hard to abandon your whole world?"

"Very hard. Leaving someone you love behind sucks." From the way her eyes welled up, I could tell she spoke from experience. She drifted, avoiding the subject, "Where are you from?"

"Ludlow, Massachusetts. You?"

"Seattle originally, but now I live in Washington, DC, and I'm back in school." She pulled a wallet out of her purse and showed me her driver's license. "Michelle Parker, that's my new name. Took me a long time to get used to it. Being on my own is the hardest. I always end up here."

Starting from scratch, what a scary thought. "Did you stay here long?"

A nostalgic smile glazed her lips. She clearly didn't consider her time here as being in prison. "About a year and a half, and Thom and Liam became my family. Thom's the sweetest and Liam," her voice softened, "Liam's a great teacher. Without him, I'd be dead. Or worse."

Worse than dying? I sidestepped the issue. "Can I ask you a question?" Her encouraging nod gave me the nerve to ask, "What kind of powers do you have?"

"It's okay to ask, Alana," she sat on the bed. "I read and influence people's feelings... to an extent."

I felt so comfortable with her... Was she using her powers on me?

"The latter totally drains me out, so I don't do it often, but," she glanced at me sideways, "I can read your feelings pretty well. I know you're confused and scared. It will dwindle as time goes on, you'll see." She crinkled her nose. "And... I can tell you *like* Thom."

The words brought colors to my cheeks.

"Don't worry. Your secret is safe with me."

"Thanks. I still don't know what to make of these feelings myself, let alone share them."

"I understand. What about you? I showed you mine," she said in jest.

"Healing powers."

"I'm jealous! It's so much more useful."

The humor helped take the edge off this stressful day as if she knew exactly what to say to comfort me. She probably did know.

She pried a big paper bag out of her luggage and deposited it in my lap. "For you."

It was filled to the brim with everything a girl could want. Lipstick, mascara, eyeliner, conditioner, hair straightener, tampons, three shades of foundation, nail polish, etc. A wave of gratitude choked me, and tears prickled my eyes. "Thank you."

Lilah was an angel.

Our conversation drifted to her adjustment to the move. She bared her heart to me, and it comforted me even more. She was living a somewhat normal life again. She had to deal with difficult courses, new friends, and recurring problems with a stalker-ish neighbor, but nothing supernatural.

Her passion for her biology major shone through her speech, and I envied her. College had been a casual relationship on my part.

"When I was younger, I wanted to be an astronaut, a detective or Jessica Alba. But I'm not her. I get queasy riding in the backseat of a car, and to become one of Charlie's Angels isn't a viable career path," I explained with a smile.

Lilah giggled. "What did you choose, then?"

"I started a major in Linguistics, but I have no clue what I planned to do with my diploma." I drummed my fingers over my mouth. "I guess it doesn't really matter now."

"You can choose a new path. One you'll be more passionate about." Her optimism was contagious, and I nodded.

"Let's go downstairs. We can cook dinner."

Lilah and I invaded the kitchen. She diced vegetables for an Asian recipe, so I helped—and by "helped," I mean I stayed out of the way and passed her the salt.

I am mediocre at cooking, but I excel at burning.

The sesame oil, ginger and soy sauce aromas rising from the pan were so enticing, I forked a bite of chicken into my mouth and hummed. "Lilah, this is amazing. I wish I could cook like that. No, strike that, I wish I could cook at all."

"I used to think toast was complicated, but I had plenty of time to learn to cook during my stay at the house."

"Maybe there's hope for me yet."

Thom joined us as I set the table.

We had so much fun throughout dinner that wine spouted out my nose, and I forgot where I was. Was it a bad thing? Did that make me a crazy person? To enjoy prison?

Halfway through dessert, Lilah gave Thom a meaningful nod. "We should visit Liam again. I want to try something."

I didn't have a smidgen of desire to see Liam, so I was relieved they didn't invite me along. The dirty dishes needed a scrub, anyway.

After I was done, I curled up on the sofa, zapping through channels for a good show. Not finding anything interesting, I hit the power button and snuggled the fluffy pillow. I missed my phone. Missed having the world available at the press of a button.

Missed my daily calls with Mom.

I bet she's totally freaking out. What did they think when I didn't show up at the hospital? I bet they thought I'd been in a car crash. It's been more than 24 hours now, so the police must be on the case. I wonder if Kelly knows I'm missing yet.

I swallowed back salty tears. Footsteps drew near. Deep in conversation, Lilah and Thom came into the living room. They did not spot me lying on the sofa.

"The withdrawal symptoms are bad. God, I've never seen him like this." Sobs raised Lilah's voice a few octaves, and snuffles trumpeted out of her nose.

"Considering the dose he took, I'm afraid—"

"Shush!" she cut him off. "He's in there somewhere, and we'll bring him back." She burst into another fit of cries.

Thom gathered her in his arms, and I got that uneasy feeling again. Intimacy seemed natural between them. Had romance blossomed? A year and a half was a long time. Maybe they'd been more than what they were now?

I lectured myself for caring. High school was over, and I was not going to pursue Thom anyway.

I sat up and made my presence known. "Hey."

"Sorry we took so long," Thom apologized.

"It's fine."

Lilah disentangled herself from Thom and joined me on the couch. She'd been so nice to me that I didn't even hesitate and gave her hand a squeeze. I didn't know what to say to ease her pain. "I'm sorry he's not doing well."

"I'm being silly. It's just so wrong to see him like this."

Thom sat with us, looking glum, and I turned the TV back on to create a distraction. We watched the screen in silence, and I'm afraid the attempt at brightening their evening fell flat.

Lilah let out an emphasized yawn. "Well, I'm beat. Good night."

A wink behind Thom's back confirmed she was giving me the

opportunity to stay alone with him. Whatever they might have been, Lilah didn't mind my crush. I'd have to tell her I didn't intend to act up on it. Not ever. Witch's honor.

The main reason I didn't want to go to bed was that Thom's presence helped push all my dark thoughts to the back of my mind. How could I trust a guy so much when our meeting led to such impossible circumstances? And why had he befriended me and not Lilah? According to her, he'd barely orbited her life. Did he feel it, too, this thing between us?

HAPPY TO FIND my muscles in normal working order the next morning, I stretched, able to flex and bend without any residual pain. I showered and shampooed my hair with my new conditioner before checking on my cut. The gash was still deep, and blood threatened to spill at the barest touch. I copied nurse Thom's work and wrapped it up in gauze again.

Growls contorting my stomach, I strolled into the kitchen. Lilah was packing a lunch and looking like she hadn't slept at all. Leftover mascara had gathered in the lines under her eyes.

"Alana," she greeted me, yawning, "good thing you came down. I have to leave, and I wanted to say bye."

"You're leaving?" I asked, surprised she wouldn't spend an entire day before driving back, especially since she seemed unbelievably tired.

"Yes, I have exams this week, and I'm teaching a class tonight." She sipped coffee from a huge thermos cup, eyes closed, like it was the most delicious beverage she'd ever tasted.

"A class?"

"I'm a ballet instructor."

It fitted her like wool on a sheep, her toned legs and petite figure the hallmark of all great ballerinas.

As a child, I'd had no patience for it. Mom had retired my cute pink slippers and switched me to jazz and hip-hop instead. I served myself a huge bowl of Lucky Charms and wondered briefly if Thom had stocked them for me.

Lucky Charms were my absolute favorite, a fact well-known among my friends. *They're magically delicious*. I chose the tiniest spoon available and separated the hearts, rainbows and blues moons from the rest, saving those for last.

"Did you study all night?" I asked.

"I used my powers on Liam, to make him feel better, but I'm out of practice. I'll be back soon. In the meantime, I'm just a phone call away."

The cereal crunched between my teeth. "Thanks. I don't know if Thom will let me use a phone, though."

"Don't worry. As long as you follow the rules, he'll let you do *anything*."

I let the insinuation slide.

The mention of the rules dragged my mind down a treacherous and depressing path. The main rule was that I couldn't contact my parents, and I wasn't sure I was ready to abide by it. "I can't stop thinking about my parents, and how worried they must be." The spoonful of sweet milk turned sour, and I set my bowl down. "If I could just call..."

Lilah shook her head in disagreement. "Alana, I wanted to do that too, but..." She took another sip of her steaming cup. Her expression was pained, and tears flooded her eyes. "Thom wasn't always so strict with the rules. Before me, Thom helped a guy named Evan. He had a wife, and he was worried about what she would go through, so he called her. She died. He died. It was a mess. Trust me."

Trust her? I wanted to, but I was flying blind. The cautionary tale had sounded forced. Rehearsed. She'd said the whole thing without taking a breath, avoided eye contact and clearly wanted to change the subject as fast as possible. I hadn't known her for long, but I got the sense she was afraid I'd ask questions about this Evan.

What was she hiding?

7

PAPERCUT

Alana

After Lilah's departure, Thom said he had some work around the house. Did he mean cutting the grass or more along the lines of repelling demons? Afraid of the answer, I didn't ask. With no phone and no Internet, sick of afternoon soap operas, I wandered into the library. Novels were my go-to escape from reality.

The volumes on the shelves had been placed in no particular order and not even in the same orientation. Some were stacked logically with the spines angled towards me, but most were on their sides, stacked half opened on top of each other, and some fore-edges faced outward.

Was this the Mad Hatter's office?

Thom's laptop sat on the desk, unplugged, a soft blue light fading in and out. Three rows of drawers on the wall were built-ins. All locked. Restlessness encircled my heart. *Nope.* Not allowing myself down that slope again.

Cardboard boxes laid, forgotten, against the back wall. A thick layer of dust lifted when I opened the biggest one. *What a mess!*

With a newfound purpose, I gathered supplies in the kitchen. A bucket of water, soap and some rags in hand, I headed back to the library like a soldier equipped to win the war against filth, grime and lazy men who don't unpack their stuff.

A loose bun tied on top of my head to get my long hair out of the way, I tackled the tedious task with enthusiasm. The familiar straightforward act of scrubbing cheered me up. I turned up the radio and sang along Bon Jovi's classic "You Give Love a Bad Name."

After all the surfaces were washed squeaky clean, the vanilla-scented detergent filling the air, I emptied a few of the boxes.

More books, more dusting.

Most of them were old—first-edition-Bible old—the hand-written pages were worn, and deep creases in the spines threatened to tear. Books are sacred, so I handled them with the anxious care of a mother cradling her newborn and decided to reorganize the collection. I grouped similar-sized tomes together, placing small ones on higher racks and big ones closer to the floor.

An ominous atlas lay at the bottom of the last box, and I had to use both hands to lift it. Leather bound, it was massive and had no title. Opening it to the middle, I gaped at the illustration I found.

A nine-legged monster—nine!?—was depicted, its ugly physiognomy detailed and lifelike. The black ink lustered under the electric light. The abomination looked ready to leap out the page and snap off my head with its pointy teeth.

A shiver ran down my spine, and I pressed the book shut. I wasn't the type of girl to be afraid during a horror movie, so my strong reaction surprised me. Ghosts and demons in fiction were funny or disgusting-looking but never scary.

When did I become such a wimp?

It was only a book with some scary drawings in it. Some sort of bestiary. I flipped through a bunch of pages, trying in vain not to squirm.

Each sheet held a title, a description, and a monstrosity. Not written in any language or form readable, the alphabet was nonetheless familiar. Thanks to my history minor and my Viking-obsessed teacher, I recognized it as old Germanic runes.

An overused thread of silk served as an old-fashioned bookmark, and I pulled on it gently. A man with dark eyes, dressed in a black cloak, glared from the paper. No doubt a Shadow Walker. I ran my fingers across the ink, wondering what the runic alphabet meant.

Thom didn't own this book for fun or to scare curious guests. These creatures must all exist, somewhere. Hundreds of different demon species at my fingertips. I used to watch supernatural teen dramas and hope I'd find my own dreamy hero. I'd never fathomed I would come face to face with a monster.

Fate's cruel twist had proved me wrong, but the skeptic part of me couldn't accept that these things walked among us, most people oblivious to their existence. How could humanity be so misinformed?

The heavy book belonged to the bottom shelf, and I put it away, opting to find something readable. A series of smaller ones had intrigued me since I started the cleanup. All bound identically, they were numbered 6 through 23. Where were 1 through 5? It bugged me.

It was a diary, some pages were torn, and some passages were indecipherable, but otherwise, the beautiful script ran like water on the paper.

Journal of Thomas Walker

Thursday, September 6, 1894

I write in this journal in secret since Father thinks it's too great of a risk and a waste of time (for a man). He confiscated the ones I wrote so far, and I can't help trembling at the possibility that he's read them. I will keep all of my writings hidden from now on and pray they will never be found.

I want to leave the South and no longer be forced to suffer his tantrums. Business is going from bad to worse with the labor shortage, and I'm afraid that Father will resort to anything to keep us afloat.

He thinks I'll supersede him, and I have not yet had the courage to tell him otherwise.

Emily is still away at Aunt Marilyn's, and I can't wait for her to return. She always seems to know the words to put Father in a better mood; he's never out of humor with her. James is anxious to see her. I don't think they've ever been apart for so long. But with Mother's death, Emily needs to be with other ladies, and I think Aunt Marilyn's company will do her worlds of good.

James finally stopped running around with those unlawful revolutionists from Thibodaux. I warned him that if father was to learn of his conduct, he would whip him to death.

Wednesday, November 14, 1894

James's tutor says he's becoming a good student and that his grades are improving.

Father hopes he's beginning to show signs of the Darkblood. My poor brother is only fifteen, a small boy. I remember how Father used to scrutinize me at his age and how unnerving I found it. Maybe that's all there is to this newfound interest in school. Emily asked me about the Darkblood curse, and I didn't know what to tell her.

Mother's death has affected her greatly, and I do not want her to worry. She loves James so much. Father thinks they are spending too much time together. I told him twins share a bound that can't be broken, but as usual, he ignored me. He talked about getting her into a private boarding school, and I begged him not to. With her fragile health, the house is the only safe place for her.

Monday, November 19, 1894

Father is gone for the week and left me in charge of the house. I haven't had any time to write. He's coming back today, bringing a distant relative to stay. James was moody all week, more so than usual, and I heard him talk to himself in his room last night. I wish Father would not bring a guest over, especially now that James is not himself.

Emily asked questions again. I told her what Father told me, that the Darkblood is a great legacy and that, if it chooses our family, we will never need for anything again. She asked then, in her melodic voice, how come we called it a curse if it was such a blessing. I admit I've been asking myself the same question.

Monday, December 10, 1894

James' behavior is more erratic than ever. He woke up last night in a cold sweat, screaming in horror. His cries brought tears to my eyes. Father smiled when I asked him about it. I cannot ignore the facts anymore. James is becoming one of *them*, a demon. He can already hear the others whispering in his mind, his link to the Collective almost complete. Father is ecstatic, so proud that his own son will "become as powerful as a God." He kept saying the Darkblood curse almost never chooses a second born as if he'd not dared hope.

I tremble for James and for what it means for our family. I also feel grateful the curse skipped me. Does that make me a bad person? Emily cried when I warned her to keep her distance. She does not understand the danger. I'm afraid losing James will prove too much to handle for her wavering health.

Wednesday, December 19, 1894

They came for James today.

I knew this day would come and yet I cannot believe it. Father beamed with happiness all day, repeating that it's a great honor to be blessed by the Darkblood. I doubt it now more than ever.

Three, they were dressed in black cloaks, just as I remembered. Father welcomed them into our home as if they were royalty. He forbade me to speak, so I just stayed to his right as they discussed my brother's future.

They negotiated a price as if we were selling him. It was nauseating. Father was promised a lot of money and meetings with very influential people. When they left, he said I could only wish my son would be worthy of the same fate.

He is not so moody anymore, though, his disappointment in my normalcy erased.

THE DOOR CLOSED with a loud bang, startling me from my cozy position on the leather couch. My eyes snapped up from my reading in alarm.

"Sorry, didn't mean to scare you," Thom apologized, peeking over my shoulders. "I wouldn't recommend that one, more than half is missing or unintelligible." He sat down next to me.

I put the diary down on my knees. A zillion questions plagued my mind. "This is your ancestor's diary, right? I'm guessing you were named after him?"

"Thomas Walker was the black sheep of the family and the one who built this house. He's dead, but my dad found a chest containing his journals. They explained how he built the place and how to access it. Without this heritage, Liam would still be in the clutches of the bad guys."

Liam would still be one of the bad guys. I bit my bottom lip not to let the words out.

I feared Thom might clamp up if I asked about intimate family stuff, but curiosity got the better of me. "Can I ask you about Liam, about how he became what he is?"

"It started with little things. I was only eleven, and he had just turned fifteen. He became twice as bright as any kid in his class. He grew stronger, smarter and faster until my parents realized something was wrong... beyond the normal teenage changes.

"When he talked to the other demons, we all thought he was talking to himself. The nightmares began, and he would get impossibly restless at night."

"He was taken from us a few weeks later. Demons from the clan came for him and didn't take no for an answer. At first, my mom hoped they could help him." A dark chuckle rasped his throat. "Help wasn't on their mind. They shaped him into a weapon. He wasn't learning anything *good* with them. It took my dad two years of pretending not to care to be admitted in their little... club. He visited the Walker's estate in Louisiana one year and came back with hope."

I sneered, "There's a posh demon country club in Louisiana?"

"Yes, my dad was raised near the heart of the Walker clan, but he moved to get away from his father. Dad was the middle child, the fourth of seven boys. None of them became a Shadow Walker, and my grandfather was furious. Seven sons and not one chosen, he disavowed them all. When Liam turned, it was a different story, and my dad became the prodigal child. An old connection helped find Liam, but it took three more years to get him back.

"We grew up in Vermont, Liam and I. My parents were big fans of hiking and skiing. After we moved here to Virginia, my mom home-schooled me through high school."

Gosh, his adolescence had been practically ruined by all this supernatural drama. At least, I was an adult—somewhat.

"What happened to your parents?" I asked with a small voice.

His face darkened. "When my parents got Liam back, Liam's 'mentor' was pissed that his 'student' was no longer under his influence. It made him look weak, so he hunted them to get revenge. It took him a couple of years to find us, but he was like a dog with a bone..."

The unshed tears filled in the blanks. A demon had indeed killed his parents and not a car accident. Thom averted his gaze and glanced around at the unrecognizable room. The fruits of my afternoon work provided a welcomed distraction. "I feel awful that you cleaned up my mess, but good job. I've been putting this off for ages."

The dryer dinged loudly from the next room.

"I'll get it." I stood up and headed for the laundry room.

Thom followed me into the hallway. "You don't have to do laundry."

"I want to. It's a good distraction."

He hesitated, but I waved him away.

Home economics might not be my favorite subject because of the cooking part, but I transcended the art of laundry.

Many think of it as a boring, repetitive chore, but I disagree. The smell of fabric softener, dividing the colors between whites and darks, splitting rough from delicate, the comforting warmth of the fabric fresh out the dryer... fantastic. Plus, you push a bunch of buttons and get an hour-long break. What's not to love?

As I bent down to retrieve the load, I inventoried the batch: shirts, pants and a tablecloth mingled in the basket.

The sight of my "Bite me" T-shirt brought bile to my mouth. Suddenly, oxygen was sparse. The retched acid burned my throat as I swallowed it back down. The cute drawing of a gingerbread man missing a bite had once been my favorite shirt, but, at the moment, its happy eyes were mocking me.

Last time I'd folded this particular item of clothing, I'd been looking through my laundry for a sexy outfit for my birthday party. I'd worn the fun shirt the next day at my parent's, not knowing it was the only piece of clothing I'd get to keep.

The chain of events that had brought me here had started with this childish piece of fabric, and its innocence affronted me. How dare it be the same—unchanged, untainted—while my life had gone up in smoke?

I felt like screaming out loud, but wouldn't that be over-dramatic? Instead, I pressed my lips into a thin line.

I'd only been here for days, but each of them felt like a decade.

I missed my tiny apartment. It wasn't fancy, but it was mine. I missed my mom and dad and our Sunday night dinners. I missed going to the movies with Kelly and sneaking into a second show. Even my pompous Study of Ancient Civilization teacher haunted me. The essay about ancient Greece I'd sweated so hard over would rot away in a dump.

What would happen to all my stuff? In a year or two, would there be any trace of my existence left in the world besides my parent's grief?

Back in high school, when I'd gotten really worked up about my exams, I'd made to-do lists to regain control. I grabbed a pen from the office and scribbled a few words down on a paper towel, already confident I had a better grip on things.

TO DO:

1. Get rid of my crush on Thom
2. Learn to control my powers
3. Ask Lilah to buy me a bra !!!

I couldn't afford to spiral out of control, so I gathered my homesickness and crammed it inside the tight seal of metaphorical Tupperware.

As if it was a disgusting insect, I pinched the shirt with my thumb and index and flung it behind the washer. It would still be there if I ever wanted it back. In the meantime, I could work on overcoming my sense of loss. I threw myself into the mindless act of folding and ignored the jabbing spikes tucked around my heart.

THE TWO-WEEK TRIAL ran its course. I passed the time reading more books and asking more questions. Lilah visited again and demonstrated her powers to me. The peace it brought me was the best proof I could have hoped for. I didn't think there was any way this could be a fabricated hoax. She was a witch, no doubt about it.

And Thom kept his promise.

I came downstairs to find his cell phone and car keys laid down on the table. He sat at the opposite end, his face damn serious. "The two weeks are up."

I nodded and rested a hand on the back of a chair.

"You can call whoever you want. I can drive you anywhere you wish. I did my best to convince you of the danger you're in. It'll break my heart if you leave, but I also know I can't keep you against your will. In the end, it's your choice to make," he said, his blue eyes pleading me to make the right decision.

I'd written a letter to my parents in which I told them I was okay but that I needed to stay away for a while. It was tucked under my pillow upstairs. I'd thought about masquerading it as a heat bill, a feat easily done if Thom gave me access to a computer, a printer, and a blank envelope. Even if they were under surveillance, I doubted an innocent heat bill would attract any attention, and I'd hide my letter inside.

It might ease their minds and allow them to go on with their lives, but, knowing my parents, it wouldn't be near enough to convince them I was out of danger. I wasn't the type to run away without saying goodbye.

Would they believe I'd had the sudden urge to go on a vacation in the middle of a semester, seconds after my father had almost died?

I didn't think so.

So many things could go wrong. I was terrified it would be intercepted or that they might give it to the police even if I insisted they didn't show it to anyone. A letter full of love. A letter that could get them killed if it fell into the wrong hands.

I didn't want to send it anymore, not if it meant risking their lives.

"I'm staying." My voice broke. It was my choice, but it was a hard one. "But I wish things were different."

"I know." Thom wrapped me up in his arms, and I welcomed the comfort.

Grief takes on many forms, and I had to grieve for my old life. The two weeks had merely been borrowed time during which I could entertain the idea of going back. A lie to ease the pain. Forward was the only option. I hid my face in Thom's chest, and it hit me how much I trusted him. His genuine sorrow only solidified my resolve as I accepted my new reality.

I couldn't go back.

8

RESTLESS

Alana

A comfortable routine settled between Thom and I in the month that followed. In the mornings, he was absent, sequestered with Liam or otherwise occupied with groceries and the upkeep of the house.

The bad habit of sleeping in infected me. When you've got nowhere to be and nothing to do, it's hard to be a morning person.

Half the library's collection of diaries—the ones in English—were piled next to my bed. I was committed to educating myself about the supernatural world.

Most afternoons, I spent countless hours in the fully-equipped gym, and the journey from couch potato to semi-competent athlete was arduous.

It would take many months for my efforts to come to fruition, but I already ran faster and for longer stretches of time than I'd ever thought possible. I was in the best shape of my life.

Running was not the only activity on the menu. I'd learned how to protect my hands and box the hell out of the punching bag dangling at the back of the gym. It was good exercise and more fun than I'd anticipated. Every day I discovered something more gruesome about Shadow Walkers and demons in general, so I'd asked Thom to teach me to fight. I never wanted to be helpless again.

The training sessions were the highlights of my boredom, and I poured my heart and soul into them. Our evenings were spent playing a game or watching a movie. Thom had also given me access to his computer, though I'd agreed with his suggestion to ban me from the Internet in case the urge to google myself or go on Facebook got too strong.

Despite my feeble efforts to the contrary, we were growing closer. I would let my head rest on his shoulder on movie nights, and he would grab my hand when I was homesick. As friends, of course. I wasn't about to let myself fall in love with the man that had kidnapped me to save my life. I wasn't completely insane. Yet.

But I couldn't hide my enthusiasm when Thom joined me early in the gym on Saturday afternoon. He was wearing a white shirt with black exercise pants, which meant he wanted to spar. He always wore shorts when he ran or bench-pressed.

"Ready to get beat-up?" I asked from the treadmill.

He chuckled. "Always."

My sensei and I dabbled in mock combat but only the basic moves. I couldn't inflict any real damage yet.

I grabbed a towel and wiped the sweat away from my face. Thom removed his long-sleeved shirt, and I watched him from the corner of my eyes, stealing a glance at his abs as his undershirt hiked up his stomach.

I looked away and stretched my arms.

His smile disappeared as he drew near. "Shit, Alana. We have to be more careful."

I followed his gaze to the flurry of bruises on my lower arm. I didn't mind the purple marks. In fact, I was quite proud of them. "Don't worry, I can barely feel them."

I didn't want him to go easy on me.

His eyes narrowed. "I find that hard to believe."

I arched my eyebrows. Was he calling me a liar?

"Fine, I won't hold back. But tell me if you need a break."

I took a defensive stance, ready for action.

We spent half an hour revisiting the different techniques to dodge a punch and deflect a blow to the stomach. I avoided almost all the punches, and Thom looked impressed.

"Are you ready for something new?" He asked as he passed a hand through his hair, the ends curling around his ears.

"Yes."

"Let's practice against someone who grabs you from behind."

"Okay." I turned my back to him.

"First one we're going to do is called a bear hug, and it's easier to escape than a rear chokehold. A rear chokehold would be higher around your neck." He closed the distance between us and put his arms around my shoulders. "I won't squeeze you for now, so you can get used to the feeling."

This trick put Thom flush against me. He was gentle and slow not to freak me out, but I wasn't freaking out. Instead of fear, a blazing heat swarmed into my chest.

"When you're ready, you're going to put all your weight to the outside, backstop my knee and try to knock me off balance," he said, his breath hot on my neck.

"Like this?" I tried to make sense of his instructions.

"Not exactly."

Not exactly was Thom's polite speech for *not at all.* He explained the whole thing again and helped me place my leg right.

"Now, you're going to strike your left elbow straight up at my face while you're pushing your entire weight against the back of my knee."

We repeated the exercise a few times. We were just rehearsing the movements, so he didn't use any real strength. It felt more like a snuggle than an attack. I took longer than needed to break free each time and enjoyed his strong arms around me. Guilty as charged.

Yes, I was sweaty, and my hair was all messed up. Yes, I was wearing sportswear one size too big and no make-up, but, as I leaned one last time into Thom to get into the correct position, my butt brushed his crotch, and there was no doubt he found me attractive.

If I hadn't been all red already from the exercise, I would have blushed crimson. I repressed the crazy impulse to back into him even more and finished the routine instead. I didn't want to embarrass him or make things awkward, so I feigned I hadn't noticed anything. We both pretended we weren't more breathless than we ought to be.

Thom took a few steps back. "Great job. We'll pick it up here tomorrow."

"Okay." I patted down my face and upper chest with a towel.

"I'll go see how Lilah's doing."

Lilah visited every weekend and on Wednesdays when she had the afternoon off from classes. She spent hours at a time in the basement, performing her feeling therapy on Liam.

Thom headed down to the dungeon. I went upstairs and set the shower water to cold to wipe any sexual thoughts from my mind.

When I returned to the kitchen, Thom was checking on the food. "Lilah should be here any second."

I set the table while we waited. After a few minutes, I grew restless. She'd never been this late for dinner before. The possibility that she might trust Liam despite Thom's warnings and get killed gnawed at me. Lilah had a selfless soul and put others before herself. Liam's recovery mattered more to her than her health. I opened my mouth to ask Thom to go check on her when the sound of her footsteps thudding up the stairs uncoiled the tension that constricted my stomach.

With huge dark circles under her eyes and ghostly pale skin, she could have been a walk-on for a zombie movie with little added makeup. "I stayed as long as I could, but it drains me. I'm exhausted." The disappointment in her voice was thick. She put way too much weight on her tiny shoulders.

"You're doing wonders of good for him," Thom said.

I echoed the sentiment. "He's right, you're awesome."

The pep talk rolled over her like rain on the umbrella of her misery. Hot tears ran down her cheeks. "It's still not enough."

Lilah missed Liam a lot. At first, I'd thought she was just being a good friend, but my instincts told me something was amiss. Liam consumed her every thought.

Even after weeks, she always rushed to his side when she arrived, worried sick that he'd regressed during her absence.

And he always had.

THAT NIGHT, I got up to get a glass of milk from the kitchen, a trick Dad used to cure my insomnia as a child. I gazed out at the night from the huge hexagonal bay window that opened on the terrace and sipped my drink joyfully.

Moon rays reflected upon puddles left by a late evening thunderstorm. Eyes closed, I pretended the drizzle tickled my cheeks. Since I loved the sun, missing the rain was a damn giveaway I'd been stuck inside for too long. I gulped down the rest of the comforting liquid and licked my lips.

A moving shadow caught my eye, and my startled gasp made it stop in its tracks. The standstill allowed me to recognize Lilah's slender form.

She tightened the sash around her silk nightgown and played with the lace hem. Dried tears were visible on her cheeks. She had gone to see Liam again.

"How is he?" I asked, hoping she would open up.

"The same," she looked contrite, as if I'd caught her doing something wrong, "and I can't sleep."

"Want milk?"

She shook her head no. "Maybe we could meditate?"

Not a New Age fiber in my body, I forced myself to keep an open mind. "Like yoga?"

"Meditation helps a lot with controlling our powers."

I would have done anything to ease her anxiousness. "Let's try it."

A small smile curved her worried pout, and she guided me in front of the couch. She sat on the plush carpet, her legs forming a flawless lotus position. I crouched down, imitating her stance as best as I could, an overgrown frog to her water lily. She grabbed both my hands and drew a few deep, calming breaths.

If I confided in her first, she might be more inclined to share her troubles. "You know, I never tried to heal my hand, I'm afraid." The admission cost me.

Fear is not an emotion I'm comfortable with. I'd take angry, disappointed, even sad over the stinging vulnerability of fear. Fear implies weakness. Uselessness. Helplessness. I hate those words.

"It took me a while to control my abilities. I was a snail compared to the others. If only I'd learned faster, Evan might still be here," Lilah said, her speech heavy with unshed tears. “Evan is my personal apocalypse. After his wife died, he—" She choked on a sob. "He cut his arms open with a razor blade."

My heart sunk, and I squeezed her hand. *That's why she avoided the subject.*

"Thom blames himself for letting Evan call his wife in the first place, but it's my fault. I knew how wretched he felt. I should have helped him. I should have stopped him. I—"

"Hey. It's not your fault."

"Thank you for saying that." She sniffled and wiped her tears with her sleeve. "I can't teach you much, but I can try to explain. There's this place in your mind that feels different. You find it and nurture it until it's easily accessible. Then, you get it to behave."

Despite the guilt and the crushing pressure Lilah inflicted upon herself, I had no doubt she'd be a great teacher. I didn't know how to begin searching for a special place in my brain, let alone nurture it, so I concentrated on my breathing. Out of respect, I swallowed a nervous laugh.

"I don't know what to look for," I admitted.

"Don't worry. You might have to wait for Liam to help you before you make any progress. With his powers, he can push you in the right direction." After a few inhales and exhales, she let out a distraught whimper. Tremors shook her hands, so I clasped them tighter.

"What's wrong?" I asked.

"He's in so much pain," she breathed, tearing herself away from my grasp. She hugged her knees to her chest and rocked back and forth, like a wounded animal, and a light bulb ignited in my head.

She didn't just read other people's emotions. She shared them, and Liam was in agony downstairs. I had been a moron not to understand the ramifications of her power.

"Don't feel bad, I kept it to myself," she said.

"Can't you turn it off?" Walking through life feeling everybody's pain and anguish sounded not only inconvenient, but enough to lose your mind.

"Usually, yes, but his pain is so fluid, it drips through the cracks."

No wonder she was always on edge.

I forced Lilah into bed and stood beside her door until I was sure she wouldn't sneak back downstairs.

Our conversation had been a real eye opener. The drawback of her powers was immense, and it got me thinking about the arduous work ahead to get control over my own. Better to start as soon as possible.

Sitting crossed legged on my bed, I unwrapped my injured hand and let it rest on my knee. The wound was expanding, an inch wider than it first had been. Unnatural. That night, Liam had consumed my powers, and it had left a supernatural scar. My best guess was that it would never heal without supernatural intervention. Good thing I appeared to have healing powers because it was time to put them to use.

My palms were sweaty; I hadn't studied for this. Where to start? I emptied my mind as Lilah had advised, on the hunt for this specific area of my brain that was supposedly attuned to this dark new world.

...

The quest was fruitless, so I massaged my aching temples, coming up with a new plan.

Instead of looking inward, I focused hard on the anomaly sliced into my hand, squinting the way they do on witches' TV shows.

Heal.

Close.

Be gone.

Disappear.

Shoo.

Did I have to speak at it out loud? "Come on, heal."

I half expected the cut to catch on fire or get bigger, like in Harry Potter when the students mess up a spell, but nothing happened. These so-called powers prevented me from having a normal life, and I couldn't use them? What a load of crap! I clicked my tongue in frustration. They were wrong; I wasn't a witch at all. At least, not a good one.

The cut was painful as ever. *Wait! Did I see one extremity curl up like it was smirking at me? No, I must have imagined it.*

Straight jacket for one, please.

I muffled a scream into my pillow.

Lilah had warned me magic had a long and fastidious learning curve, but I didn't want to spend months cooped inside.

I'd healed my dad without any effort, after all. Thom had explained the powers had been dormant for years, waiting for the right moment.

And the right moment was over.

I got out of bed and searched the library. All the volumes I'd read had mostly been diaries about the inner workings of the Shadow Walker's hierarchy and their *modus operandi*. While interesting, I needed a more concise reference about witches. I flipped through a few and found something promising. The glossary had a preface, translated from Creole by Thom. I recognized his neat penmanship. The original entries were in alphabetical order and mixed English and Creole throughout the whole volume. Thom had scribbled notes in the margins, but they were far from thorough.

I grabbed the Creole to English dictionary, opened a blank notebook and started a proper translation. It took me the rest of the night to decipher the entries regarding witches, but, between my efforts and Thom's notes, I ended up with a coherent definition.

***Sòsyè - Chans.* Witches (randoms).** *Random witches are born out of non-*

magic parents. They activate anywhere from a couple months to seconds before midnight on their twentieth birthday. They are usually less powerful and dangerous than proper witches, but it might be because the latter are trained since birth. They are left to their own devices. Easy to identify as most do not know how to mask their flare and auras, they sell for a nifty price on the slave market.

Sòsyè – Reyèl. Witches and warlocks (true). *Proper witches belong to covens. They hide within society, craft potions and cast powerful spells to remain hidden. They breed between themselves and train their children from infancy. Captured, they will kill themselves to protect the many. The ones that threaten their secrecy die. It is unknown how many members they have, or how many covens there are. Stay away.*

Shadow Walkers. *Powerful half-demons excelling in trickery, mischief and deceit. Only males. They mingle sparingly with other demons and half-breeds. Obsessed with consuming witch blood since the late 1900s, they fight fiercely for every drop available on the dark trade. Can regenerate quickly from wounds, though are susceptible to aconite, killed by evil bones and neutralized by large quantities of iron. They share a mental link through what they call the Collective, though the details and the extent of the connection are unknown.*

Aconite. *Sometimes called wolfsbane, monkshood, or Queen of all Poison. Can be distilled to make a highly efficient poison that hinders the powers of a variety of demons and half-breeds.*

Evil bone. *Bone harvested from an original demon's skeleton. The few pieces that still exist were shaped into weapons or jewelry. Priceless. Kills all kinds of demons.*

. . .

Silver. *Silver is used as a powerful ingredient in healing potions. It's also the only metal known to harm shifters.*

Shifters. *Shifters are demons able to transform their entire being or a part of their body into a human or animal shape. The shape depends on the sub-species.*

9

THE WOLF

Alana

Another month passed before Thom and Lilah showed muted optimism about Liam. Thom and I were playing Scrabble at the kitchen table one evening, and something was eating away at him. He'd spelled 'WORRY', 'FAILURE' and 'FEAR' one after the other.

"Alana, I need a favor," he said after he suffered a crushing defeat. His stare played cat and mouse with mine. "It's time to test Liam, and I need your help."

Test Liam? How? A bad feeling thumped in my veins. My intuition told me this *test* would not go well, and I wished I had to sit down for my SATs instead.

I stared at the board on the table and let my hair fall over my eyes. "Shouldn't Lilah be here?"

Whatever he hoped I could do to help test Liam, Lilah would do a hundred times better. I would have preferred to stay out of the rehab loop.

"No." Thom's tone was categorical.

"Why not?"

"Because it might fail..."

Gosh, he was right, and I was a selfish idiot. If it failed, and I had no doubt it would, Lilah would cry herself to sleep even harder than usual. I didn't want that, so I nodded in agreement.

We climbed down the stairs. Always the gentleman, Thom opened the basement door for me. I hesitated on the first step. The paint peeled off the walls, the centennial wood exposed.

A foreboding sense of doom constricted my chest. I avoided the spider webs as best as I could and climbed down the creaky stairwell. It led to a small antechamber, where another door waited for us.

And what a door!

The arched entryway was massive, the kind you'd expect to find in a nuclear bunker. Long streaks of rust freckled the steel door, the bright orange sticking out against the darkness of the metal. Thom used all his strength to open the way, his biceps straining against his long-sleeved shirt. The hinges creaked as the door reluctantly gave way. Clouds of dust rose, and I sneezed. The sound reverberated in the cavernous vault as we walked in.

The basement had a definite dungeon vibe. Long, narrow-gaped bars separated the main room in half. These delicate bars were all that prevented Liam from killing us? I'd imagined an armored plated wall with a tiny window to pass food. Bulbs of light dangled from exposed wires at regular intervals, but their feeble glow didn't reach the nooks and crannies. The lights on the prisoner's side had been smashed flush against the electrical plates.

Every hair on my body stood up to attention, and my ribs felt like they might shatter. Shadows roamed free where Liam stood, a dark shape in a darker corner. A dangerous panther pacing its cage.

My muscles were made to walk, eat and play. His existed to pounce, maim and kill, and they undulated with grace under his black shirt, each feline movement sharp, calculated. Barefoot, his toes dug into the carpet under his feet, ready to get traction if needed. He hadn't shaved since that night, and the untamed beard polished his savage look.

Last time I'd seen his serious face, it'd been smudged by the burgundy shade of my dried blood. His eyes were not as dark, but the intensity behind them was the same.

This demon would kill me without a second thought.

A rudimentary bed stood in the corner of the cell, the sheets in knots over the mattress, and a separate bathroom was nestled in the back. Everything had been done to make it comfortable.

Thom whispered in my ear, "He kept his face straight. That's very good. Last week, he would have gone crazy just looking at you."

Last week? What were we doing here? Weren't we jumping the gun?

"Can't he use his powers to come out?" I asked. After everything I'd been told, I was positive bars weren't much of an issue to a Shadow Walker.

"The cell walls and bars are entirely made of iron, the one metal that weakens his powers."

I had read about this in Thomas Walker's diary and the glossary, but I didn't understand how something so trivial could hurt them. "I thought the iron thing was a myth."

Thom's eyebrows raised in question. "Why?"

I shrugged, "I don't know. It's just so common."

He cracked a mischievous smile. "You expected silver?"

I gave his shoulder a playful slap. "I don't think he's a werewolf."

He chuckled, and I rolled my eyes, secretly loving these quarrels between us.

"You guys are so cute." Liam's low baritone sliced through me and resonated like a gong in every fiber of my body. "Not that I don't enjoy the show. Few distractions are available at present, but are you here to flirt or to set me free?"

A vicious blush crept up my chest. *Nobody should have a voice like that.*

Thom considered the question while he observed his brother's reaction to my presence. Liam's wolf stare flicked over to me every few seconds, and I was skeptical of his recovery.

Thom passed me his pocket knife. "We need blood."

The first cut on my hand still hadn't healed and burned like hell, so I hesitated.

"Oh, come on, man. Don't make her cut herself," Liam said. The sugary compassionate tone convinced me, and I cut the same hand, just below the gauze. Blood formed small droplets in my palm, and I made a fist to let them fall to the floor.

A deafening thunder slammed the air, and the ground beneath my feet quaked as Liam threw himself against the bars. The force of impact between his body and the iron stripes sent him tumbling down, but he sprung back up with the ease of a master in gymnastics, his blurry shape difficult to follow. The white of his eyes had disappeared, his mouth deformed by a hungry grimace. A mad man's shriek echoed around us as he tried to reach me through the bars, his hands clawing at emptiness.

Thom cringed but remained silent as we exited. Once the heavy door was back in place, his shoulders sagged. "It's a good sign that he fooled me for a second. I thought it was worth a shot."

The saddest puppy dog look creased his handsome face, and I knew a quick fix was impossible. It cost him to keep his brother in a cage. What could I say? I rested my head on his shoulder and entwined my fingers with his.

Heat pooled in my belly when he rubbed slow circles on the back of my hand with his thumb. I raised my gaze to search his, but he was staring dead ahead with melancholy.

THE SIGHT of Liam brought back in full force the memories of that fateful night, and I spent the rest of the day banishing them to the back of my mind.

But, as I laid alone in bed, I relived it all.

I couldn't think about anything other than the crazed look on Liam's face when he'd pulled me close in that alley. I recalled vividly the fire in his eyes as he'd kissed my wrist, and the choked whimper that had fallen off his lips as he'd buried his face in my neck.

My heart ran, a wild rabbit in my ribcage, and I didn't feel safe anymore. What if Liam escaped the basement? What would he do? Would Thom be able to stop him? The answers that came to mind sent a myriad of pessimistic outcomes tumbling behind my eyes, full of blood, screams and tears.

I had a nightmare.

I was walking hand in hand with Thom in a forest. The light shone through the trees and fanned in distinctive rays across the kaleidoscope of colors blanketing the earth. Autumn leaves cracked under our footsteps.

Laughter died in my throat as his knuckles caressed the side of my face. Eyes closed, I waited for the kiss I knew was coming. Soft lips brushed mine, and I held my breath, the sweet rush of a desired first kiss spiraling in my bones.

The air chilled around us. The gentle touch turned to icy stone, and a hand clasped around my throat in a tight, unforgiving hold. Thom had disappeared, replaced by his demon brother.

Airways crushed, I couldn't breathe, and my vision blurred as if I was under water. Strong spasms shook my ribcage, and my lungs burned for air as they tried to expand despite the lack of oxygen.

Another figure stepped close, then another, and another until five black cloaks laughed in a circle around me as I died.

Dreams were an intricate part of my nights since childhood, but they revolved around boys, my favorite TV shows and school. Bad dreams had me fail my driver's license test or lose all my teeth, but nothing like *that.*

Shaken, I combed my hair away from my face and got up. A light snoring sound tickled my ears as I passed Thom's room. Careful not to startle him, I walked into his bedroom and breathed, "Thom?"

Unintelligible grunts answered me.

A grin tugged at the corner of my lips. "I'm having trouble sleeping. Can I stay here?" I asked, blood gathering on my cheeks. Thank the heavens we were in the dark. I felt silly, but I was desperate for a few hours of calm, and I knew he wouldn't say no.

Complete darkness blinded me, but I heard him shift around. "Of course, I'll make us coffee, and we can talk."

"Or I could sleep here for a while?"

A soft "okay" made my heart flutter.

Not willing to cast down all boundaries, I laid over the covers and closed my eyes with nothing but Thom's smile on my mind.

AFTER A DREAM-FREE, restful sleep, I took advantage of the mere inches separating our faces to study him. There was a softness to his features I hadn't seen in a while.

He was lying on his stomach. His naked arms were tucked underneath his head, and his white shirt hiked up to his lower back, giving me a sinful view of his golden skin. A rush of heat squeezed my stomach, and I bit my lips, grateful I was wearing a thick long-sleeved shirt with pants.

His lips curved up, and he blinked. *Busted.*

I fumbled with the edge of the pillow. Did he remember our quick conversation last night? Either way, he could get the wrong idea. "Sorry, bad nightmare."

"No problem." He yawned and laid on his side. "Was it because of Liam?"

I nodded and avoided his gaze.

Thom let out a small sigh. "I was sixteen when a man—my dad never admitted it, but I'm sure he was a demon—delivered Liam to us here, chained into an iron casket. The man put him in the cell and opened the lid. Liam was rabid, eyes all black, and it scared the shit out of me. I didn't recognize him. My mother cried her eyes out, and I didn't sleep for days.

"I was almost seventeen when I saw my brother again, but he wasn't the same guy I knew." Thom scratched his stubble before shaking his head as if to rid himself of the memory. "He got better, bit by bit. After a while, he was somewhat Liam again, but what they did to him, what they made him do, nobody should go through that..." There was a long pause before he added, "It could have been me."

I was so glad that it wasn't.

"I feared this day would come when Liam would relapse," he said on a sigh.

I echoed Lilah's adamant mantra, "He'll get better." I had no idea what I was talking about, but it seemed to ease him just the same.

"I have a confession to make." He had the sweetest boyish expression on his face, and my heart skipped a beat. He went on, "Of course, I wouldn't wish this life on anybody, but there's a part of me that's happy you're here, that I'm not alone in this huge house for God knows how long. Can you forgive me?"

Could I forgive him for being happy I was stuck here? The answer was as surprising as it was honest. "Yes." Butterflies took flight in my stomach, and I caught myself snatching a glance at his lips. The air around us crackled, and I was almost sure he would lean in and kiss me, almost sure I would let him.

Except he didn't. The applause from my rational mind was deafening. Too much, too soon. Here I was lying in bed with him, although I'd promised myself to keep my distance. I had never been in such a tiff with my heart. "*The heart has its reasons of which reason knows nothing.*" Well, my heart better get in line and quick. Its reasons wouldn't have to glue back together the broken pieces left by this doomed romance. I would, and I didn't care for messes.

10

ONCE UPON A DREAM

Alana

Summer was in full bloom with longer days and shorter nights, and I had to observe the changes from afar, unable to *live*. The heartache of being idle, as if placed on a shelf for later use, grew each day. Red flowers in the planter next to the kitchen's bay window taunted me with their joviality. Squirrels chasing each other through the trees annoyed me with their sense of fun.

Cabin fever makes you moody.

Patience came at a higher price, and shortcomings in my supernatural education with Lilah were multiplying like bunnies in spring. Meditation frustrated me, and I had no talent for magic.

I lounged in the breakfast nook for hours on end and sulked.

My shoulders rested against the glass and absorbed what sun rays I could, a fragile flower safely tucked in her greenhouse. I was sick of being fragile; I wanted to be strong.

Thom slammed the basement's door opened and entered the kitchen with a radiant smile. "Are you hungry? I'm starving."

"Liam doing well?" I asked, surprised to see him so chipper.

"Great, we played cards. He's bored out of his mind."

Not pitying the bored demon, I glowered, "Aren't we all?"

"Someone's grumpy."

"I'm not grumpy."

He grinned. "Says all grumpy people."

He was right. "Sorry, just tired."

Tired of standing still. Tired of reading depressing books about my slim chances of survival.

I rose to my feet, and he wrapped an arm around my shoulders. I rested my head on his chest, grateful for the comfort. My heart swelled when he pecked my forehead. "You're in a good mood."

"Liam is ready. I need your help again, but let's have lunch first."

Another cut. Ugh. "No problem," I lied.

We made sandwiches, but the ham and lettuce held a bitter aftertaste of apprehension. Thom was a nervous mess. His fingers kept scratching at his neck, and I could feel the vibrations caused by his jittery legs through the table.

I abandoned my plate in the sink and forced a neutral expression on my face. "I'm ready."

"Okay."

As we returned to the dungeon, the weight on my heart pulsed, the flutter of fear licking my ribs.

Liam was slouched in the darkest corner of the sterile cell, his back against the wall and his knees propped up. He was throwing a ball on the opposing panel and catching it as it bounced back to him. He looked as though he'd been doing this for hours and didn't spare a single glance in our direction. His knuckles crushed the ball at our approach, the repetitive chain of movements broken.

Silence stretched on. His shimmer splashed around the edges of his body, the shadows harnessed by the skin, struggling to break free.

With a reproachful scowl directed at Thom, he finally said, "I told you not to bring *her* here." The word *her* fell off his lips like a curse word.

"It's been a while. You're better." Thom's faith was palpable as he rebutted his brother's biting tone with calm encouragement.

Liam peeled himself off the floor. "I am not." Muscles rippled under his dark shirt, ready to pounce. Even though I avoided eye contact, I could tell the precise moment his gaze roamed over me. I was dinner.

Content to keep the beast in the cage, I was more than willing to agree, but Thom's features were lit with determination. "We'll use Alana's blood, and you'll know I'm right." Thom passed me the knife and waved for me to proceed.

God, I longed for a future in which cutting myself would not be needed ever again.

As I executed the dreadful task, I watched Liam, expecting him to go berserk. He gritted his teeth together and gripped the steel bars with both hands. Ragged breaths heaved his chest, all because of the freckles of blood peppering my palm.

Rattled at how potent these tiny red dots were, I wondered how it felt to be unraveled by such a trivial sight. *Not good, I bet.*

"Put your hand through the bars," Thom asked.

Liam consented. I noted his cut was healed whereas mine nagged me with its indifference to the basic rules of biology. Thom pressed into the fresh nick on my hand and gathered a few drops on his finger. He walked to Liam and smeared the blood in his brother's trembling palm.

Liam cringed, and his hand twitched. From the top of his raven hair to his toes, his body stilled, transformed from hot-blooded predator to marble statue. The air buzzed with electricity as he cracked one eye open, then the other, and wiped the blood on his pants. "I guess I am better," he breathed, surprised.

Thom's frown melted into a luminous smile, and the tension evaporated. "Welcome back, bro." He opened the jail's door.

The two boys crashed into a heartfelt man hug, patting each other's back, but their joy at being reunited didn't quite reach Liam's eyes. I took a careful step backwards. Was it safe?

Liam stiffened when I skirted away from him. "I need to take care of stuff," he said before he disappeared in a blur.

Thom gave my fingers a reassuring squeeze. "Don't worry," he seemed to think for a moment and added, "just don't cut yourself by accident, okay?"

I answered his humorous plea with a grave nod, not feeling better about the situation. Impatient to leave this creepy basement, ideally forever, I hurried up the stairs. Once in the kitchen, the knot in my stomach loosened.

Thom rubbed his hands together. "Want to help me cook a good reunion dinner?"

"Sure."

He got a knife and handed it to me but pulled away as I went to grab it. "That was a test. No sharp objects, remember?" A big goofy grin stretched his lips. "I'll chop the onions. You can get me a large pot and a pan."

I stuck my tongue out at him. He chuckled and grabbed a cutting board.

As we made dinner, he made a huge deal of *helping* me with all the things I could remotely hurt myself with, like the can opener and the grater. He was totally yanking my chain. I huffed and rolled my eyes, but I was secretly beaming.

An incredible change had taken place. A huge weight had been lifted off Thom's shoulders. The carefree guy from art class was back.

He was scrubbing the counter when I plunged a spoon into the sauce and blew on it to cool it down. He watched expectantly as I tasted the fruits of our labor. It tasted great, but I grimaced.

His brow pulled together. "Is it bad?"

"Taste this." I got a goop of sauce with a new spoon and held my hand under it as I raised it to his mouth.

At the last second, instead of aiming for his mouth, I smeared the sauce across his cheek. "Ah. Got you!"

He dragged his thumb across the tomato stain and licked it. "Yum."

We both erupted into a fit of laughter, and I was gasping for air when Liam walked into the kitchen. His arrival sobered me up quicker than hearing my parents come home early while I made out with my first boyfriend.

Jet black hair wet and jaw shaved, he looked less scary. Maybe ninety-five percent scary, five percent human. Or ninety-six to four.

"Alana made spaghetti. We should celebrate," Thom offered, pointing to the sum of our efforts simmering in the pot.

Liam's sharp look traveled from my arm to the tip of my head, and my insides curled. Eyes glued to the ground, I resisted the pull to meet the beckoning stare.

"Not hungry, thanks. Going for a run." Liam turned on his heels at normal human speed.

Why would he leave so quickly? I couldn't help but feel responsible for his sudden change of heart.

THOM AND I ATE, washed the dishes, and spent the rest of the evening playing Scrabble.

"Who's kicking whose ass?" I teased after winning my second game of the night.

"Yeah, you rock."

Amused at how frustrated he sounded, I grinned, but my playful smile morphed into a yawn.

Thom put the board away. "Let's call it a night."

I couldn't put it off forever. We'd flirted all evening, his mood elevated by the events of the day and my inhibitions lowered by the alcohol I'd consumed to calm my nerves.

He walked me to my door, and I let my back rest against the wood. This was the closest to a real date we'd ever gotten.

My stomach fluttered when he bent down and kissed the corner of my mouth. "Good night, Lana."

My emotions had gone up and down like a roller coaster all day, and I didn't trust my judgment enough to angle my lips to his. "Good night."

The cool doorknob twisted open to reveal an equally cold room. Strange. Goosebumps scattered across my arms, and a tingle pinched the back of my neck. I glanced around the silent room, but nothing was out of place, so I hurried and crawled under the heavy covers.

The sheets were itchy under my palms, and the dark ceiling crept down on me as I clicked off the bedside table lamp.

I tossed, turned and gnawed at my nails. If only Thom's room acted as a buffer between mine and Liam's, it might have been easier to relax. What if the demon fancied a midnight bite? The coppery tang of blood invaded my mouth.

Oh, stop it! I hugged a pillow to my chest and forced my mind to go blank.

I MUST HAVE FALLEN asleep because, next thing I knew, I was dreaming.

A cloaked figure hunted me through the house. I couldn't run. I couldn't scream. The world turned upside down, and I couldn't even move.

Wrists tied above my head, I laid stark naked on a bed of black sheets. The silk caressed my buttocks as I shifted. A halo of light rose from my white skin, preventing the opaque darkness to swallow me. Shadows moved, and I tugged on my restraints, my arms weakened by fear. Crimson toenails caught my eyes, matching my fingernails. Locks of red hair covered my breasts, darker than it should have been. Bloodier.

The shadow came into focus as it closed in on me and stepped into my glow. Serene, Liam stood next to the bed as he hummed a soft tune. He snapped a few pictures of me, and I tried to squeeze my legs together, but I was paralyzed.

He set the camera up on a tripod and sat down next to me. I watched as he drew lazy patterns across my clavicle with the tip of an antique wave-bladed dagger. Droplets of blood rose in its wake, and he licked them with fervor.

He was oblivious to anything else, his hungry stare glued to my skin, and I was soon branded by a row of red tattoos. I tried to speak, but my vocal cords were numb. Shaking from the effort, I hiked a knee an inch higher.

Liam was startled by the movement, and his gaze snapped up to meet mine. Smooth as mirrors, his black orbs reflected plump carmine lips and scarlet irises. Blood trickled down my arms as I fought against the metal cord snared around my wrists.

The demon trailed sloppy kisses from my collarbone to my earlobe, his stubble scratching my skin. "God, I want to bathe in your blood." The pant crackled with unrepentant gluttony. He blanketed me with his body and kissed the hollow of my neck.

I gulped. The weird blade pushed against my navel, and, with a wink, Liam plunged it deep into my stomach.

I YELPED and found myself in my bed, wearing my pajamas. My pulse echoed at my temples, and I shifted on my side to turn on the bedside table lamp. It clicked, and I pressed my fingers to my eyes, trying to rub the vivid images out of my brain.

I pushed the covers aside and fanned myself with my loose shirt, my whole body on fire.

The bulb on the nightstand flickered. Once. Twice. It emitted a curt buzzing sound before it burned out. The sudden weight of a man pinned me down to the mattress.

With a cruel and disgusted grimace, Liam strangled me with both hands. "Get. Out."

COLD SWEAT TRICKLED against my chest and neck as I woke up. *What a fucked-up dream!* God, I hated false awakenings.

I combed my hair away from my face and drew a deep breath, but it failed to calm me.

Black eyes flashed in the dark, a remnant of the lifelike dream, and revulsion quaked my body. I scrambled out of bed and raced out of my room like Lucifer was on my tail.

As I passed Liam's bedroom, fear glued me in place, and my legs almost gave out underneath me. Was I still dreaming? A gush of air at my back spooked me, and I spun around, my chest heaving. There was nothing but shadows.

When my legs obeyed me again, I ran to Thom's room, breaking yet another resolution.

Out of breath, I shut the door behind me and rested my hands and forehead against the wood. A line of ants climbed up my knuckles, and electricity arched from my palms. I couldn't shake the feeling that there was a presence on the other side. A menace. A shadow.

I forced a deep breath down my lungs and exhaled slowly. Thom's light snoring made the nightmare seem absurd and diluted the hold of the dream. Within minutes, I could breathe again. Nothing and no one roamed the hallway.

My heartbeat slowing down, I joined Thom under the covers and snuggled into a pillow, thankful he was not a light sleeper. Morpheus claimed me sooner than I expected.

WHEN I WOKE UP, Thom's hands lay flat against my stomach, his heat delicious against my skin. A hint of daylight seeped through the blinds. *Should I stay? Should I go?* With a sigh, I opted for caution and extricated myself from Thom's sleepy embrace.

I tiptoed out of the room. A few steps down the hallway, I noticed Liam's door was wide open. Fear coagulated into a stone in my stomach.

"Hi," a throaty voice greeted me from behind, and I jumped, coming face to face with the devil. His head slowly tilted to the side. A cat contemplating a bird.

The stare bared me. Silence pressed like an elephant doing acrobatics on my chest. "Need to get dressed." I scurried to my door.

"Wait."

I gripped the doorknob, knuckles white, and summoned the courage to check if his eyes were black. They weren't. Bluish gray, almost silver, they glistened in the morning light.

He hesitated, his gait shifting from one foot to the other. "Let me see your hand."

Unable to stop staring, I put my palms up in front of me. The night of my birthday, his eyes had been brown. Such an unusual color would have caught my attention. He moved forward, and my pulse quickened, but I didn't budge. In fact, my body was not responding to any commands.

Was he hypnotizing me? Layers of bandages fell at our feet as he undressed my wound. Despite trying hard not to, I flinched when his fingers grazed the cut.

Flashes of the past filled my mind.

A younger version of my parents towered above me, snapping pictures. The flash blinded me. Today was my first day of school. I was eager to go but terrified. What if I didn't make friends?

A small spectacled teenager stood in front of me as I leaned down to give him a quick peck on the lips. My first kiss. The boy turned maroon, and I giggled.

The vividness of the memories did not spook me as much this time around. Somehow, I felt more in control. Beyond the images and feelings assaulting my senses, a web stretched around me. I threaded carefully and tugged on a string. Could I conjure something specific instead of the random childhood memories? I concentrated hard on Thom.

"Hi, I'm Thom." The cute blond sitting on my right introduced himself, and I shook his hand. Wow. Art class would be even better than I'd imagined, and I'd had high expectations to begin with. I congratulated myself for taking the time to brush my hair and dress, remembering how I'd almost come to class in sweatpants.

It was working. Excited, I pulled hard on the next string. Too hard. The images swirled in a tempest, and I braced the storm down an unbeaten but strangely familiar path.

I saw myself, hair frizzy from sleep and skin pale in the gray light. I was seeing through Liam's eyes, as he/us stared deep into my green irises. His version of me had dilated pupils and a frazzled heartbeat.

A strange, bitter voice glazed over the scene. *Look at her. She's terrified of me.*

The flow stopped as suddenly as it had started, and I was facing Liam again. I blinked to regain focus and looked down at my hand. It was healed. "How?"

"Your powers are not out of my system, yet. I gave you a nudge."

"Did you see anything?" I blushed, afraid he'd been in my mind too.

The other voice had been his. I had read his thoughts. Had he read mine?

He frowned at my question. "What do you mean?" Either he was a world-class actor, or he had no idea what I was talking about.

"Never mind."

He released my hand and walked away.

"Liam?" The sound of his name halted his stride. "Thank you." The words felt right. I couldn't believe I hadn't thanked him for saving my life.

The silver orbs softened. "You're welcome."

Without his demon senses, I'd be dead. Not only had he saved my life, but he'd risked his sanity to do it. To show fear was cruel, and I had to learn how to keep my emotions in check.

I kept the *ride-down-memory-lane* side effect secret. Somehow, I knew it would land me in trouble.

11

THE DEMON, THE WITCH, AND THE WARDROBE

Alana

The next morning, I sat crossed-legged on my bed, brushing my hair, when voices rose from the backyard. I'd made a habit of leaving my window opened to breathe in every whiff of fresh air I could. The curtains hung agape, and I peeked through the sliver of light between them.

Thom and Liam were playing basketball in the backyard.

Dew glistened on the vibrant green grass, and birds chirped from a safe distance. They were eying the feeder next to the hoop, their feathers ruffled in frustration, angry to be disturbed in their morning routine by two loud mammals in shorts.

I observed the boys without being seen. They looked more alike than I'd first thought. Same symmetrical bone structure, same strong jaw. Both Thom's tousled ashy blond curls and Liam's black hair complimented their complexion.

Thom was naked from the waist up, a distracting habit of his, and wore white shorts while his older brother wore black from head to toe. They had a definite yin/yang situation going on.

On a game perspective, Liam was quicker, and won the game without a sweat as he landed shot after shot.

Thom looked bewildered before his eyes narrowed, "You're cheating."

"I'm not," Liam answered with a mischievous grin that wasn't fooling anyone.

Thom chuckled before throwing the ball hard in his brother's chest. "Let's do an honest one."

The second game was riveting. Equals, they scored one after the other, unable to get the upper hand. They teased and taunted each other. The way they tussled and scuffled, anybody could have guessed they were brothers. At an impasse, the boys decided to go to sudden death. Next one to score wins all. My sight wandered over Thom's body as he played. Inappropriate thoughts crossed my mind. *Damn, those arms...*

Thom managed to land the shot and did a little dance. A quiet laugh escaped me.

Liam cracked up, too. "Okay, you win, I suck at being normal."

"Told you so," Thom gloated as he picked the ball from the ground. "Let's eat. Maybe Alana's up by now." He disappeared from view.

Liam paused. Silver eyes jerked to my window for a brief second and met mine. A nervous hiccup climbed up my throat as I jumped away from the window. I changed into day clothes and fluffed my hair. The smoothed curls roamed loose, and I put on lipstick before I joined the guys in the kitchen.

"Good morning," Thom said as he cracked an egg into a pan. Thank God he'd thrown a shirt on.

"Good morning," Liam repeated.

I sat beside him on purpose, wanting to show trust.

Thom got a spatula from the second drawer next to the stove and shot me a glance. "You slept late."

"Yeah."

Liam scoffed.

"What?" I gave him a puzzled look.

"Liar," he whispered so Thom wouldn't hear.

Bacon fell in a second pan, and Thom asked, "What's going on?"

"Nothing," I replied, my face tomato red. Being a faired skin redhead has its drawbacks.

"You were drooling," Liam said, amused.

Was he serious? My five-year-old self showed its head. "Was not."

Liam hadn't evolved past three. "Was too."

Were we having this conversation for real, or had I banged my head and woken up in the sitcom version of my life?

Thom's eyes drifted between the two of us. "Am I missing something?"

"Alana has dirty thoughts about you," Liam said, and I gawked at him.

He did not just say that. Shouldn't they have warned me Liam could read minds? I stabbed an accusing finger in the demon's direction. "It's not fair. This guy can read my thoughts."

Liam snorted, and I glared, more angry than embarrassed.

Thom scratched his head. "Err—Alana? Liam can't read thoughts."

Stupid girl. Liam had been fishing. The smugness on his face grated like nails on the chalkboard of my humiliation. I could learn to hate his ass.

But I'd had a somewhat normal—though unpleasant—social exchange with the devil. That thought calmed my boiling nerves. Thom brushed the subject aside to talk about his plans for the day. Now that Liam was back, the search for new potential witch could begin. They talked about a bunch of other stuff I didn't pay attention to, my cheeks still burning hot.

Mind reading and telepathy. *Most supernatural beings can communicate telepathically. Reading thoughts and the inception of fabricated thoughts into a healthy mind is a rare and unreliable skill. Inception is not to be mistaken for possession or the replacement of one's mind by another entity such as parasitic demons. See* ***Furias****.*

. . .

Furias. *Parasitic demon who takes control of its host by short-circuiting its nervous system. Humans and animals are perfect hosts. Weakened demons might also be susceptible.*

LIAM WAS NOWHERE to be seen that afternoon. As Thom and I sat down to eat without him, I asked, "Where's Liam?"

"He's meeting Lilah halfway."

Lilah. Good. She'd be ecstatic to see him. I pictured them meeting in a pub or bistro. The constant sorrow that had plagued Lilah for the last few months would vanish as they hugged. I bet the restaurant had those pretty champagne flutes, and they'd crack open a bottle to celebrate Liam's recovery. They'd take a walk after the meal, along flowered streets, the weather nice and warm.

God, what I wouldn't give for a night out on the town, eating professionally prepared food and leaving the dishes to someone else...

Engrossed in my daydream, I didn't notice Thom's tensed face before he said, "Lana, Liam has a lead on a new potential. I need to go to California."

He couldn't have gotten me faster out of my reverie if he'd punched me in the face with the frying pan he was holding. "You're leaving? When?"

"Tomorrow. We're already playing catch-up, so there's no time to waste if we want to save him."

It made sense, Thom had a job to do, but selfish jealousy engulfed me. I didn't want to stay here alone. Why couldn't I go to California, too? "How long will you be gone?"

"At least three weeks. Liam will stay with you for now."

The news loosened my jaw. I'd assumed they were both going. California was on the other side of the continent, and Liam had only been *cured* for a minute. "Is it really safe?"

Liam chose this moment to erupt into the kitchen, and his timing was too inopportune to be a coincidence. Why was he back already? Why wouldn't he enjoy his freedom?

"Big bad wolf won't eat little red riding hood." He rummaged through the fridge and came up empty handed. "Thom, when did you last buy food? There's nothing left in here. Couldn't tear yourself away?" He grabbed an apple on the counter and bit down on it noisily. "I may have to eat her, after all."

I rolled my eyes at Liam's sarcasm—this guy possessed a special talent to get on my nerves—and sighed. Why was Liam staying, and not Thom? The demon was supposed to teach me how to use my powers, but I was skeptical.

"Did you figure out her heritage yet?" Liam asked his brother. When he spoke about me in Thom's presence, he directed the question to Thom. Always.

"Heritage?" Thom and I asked in unison.

Liam chewed before adding, "She's not a random. She's a witch through and through, probably on both sides."

"How do you know?" I asked.

"I can tell." Hunger flashed in his eyes, and I avoided his direct stare.

I tried to focus on anything but the swelling fear in my belly and noticed his black hair was shorter. The haircut reminded me of the day I'd met him.

I pressed my lips together. "I'm adopted. Closed adoption, my parents knew nothing," Liam's frown made me pause. "Is that so difficult to believe?"

"Very. Your bio parents were idiots."

I arched an eyebrow at Thom for a less judgmental answer.

"What Liam means is that leaving you with normals was careless and dangerous. Randoms turn right before they're twenty, but full-blooded witches can activate at any age. You could have developed powers in diapers, and your adoptive parents would have been sitting ducks, waiting for you to be taken. Either they had no other choice, or there's a catch. If they belonged to a coven, they should have left you with another member."

"Shouldn't we look for one of these covens? They might have answers," I said.

Thom shook his head. "Covens are deadlier than demons when they put their minds to it. They don't like to be disturbed, and they don't care about anyone but their own."

I could tell from Liam's solemn expression that covens of witches were to him what clans of demons were to me. The proverbial bogeyman.

I'd never harbored more than mild curiosity regarding the identity of my biological parents. Adopted children are supposed to go through this whole phase during which they feel sad and unwanted. Mom had pestered me my whole adolescence, afraid I hid this complex beneath layers of bravado, but no. Mom was infertile, so they had adopted. I was her precious little girl—no question. A piece of my identity hadn't been missing.

But Liam's revelation tickled my curiosity. My birth parents were witches? Where were they? Could they still be alive?

For the first time in my life, I was torn between a desire to meet them, and a fear that they'd abandoned me because of what I was. Maybe there was something wrong with me? A baby witch surrendered to normals, exiled from her coven for obscure and mysterious reasons… I hated the idea. I was no special snowflake. There must have been a logical explanation.

ORANGE SLIVERS CLASHED against the deep blue night when I got up at an ungodly hour to say goodbye to Thom. Peppered with clouds, the sky promised a fresh start and a beautiful day, but my body was stiff from the lack of sleep and the prospect of living in this house—this *other*world—without Thom. This dawn tasted like sunset. Like the end of a reprieve between two dark spots. The stuffed bag at his side reminded me that he didn't expect a quick trip. Liam made himself scarce, and we lingered in a heartfelt hug.

"I'll miss you," I whispered against his skin. Thom was the sole reason I hadn't imploded, yet. I wouldn't fare well without him. My instincts told me Liam wouldn't play Scrabble or cook me dinner.

"Liam will behave, I promise."

He should have defined the word *behave* in more explicit terms. Thom and Liam had different views on what constructed proper behavior.

I gnawed on my thumb. "Are you sure it's safe?"

"If I had a drop of doubt, Liam would still be locked up downstairs. I didn't make the decision to let him go lightly."

"I know, but—"

"Alana, I'm flattered you feel safer with me around, but I'll be honest. If Liam wanted to attack you, I'd be helpless. But he doesn't. He's a good guy, and he only did what he did to save your life. That's why I want him here, where nothing bad can happen. Give him a chance."

I played with my fingers as I considered his plea. "If you're sure."

"I am."

His certainty cheered me up. A bit. Maybe.

AROUND NOON, Liam erupted into my room without knocking, and I yelped. "Get dressed. We're going out."

"What?" I asked, shocked.

"We're going out."

"I thought that—"

"Don't you want to get out of here for a few hours?" Truer words had never been spoken.

"Yes."

"Then hurry."

The door closed behind him, and I whisked off my sweatpants. One leg inside the jeans I planned to wear, I froze.

Thom had been clear I was never to leave the house. Was Liam taking me somewhere dangerous? Did I care if it meant I could rejoin the world for an afternoon?

Excitement tightening my nerves, I tied my hair back in a glamorous pony tail and let a few strands fall around my face. After I applied red lipstick and mascara, I joined Liam in the living room.

"Where are we going?" I couldn't have sounded more eager.

"Grocery store. There's nothing left to eat."

A nervous chuckle flew out my mouth. It sounded so normal.

"Also, Thom made me promise to take you… shopping." The apprehensive tone made it clear it was torture to tag along for such an activity.

The front door materialized into existence as we drew near. I'd never get used to this. Skittish, I paused over the doormat, almost expecting an alarm to go off, and took my first steps outside the house since my abduction. Warm air filled my lungs as I breathed deep.

The harsh light of the midday sun assaulted my retinas, but I rejoiced at the smell of freshly cut grass. I kicked off my boots—extremely out of season—and yanked off my socks. My naked toes dug into the stark green lawn, and I hummed in unbridled joy. I loved summer. Liam's lips twitched with humor.

A sleek sports car waited for us at the end of the driveway.

"Liam?" my voice trembled over his name, "I thought I couldn't leave the house, that it was too dangerous."

He opened the driver's side door. "You can't alone, but nothing can happen to you while you're with me."

The devil-may-care tone wasn't enough to reassure me. I wanted him to explain why. Thom often went too fast in explaining details, but Liam was a closed book.

I gawked at the fancy interior of the vehicle, without a doubt the most expensive one I'd ever seen. Liam put on sunglasses and shifted the car into gear. My questions blew out my brain as he sped up. The speed limit apparently didn't apply to him.

Nor did all other laws—laws of society, laws of criminal justice or the simple laws of physics. When the meter crossed a hundred miles an hour, I was beyond freaked out, and ready to throw up.

"What the hell are you doing?" I screamed, trying to knock some sense into him.

He chuckled before accelerating again, and the scenery blurred. I flattened my back against the seat, swallowing back bile. Liam noticed my queasiness and eased up on the pedal, but we were still racing twenty miles over the limit when we crossed paths with a patrol car.

What did he hope to achieve by getting arrested with me in his car? Without a doubt, I was reported missing. Milk cartons were not the standard for disappearances anymore. Officers had access to a bunch of records through their car's computer. What if they recognized me?

We glided past the police. "How?"

"They can't see us, Alana," Liam explained as if he was talking to a preschooler.

A bit of breakfast rose into my mouth, and I didn't dare to speak further. Explanations would have to wait for solid ground.

Liam parked next to an outdoor shopping outlet. I put my wobbly feet on the pavement and considered kissing it. Catching my breath, I glowered. "Was it necessary to drive so fast?"

"No, but it was fun," Liam said before his expression darkened. "Don't throw up in my Vanquish." He marched onward. The conversation was over.

I caught up with him and grabbed his arm to force him to slow down. As soon as my fingers grazed his wrist, he yanked his arm away as though my touch had burned him.

My brows furrowed in confusion. "Please explain why they didn't pursue us."

"Because I made it so."

"How?"

He pointed to the store's window, and I gasped when I caught my reflection in it. It wasn't me.

Short brownish hair fell right over my shoulders, I had a bigger nose, and my eyes... I had seen them before, but not on me. They were Lilah's, the piercing shade of a clear summer sky.

"Oh my God!" I ran my hands on the estranged features.

In a blink, the illusion dispelled, and my face reappeared. *Thank God.* "You can make me—or anyone—see anything?"

My question was met with blatant indifference. "Let's get this over with."

Unease crept into my heart. He was incredibly powerful. Was he the shadow roaming the hallway the other night? Had I sensed him, somehow?

A grim line formed at the corner of his mouth like he'd followed my accusing train of thoughts, so I wiped the worried grimace off my face. He had done nothing to warrant distrust. Technically. He could do whatever he wanted, and, yet, he'd risked his life to safe me. The hallmark of a good guy. But *good guy* and *murderer* had always been mutually exclusive in my mind, and it was hard to reconcile the two.

My thoughts were blown away by the animated chatter of shoppers walking past us, their voices music to my ears. I hadn't seen or heard anyone but Thom, Lilah and Liam in too long. On the other side of the curb, the AMC beckoned. I hadn't been to the movies in forever, but it was too early for movies. Maybe we could go with Thom when he came back?

The trees on each side of the central walkway between the shops were impressive. Their leaves casted a welcomed shade on the path made tortuous by round fountains.

Liam let me take my pick of the various stores. Tired of the clothes that didn't quite fit me, I missed dressing up. I chose a big chain that sold a bit of everything. A stack of beautiful items, including shoes, massed in the changing room at an alarming speed.

I was having so much fun I'd forgotten a tiny detail. How could I afford all of this? I pulled the curtain aside and peeked out. Liam sat on a chair a few feet away, typing on his phone.

I bit my bottom lip. "I don't have any money."

He didn't look up from the screen. "You can take whatever you want, obviously."

"You expect me to steal?" He threw me a questioning glance, blind to the issue. I raised my eyebrows at him in return, "I'm not comfortable with that."

"Where do you think your other clothes come from?"

"I don't care. It's not right."

He rolled his eyes. "It's all the same to me if you wear the same dingy shirt day after day. If we frowned upon stealing, we would've been too busy working to save your life." Why did all his answers sound like he was explaining two plus two to a difficult child? His cold logic was wrapped in condescension, and I hated that it made sense.

I clicked my tongue and returned to the booth. The pile of clothes was enticing, but I restricted myself to the essentials, if only to show Liam one of us still valued integrity. I kept all the underwear—just because—but limited myself to a pair of pants, a pair of flats, a pair of pajamas and three shirts. I changed back into my old clothes.

Dingy shirt. I scoffed, looking down at my chest.

True, it was bigger than needed and not the most stylish cut. I hesitated before switching it for the only fancy one that I'd selected—a black halter top with lace above the chest and upper back. Staring at my reflection, I indulged in a moment of vanity. The black lace contrasted with my fair skin, and it hugged my curves in all the right places. Sexy, but not provocative.

I grinned. It's crazy how a good outfit can affect your mood. The discarded shirt stayed on the floor when I left the changing room, my *purchases* balled in my arms. "I'm ready."

"Amen." Liam made sure I knew he was bored out of his mind.

After we walked out the shop, unseen, Liam brightened up. We made a round-trip to the car to get rid of my stuff and entered the grocery store.

Liam grabbed enough food to feed an army for a month. Chips, chocolate, you name it. He had a soft spot for junk food. Demons must have a strong metabolism.

I ogled the crap in the cart. "You know, we should get vegetables."

"I don't care for them," he said, his nose creasing up in disgust.

I added healthy choices to the pile. "Well, I do, and Thom does too."

Liam chuckled under his breath, "Thom would eat dirt if you cooked it."

That remark had me catching a giddy smile from surfacing on my lips. Twice now Liam had implied Thom liked me. Was he being an annoying older brother, or was he right? Bet it was a bit of both.

When the cart was ready to fall apart, Liam pushed our food past the exit, and the cashier looked right through us.

"Now, princess, let's get you back to your castle," Liam said.

I paused in the middle of the parking lot. "Did you just call me princess?" I hated those nicknames, and he had no right to call me that. I wasn't difficult *at all.*

"Yes."

"Well... don't."

"As you wish, princess." He snorted and opened the trunk.

What a child! I couldn't believe a few days—no, hours—ago, I'd been afraid of him. I got into the passenger seat and crossed my arms. He could deal with the food alone.

ON THE RIDE BACK, I lowered my window so that the wind would help my wavering stomach. Fields of corn alternated with bright green pastures and darker-colored tobacco crops. Heifers fooled with young bulls near centennial farms, flanked by authentic colonial houses. "It's beautiful."

"I love it here." A relaxed hand on the wheel, he gazed at the road with a hint of a smile. It was the most honest thing he'd said so far, and I could tell he was the kind of person to drive for pleasure.

I spied at him from the corner of my eyes. A dark leather thread around his neck intrigued me. He hadn't been wearing it in the dungeon, and he wasn't the type of guy to accessorize. An attached pendant pulled the strand beneath the neckline of his shirt. Without thinking, I hooked my index finger beneath the cord and pulled.

Curiosity has always been my number one sin.

A small silver key and a dark ring flashed into view before the car swerved as Liam's hands cramped around the steering wheel. With lightning reflexes, he rectified our course, and we avoided the ditch.

The seat belt dug into my waist and chest before I recoiled back against my seat. We exchanged a look, but he quickly averted my confused stare. I pressed my lips together.

I'd been insensitive. He had to be jittery around me because of my blood, and it explained his reaction from before, too. He was struggling. It reminded me of our predator/prey dynamic. The image of a little bird chirping in a lion's mouth came to mind. Now, I knew for a fact the lion had to concentrate hard not to bite down and chew.

Relief showed on Liam's face when we got back into the house, and he bolted as soon as the door closed behind us. I ate my supper alone in the kitchen, watched a movie, and retreated to my room.

To my stupefaction, a mountain of clothes laid on my comforter. It contained all the discarded items I'd left behind at the store, and the underlying message was loud and clear.

Liam didn't intend on shopping with me again.

12

I MISS YOU

Alana

On a rainy Monday afternoon, the punching bag was thrashing around under my assaults when Liam entered the gym. He was wearing a black shirt and black sports pants. The demon had a serious love affair with black. Besides blue jeans, I hadn't seen a hint of color on him. Dark gray was the ultimate compromise.

"What's up with you and black?" I asked the question without thinking, not expecting an actual answer.

"Blood is a pain to wash off lighter fabrics."

Yikes.

Thom had been gone for almost two weeks, and Liam wasn't the best roommate. He popped in and out of the house or disappeared for days at a time, and I never knew when or why he was absent.

Liam walked over to me and grabbed the punching bag, steadying it. "Thom told me he was teaching you to fight." A wry grin curled his lips.

I halted my movements, annoyed, and served him a dose of his own medicine. "I'm getting good." I tilted my chin up, challenging him to say otherwise. Sure, I wouldn't win a wrestling championship anytime soon, but I wasn't the defenseless girl I used to be.

He crouched into a fighting stance. "Show me."

Uncomfortable, I paused. The nightmare with the bloody tattoos recurred almost every night. My subconscious was bullying me to keep the distrust between us intact, but I'd die before admitting he intimidated me. I threw a few sloppy punches his way. He blocked them with ease, a knowing smirk on his face, like he expected me to suck.

My eyes narrowed, and I channeled all my self-confidence. I increased the rhythm, added my best footwork and combined left and right hooks. He met my assaults toe to toe and pressured me to switch it up. The technique consumed one hundred percent of my focus, and I forgot I was weary. Sweat accumulated on my forehead.

Thom and Liam trained together. They had the same style, but Liam's execution was flawless. The precise movements showed impressive control. He could probably catch a fly mid-flight between his index and thumb and hold it there without squishing it.

"Thom taught you his favorite moves," he said as he went on the offensive.

He forced me to block a few mellow hits, not using as much strength as Thom. He underestimated me. I evaded his attempts to grip my arms and retaliated.

To my extreme pleasure, a low kick scraped his knee, and surprise showed on his face.

"I told you I'm good." I spun around and headed towards my water bottle.

Without warning, he grabbed me from behind in a rear-choke-hold. His forearm ensnared my shoulders like Thom used to do to practice.

As I met Liam's dangerous glare in the mirror's reflection, my entire body trembled. It wasn't the same. His hot breath on my neck reminded me of my nightmares, his touch electric, unnerving. My stomach flip-flopped.

What happened to avoiding physical contact like the plague? Can we go back to that? I committed all my strength into a quick thrust to twist out of the compromising position, but barely moved. His left arm encircled my waist, and my mouth hanged open. It was like being strapped to a rock. Thom and I never had practiced *this*. A smoky citrus scent invaded my nostrils, combined with something darker and fresh like the caress of a thick, early-morning fog.

Liam's lips inched closer to my ear. His darkening silvery stare never left mine as my heart played world championship yo-yo in my chest.

His voice came out rough as he said, "These tricks are fine, vital even, but against demons they're rubbish. Don't forget that." As a puppet on strings, he flipped me to face him. "The fight you'll have a chance to win will go on in here," he poked my head with his index finger. "We start tomorrow."

He let me go, and I stumbled to the floor. He didn't look back as he exited the room, and I stared at the door for a minute after he left.

My legs were shaky as I peeled myself from the ground. I felt like I'd been… mugged. The comparison sounded harsh, but my cells were vibrating in trepidation. My skin pulsated where his hands had been, and the tingles served as a reminder of *what* he was. No matter what, I couldn't fight on his level. He belonged on a higher shelf. Against his kind, all my fighting skills would never count, never be enough. I was helpless.

Damn him! I bet he got off on scaring me. I was seething, but in the back of my mind, I knew it was wiser to remember the warning.

WHEN I FINALLY GATHERED THE courage to leave the gym, Liam was nowhere to be found. I took a long shower and went on with my day. I ate, read and watched TV to cast away the effects of Liam's *lesson*, but the more I tried to forget about it, the more restless I became. Vivid images from my nightmare looped in my mind. If I went to bed now, I knew I'd dream of it again. Why had Liam rattled me like that? What was he hoping to accomplish?

The need to blow off steam became imperious, so I returned to the gym. I took the edge off by beating the punching bag to a pulp, imagining it was Liam's face. But Liam wasn't entirely to blame for my grumpiness. All day, I'd been trying to forget one other thing.

The next day was my Mom's birthday, and the homesickness had crept in uninvited. If none of this had happened, I'd be looking forward to a girly day at the spa, and a delicious dinner cooked on the grill by my dad. We'd laugh and relax by the pool. Dad would tease me and ask when I planned to bring a boy home. I'd be happy and loved.

Instead, I was stuck with a half demon who didn't give a damn about me.

My punches lost momentum as icy tendrils ensnared my throat. I sank to the floor and hid my face in my thighs. The terrifying truths, the weird rules, the brave smiles... Without Thom, I was drowning. Drowning in frustration and disappointment. Drowning in a life I didn't want.

I hadn't made a lick of progress in the witchcraft department. I didn't care about witchcraft. *Fuck witchcraft!* I balled my fists and rested my head against the wall, staring up at the ceiling. A sourness rose to my mouth. I could have had it much worse. I could have been dead, and yet, I complained anyway.

The black hole in my soul grew bigger every day, and a part of me wanted it to swallow everything. My parents, my friends, my classes, along with all the simple things I had underappreciated... They were unbearable. An invisible force was pushing on my ribcage from the inside out. It crawled up my throat and forced itchy tears down my cheeks.

I didn't let myself cry much. It was a waste of time and energy. But that night, huddled against the wall of the gym, I wept. I wept for all those days I hadn't wept. I cursed life for all those times I'd managed to rise above and stay positive. I screamed for all those nights I'd kept silent.

The sobs eventually fizzled out. All things, even desperation, can't last forever.

I splashed cold water on my face and met my puffy red eyes in the mirror. Weakness and self-pity wouldn't help, so I made a solemn promise to find a way out of this mess. And if I had to kill all the demons in the world to get there, then great.

I wouldn't live here forever, a princess locked away in her tower. I didn't have to be a great witch, or even a good one. I just had to get this beacon thing under control and get the heck out.

Lilah would take me in, and I'd go back to school. I'd make new friends. Starting over was hard but staying in limbo was worse. I was ready to learn.

13

HYSTERIA

Liam

I'm about to jump out of my own skin when Lilah finally appears. At once, I feel her working her magic. The rumbling emotions inside me fall flat like a stormy sea liberated from the wind, and I can breathe again.

I texted her an hour and a half ago, about to lose my mind.

I need you. I need to meet.

Her answer was quick.

Of course. Same place. Breathe. Don't do anything stupid.

She meant *get your shit together and don't kill Alana.*

Shivers brand my body despite the humidity. "I can't train her, I can barely breathe around her, and I definitely can't touch her."

The last few weeks, I hugged Lilah and held her hand whenever possible to desensitize myself from the scent of witch blood. It was going well, so I tested my self-control.

Touched Alana. And it was bad. Real bad. *Almost-ripped-her-open* bad.

"What happened?" Lilah asks.

"I offered to spar with her, thought it'd be the perfect test. Baby steps. Faint touches, my skin barely brushing hers as I blocked her punches. It worked until I derailed and went off script." Her scent was too tantalizing, and I lost my grip.

Lilah grabs my shaking hands, but I flinch. Her blood is also difficult to resist right now.

"Come back with me tonight. I'll help you."

"I'll be okay." I don't trust myself around Lilah either. Not tonight. When she sleeps, she can't use her powers to dampen my... need. I meet her big blue eyes, ready to make a demand that has burned my lips for many weeks now, one I know she doesn't want to hear. "Cut this bloodlust out of me."

Her aura darkens. "You know I can't."

She's lying. She can but won't.

Lilah's powers are immense, but she shies away from them. Planting a feeling or removing one completely can be dangerous. It could mess with the essence of me, but I don't care. She could erase me and leave a stranger in my place if it freed me from this hunger, and I would be fucking grateful.

Her powers wrap me up in a calm cloud. "I'll come early tomorrow, be your witch-patch. You'll be better around Alana in no time at all."

She said that two weeks ago, and it still hasn't worked. But that's Lilah, the eternal optimist. I suspect she'll be patting me on the back as I kill her.

If. I mean *if* I kill her.

I GET HOME late at night. The atmosphere in the house is heavy like she's holding her breath. I like to think of the house as a she, for it certainly has a soul. Bewitched to protect her owners, she has a temper against intruders. She struggles with newcomers like a protective mother worried for her children.

She used to whisper to me in the cellar. A rush of warm air blanketed me in the dead of night as she begged me to hold on.

She's sad now, and I wonder why. I walk through the living room where a sharp sob pricks my ears. My first instinct is to look for trouble, but the house is too calm for that.

Alana. She's crying.

I can't smell anything, so she's not bleeding. Thank the Lord for small miracles.

I hesitate as I pass in front of the gym, but I decide to check on her. Just in case. She's huddled against the back wall, cheeks sticky with tears. Her red mane hides part of her face; her hands are still wrapped. I can tell from one look she hasn't hurt herself. She's homesick, I guess.

She hasn't cried much. Had me wondering if she had a heart at all. The other witches we helped wept for days in the beginning, even the boys.

Even though I couldn't use my powers when I was trapped downstairs, I could still follow her movements through the house. Not hear her speak, or anything like that—but every breath, every heartbeat, that I heard. My soul was attuned to her so completely that I almost lost my mind.

At first, I wanted to kill her. But the vapors of withdrawal cleared, and the shame of what I had done—of what I had once again become—made its way back into my fogged mind.

I wanted to drown in her.

Tonight, I could drown in her tears. For the first time, her blood doesn't smell as sweet. It reeks of regrets and sorrow. I stay in the shadows as I sit a few feet from her. I should really leave or go out and re-enter to make my presence known. Maybe she needs company.

I dismiss the thought immediately. She's afraid of me, so it's not like I can comfort her. She's a proud girl. She wouldn't like to know I've seen her at her most vulnerable. Plus, I might lose my grip and bleed her to death, so I place my hands firmly on my thighs and sit still.

But every fiber of my soul is begging me to wrap my arms around her and hold her tight.

And I'm afraid.

14

WITH YOU

Alana

The next day, I cooked slightly-burnt chicken with a side of nothing for dinner and enjoyed it in front of the latest Netflix series. TV binge-watching was one of the few guilty pleasures I could enjoy.

Liam had been gone all day. He hadn't invited me along, hadn't mentioned he was leaving, or how long he would be out. But I remembered his promise—or rather warning—that he would start to *train* me.

As I put the last utensils in the cupboard, my elusive roommate appeared out of nowhere, a hateful habit of his. I swallowed back a yelp of surprise, my heart beating like a drum. He motioned for me to take a seat in front of him. There was no greeting or politeness involved. He was ready to begin, and I had to go along with it.

I wanted to show him his little display of power from the day before hadn't affected me, so I spun the chair next to him around until its back faced Liam and met his stare head on as I straddled it.

Something was different, though. Hazel eyes met mine. Unremarkable, they contrasted with the bluish silver ones I suspected were real. I'd never asked why his eyes changed colors. I wanted to, but I knew better than to ask Liam Walker any form of a personal question.

He sat eerily still as he maintained eye-contact, and I couldn't look away. Thom and Lilah had both assured me multiple times the demon couldn't read my thoughts, but his gaze wasn't harmless either. He wasn't just looking at me, he was looking *through me*. Like he could see me *better*.

"Are we just going to sit?" I asked, unnerved by this ogling contest.

He blinked, and the weird hypnotic pull subsided.

With the distinct facial expression of someone about to take on a disagreeable chore, he asked, "What's your favorite cartoon character?"

"My favorite cartoon?" I frowned. Where was he going with this? How did it relate to training my mind against demons?

Garfield came to mind, but I went another way. I didn't want my actual favorite to be twisted by Liam's mind. "I don't know, Tweety Bird?"

"Charming." A three-dimensional Tweety Bird, in all its bright yellow glory, materialized on the table. Real feathers puffed around him, topped off by those characteristic big blue eyes and long lashes. "Recognize the lie, and you will see beyond it."

Wings flapped as Tweety eyed me with joy. "Oh my god! He's so cute!"

"Christ, Alana! That's beside the point. Concentrate on it, tell yourself it's not real."

The undeserved cussing pissed me off. I pouted but followed the instructions anyway. I focused all my attention on the little cutie, and it poof-ed. "It's easy."

Liam rolled unimpressed eyes at me.

"It is," I insisted.

"We're talking about a three-inch-tall cartoon bird, of course it's easy. The concept is what's important. I'll test you, and you'll see how hard it can get."

My eyes widened. "Test me?"

The barest hint of a smile flickered over his mouth, and I could tell

I would not enjoy the lessons. He didn't answer the question before he whooshed out of the room.

READY TO CONTINUE my TV marathon, I found Liam reading on the couch. I browsed around for the remote. It sat in his lap, and I was not that brave.

"Can I have the remote?"

"Yes, princess." He passed it without tearing his gaze from the book.

I pressed my tongue against the roof of my mouth. "Will you stop calling me that?"

"Nope."

"Why not?"

A genuine chuckle escaped him. "Because you hate it."

The casualness had to be a facade. I was amazed he could be intense and mysterious one moment and still manage to come off as an obnoxious toddler the next. I envied his poker face.

As the next episode began, I threw him nasty sideways glances. He ignored them thoroughly. The novel in his hands grabbed my attention. It was the last Harry Potter, my third favorite of the series. "*You* read Harry Potter?"

"What's not to love?"

I sank into a more comfortable position. My head rested against the decorative pillow, and I lost track of time. A gush of chilly air made me shiver. I reached for the wool throw without opening my eyes, and an eerie feeling gripped me. The soft weight of the blanket prickled my legs, but I could swear fingers had scraped my hair. I glanced in Liam's direction, but he'd disappeared.

My imagination was playing tricks on me.

I turned off the television and went to my room.

Among all the books I'd read in the last few months, my favorites were the Thomas Walker diaries. The first few volumes had been harder to decipher, but the later ones were riveting, and his hectic life provided a welcome cure to my boredom.

I felt like I knew him. He had endured so much to live the way he wanted, and he'd gone through more hardship then I could've imagined. The saddest bit of his history had to be the fate of his sister, Emily.

Journal of Thomas Walker

Tuesday, March 19, 1895

A peculiar incident happened today. Emily swears she saw James in the gardens this morning. It's simply impossible, so I'm afraid the loss of her dear twin, added to the lack of sleep, are playing tricks on her fragile mind.

Friday March 29, 1895

Emily has been talking in her sleep to James for days now, as if he were there. When I asked her about it, she didn't recollect anything, so I let it go not to scare her.

Wednesday, June 12, 1895

Sometimes she just stares into space repeating the word *blood,* and it scares my wits out of me. The maid's eighteen-year-old son started calling her a witch, and the children in town are now afraid of her. She is letting herself waste away, her weight evaporating like butter in the sun.

Wednesday, June 19, 1895

Dear God, save us, for our family is damned. My poor sister wandered in her sleep last night and killed the maid's son with a kitchen knife. She denies it, but there was blood on her nightgown and on her hands. And yet, I believe she does not remember it because she fainted when she saw the blood.

My father paid largely for the funeral and the family's silence, but I'm afraid we can't ignore the fact that Emily's mind is not quite right anymore. Father talked about sending her to one of those atrocious places they call a sanatorium, and even though I opposed myself to it, I know she is not the girl she used to be.

Thursday. September 26. 1895

I'm ashamed to say I have been blind until now. Emily is pregnant. I suspect the maid's son raped her, and it explains so much. I should have killed the boy myself. My father is sending her to the abbey. The sisters have promised to offer her a better life.

But there had been no better life as Emily had died in childbirth. Thomas was married by then and had insisted on keeping the little girl, Clara. He'd raised her alongside his own son until the age of nine. He'd found his brother James in the girl's room one night, and the young demon had begged his brother to send the girl away and make her disappear. Thomas thought his brother couldn't stand the sight of her because she looked too much like his dead twin, Emily, but I found this explanation odd since I assumed James wanted his niece to have a good life.

Maybe it was because his twin had been raped, but, most likely, James had suspected that demons would come for Clara.

Thomas had ignored James' pleas, and, one night, two Shadow Walkers had come and taken her without a word of explanation. Sick and tired of having loved ones ripped away from him by demons, Thomas had researched spells and rituals to build himself a new home, a haven from supernatural forces. That's how the house we were living in had been built.

Clara Walker had never been seen again.

LIAM'S first test came the morning after.

I was painting my toenails with a shiny teal color on the white couch—a dauntless task, I like to live on the edge—when a bright light blinded me. I squinted, my pupils adjusting to the sun, feet digging in the white sand of a pristine beach. Wide-eyed, I took in the incredible scenery.

The sea sparkled, its warm turquoise water licking my ankles. Coconut trees danced in the wind and projected playful shadows on the sand. Pelicans' high-pitched quacks echoed above me, and I stood up, surprised to see I was wearing a white two-piece with frilly edges.

Liam appeared beside me, his black frame sticking out like a sore thumb amongst the colorful backdrop.

"How come it feels warm?" I held my arms out and looked up at the sky, the rays of sunshine hot on my skin.

"I imprint the images of the beach and the sea, and your mind patches the inconsistencies."

"Really?" My mind had delightful taste.

Dolphins jumped over the waves, and I longed to join them, curious to see if the ocean would feel as real as the sun, amazed at the potential for beauty in Liam's power. "Can you see what I see?"

"If I want to, yes."

"Does it feel real to you too?" Not waiting for an answer, I walked straight into the waves.

The paradise flickered out of sight, and I plunged headfirst over the coffee table and into the floor. *Ow.* The teal lacquer was now sprinkled all over the decorative carpet and peppered my clothes. "Look what you made me do."

"Why would you go for a swim? You knew it wasn't real."

Touché. I patted the bump on my forehead. "The illusion is dispelled if I move?"

"Not necessarily."

The front door opened, interrupting the lesson. Lilah was home earlier than expected, as it was only Thursday, but I wasn't about to complain. Radiant in her white sun-dress and matching roman sandals, she pranced to us. I got instantly jealous of her gorgeous tan. A grin on her face, she asked, "What happened here?"

I peeled myself off the floor. "Went for an impromptu swim in a fake ocean."

Liam wrapped an arm around her shoulders, pulled her close and whispered something into her ear. She giggled.

While she recounted her work week, I fetched polish remover for the carpet. My nose wrinkled at the smell as I dabbed the tainted areas with acetone and placed paper towels on top of them. I'd have to rinse and repeat a few times for the color to go away. Oh well, I had to learn to navigate Liam's illusions one way or another. If a stained carpet was the worst collateral damage, I'd count myself lucky.

Lilah and Liam disappeared into her room, and I wondered if they did more than *train* together. They'd looked awfully chummy earlier. I shook the idea out of my twisted brain. Lilah would have said if something of that nature was going on between them.

I cleaned my clothes to the best of my abilities and headed upstairs to shower. The hot jet of water rinsed out my shampoo, and a fresh citrus scent floated in the steam, tickling my nostrils. I grabbed the bar of soap and enjoyed the silky brushes against my skin. My shoulders and neck were stiff from my face dive into the hardwood sea of living room island.

I turned the water off and squeezed my hair. About to step out, I spotted a weird shape behind the glass, blurred by condensation. I swiped the transparent door with my hand and about died when I saw Thom standing there. Out of instinct, I cried out and covered my breasts with one arm. But I wasn't fooled.

"Are you kidding me? I'm *naked*." I screamed at the apparition, and it disintegrated.

Liam's muted voice answered, "The element of surprise is the whole point. Demons won't wait for you to be ready before they sneak up on you. Besides, I'm not looking, I'm on the other side of the door."

Was he lying? How could he be on both sides of the door at once? I was almost positive he was lying. I quickly wrapped a towel around me and opened the door wide. I wanted to bite his head off, but I also had many questions. "How?"

His face was freshly shaved, and his hair was damp like he'd just hopped out of the shower himself. "I heard the water running and projected Thom on your side," he explained without batting an eyelash.

Maybe he was telling the truth, but I had no way to tell for sure. If he wanted to see me naked, there was absolutely nothing I could do to stop him.

"If you project things that aren't there, does it mean your mirages don't have an actual physical presence?" It would be easier to distinguish between real and not real if I had this right.

Liam's tall frame melted into a perfect copy of myself. Every detail, down to the way each wet curl hugged my skin, was on point. My voice answered the question. "No, it doesn't. If I project a glamor around an object or a person, you will be able to touch it without breaking the spell."

I pinched the false me on the arm and stroked soft feminine skin. My skin. "It's super creepy."

Liam could rule the world if he desired. Pass himself as the President, replace nuclear warheads with confetti, play every role in a movie... the possibilities were endless. I knew a few politicians who could easily be demons.

"Your species could rule the world," I said.

Liam's sardonic smile appeared on my lips. "Who says they don't?"

It was no longer as if I was looking in the mirror. It was distinctly Liam wearing my skin. I'm pretty sure I'd never looked so smug in my entire life. *This is what it must feel like to have an evil twin.*

Before I could decide if he was kidding about Shadow Walkers ruling the world, his phone rang. The evil Alana melted into Liam's form and headed out. I pulled out a bra, tank top and underpants from my cabinet and slipped them on.

Liam erupted back into the room. "Here she is, make it quick," he handed me the phone, "Thom wants to speak to you."

I clawed it out of his hand and brought it to my ear.

"Hi," I motioned for Liam to get the hell out. The peep show was over. He sized me up with an evil glint and mouthed, "*nice panties.*"

I was wearing Sponge Bob Square Pants underwear, the big teary eyes molding my butt. Angry and embarrassed, I threw a book at Liam's head, but he disappeared into thin air. The book hit the wall and fell to the floor with a faint thump. At last, I was alone. *Hopefully.*

"Lana?" Thom asked.

I hadn't listened to a word he'd said. "I'm sorry, what?"

"Things are not going as smoothly as I'd hoped. I need Liam's help."

My stomach sunk to my feet. "I can't stay here alone. I'll lose my mind." I couldn't believe I was implying Liam's company was better than none. Jury was still out on that.

"Sorry."

The way he said the word made my heart squirm. "Why can't I go?"

He hesitated, "I'd love to see you," I could sense the "but" coming a hundred miles an hour, "but it's too dangerous."

My brain-hamster raced its wheel to find a way to make this happen. "Liam said he could protect me from anything. Was he lying?"

"No, but still..."

I had a hunch that Thom didn't need much convincing. He wanted me to come, but he was afraid his decision would put me in danger. Didn't he get it? It wasn't his decision to make. I wasn't an ornament but a person. If I had all the information and decided to go, so be it. My soul was suffocating in here.

"I'm not a child. You have to respect my choices. Plus, Liam's absence will set me back weeks in my training."

I could almost hear his guilt eating him up over the phone line, "I'll ask Liam."

Yes! I peeked into the hallway and found Liam waiting. I handed back the phone, returned to my room, and closed the door. Silent, I pressed my ear to the wood.

Don't get your hopes up. Liam will say no. He'll be happy to get a break from you and has the final say in all of this. But my heart hoped for a positive answer, and anticipation coursed through my veins. California... Actual palm trees and beaches, vineyards and movie stars...

Liam's voice shattered my daydream. "No way."

Just as I'd thought. My face fell. Why did he sound furious at the sheer idea of me tagging along?

"I don't give a fuck that she's lonely."

I stuck my tongue out and backed up to grab a pair of shorts. That settled any illusions I had that Liam and I could become friends. He hated me. Why? I'd never been rude to him, not on purpose. If anything, he'd been rude to me.

A minute later, Liam entered and threw a leather backpack on the bed. "Pack your bags, princess. We have a seer to kill."

15

CALIFORNIA DREAMIN'

Alana

Liam and I glided through the airport. We ignored the checkpoints and did not bother to buy tickets. Demons didn't have to pay to fly American Airlines, and neither did their date. Not that I considered myself Liam's date.

Liam grabbed a novel from the airport bookstore. I pictured myself relaxing under the Californian sun while reading a good book. *Yum!* My glossary of the supernatural wasn't exactly *light* reading.

I traced my fingers over the row of spines. Thriller? *No, thank you.* Romance? *Yikes, like I need to put more ideas into my head.* My stomach was already in shambles at the prospect of seeing Thom. Desperate for something that would not parallel my life, one title grabbed my attention. *The Curious Charms of Arthur Pepper* was the story of an older man traveling the world to discover his late wife's secrets. A safe bet.

The second problem on the menu was that I didn't own a bathing suit. I thought regretfully about the cute polka dot two-piece stuffed in a box in my old room. It would have turned a lot of heads. Definitely Thom's.

I gripped Liam's sleeve between my fingers and dragged him to a store. He followed my lead, too engrossed in his phone conversation with Thom to care.

I selected a curve fitting red bikini. Redheads must be careful with fiery tones, but this shade complimented my hair. As I put it on, I was happy to discover I'd lost most of my flabby tummy. With all the work outs I'd sweated through, I deserved it. I might have looked hot, but my skin was ghostly pale. I needed some sun, and I needed it yesterday.

Excitement bubbled in my blood, and I kept the swim suit on underneath my clothes. A girl can never be too prepared.

THE AIRPORT TERMINALS WERE BUSY.

Liam's powers allowed us to go anywhere unseen, so I sneaked behind the counter at the Apple Store to grab a new iPod. I was careful not to brush the store's cashier as I looked over his hunched shoulders to see what he was doing. *Watching porn at work? Ew.*

I felt bad for stealing, but I admit it was fun. Who has never wondered what it would feel like to be invisible?

We sat in a coffee shop as we waited for a last call to Los Angeles. I was sipping on my cup of coffee when a teenager eyed me with interest as she walked past and turned bright red.

"What's happening?"

With a grin that was miraculously not sly, Liam said, "This is my version of twenty questions."

Had he just offered to play a game with me? For fun?

"I glamored you. You look like a famous person, and you have to guess who."

And he was explaining the rules? Had hell frozen over? "What if I win?"

"I stop calling you *princess*."

"You're on." I observed the passing crowd. Most people were in a hurry to catch their planes, but a few stopped to stare. Mostly women. "Am I a dude?"

"Yes."

"Am I a movie star?"

"Yes."

My mind flew over the names of popular actors. "Am I Brad Pitt?"

"Do you think I want to create a riot? No."

"What kind of movies do you watch?"

He shook his head. "Only yes or no questions."

After nineteen questions, my only clues were that I was both a TV and movie actor, and had starred in a series of superhero movies. *Damn, I'm losing.*

"Only one question left," Liam reminded.

I bit my lips.

A woman in her early twenties approached me. "Hi," she said nervously.

I felt wrong passing as someone else, but what harm could it do? "Hi."

"Can I get a quick picture with you?" I nodded, and she got her smart phone from her purse. "I really love your movies."

"Thanks," *Yes! Talk about my movies.* "Which in particular?" I took the phone and gave it to Liam. Were his powers able to fool a lens? I guess I was about to find out. He snapped the picture.

The woman was pleased. "I have to say *127 Hours.*"

She left, thanking me for being so nice.

I grinned from ear to ear. "Am I James Franco?"

"You cheated, you know."

"I did not!"

"Did too."

"What about the photo?" In this age of social media, this picture would end up on the web in less than a minute.

"Haven't you ever heard of a doppelganger? And why do you think there have been so many Elvis sightings? I'm not the only one who likes to play pranks on the normals."

The announcement we'd been waiting for resonated overhead. We gathered our things, and Liam dropped the glamor.

We glided by the lady checking for ID and tickets and went

straight to the walkway leading to the plane. As we took a spot in the line of people waiting to board, Liam told me to wait and went inside. Most people unconsciously made way for him, even though they didn't see him, and I wondered if they would do the same for me.

"What were you doing?" I asked when he came back.

"I selected our seats."

"How?"

"You'll see."

We walked down the narrow hallway and immobilized near the fifth row of first-class seats. Liam called a flight attendant over. "I'm sorry, but I think those two men are in our seats." He showed two make-believe tickets to her.

She nodded and spoke quietly with the two passengers already sitting down. They insisted they had the right seats and showed their tickets as well. Of course, by the evil glint in Liam's eyes, I knew their tickets said whatever the hell he wanted.

The young hostess looked flustered. "I'm sorry gentlemen, but you haven't been assigned a seat, yet. I'm sorry for the inconvenience, but, if you'll come with me to the front and wait, I'll clear this up."

They protested and grumbled, but, as a second attendant made it clear they had to follow the rules, they stood and grabbed their carry-ons.

I leaned into Liam and whispered, "Why them?"

"They were being assholes to the stewardess."

The flight attendant was about my age. Cute as a button in her uniform, her shiny blond hair was twisted into a glamorous bun. She shot Liam a timid grin.

He smiled back and said, "Thank you."

Of course, he'd be polite and nice to *her.*

The two men ended up in coach, and I waited for some amount of guilt to kick-in, but I really didn't care if they had to squeeze in smaller seats. I stowed my bag beneath my feet. "Thom needs your help with what, exactly?"

"He identified the seer, but he needs me to get rid of him. The man is a well-known businessman, so Thom can't shoot him dead without risking too much attention. We don't want trouble with the law. Demons have eyes there."

My optimistic outlook on the trip went up in flames. We were assassins, not tourists.

The plane rolled away from the gate. A cousin's wedding in Chicago and a school trip to New York summed up my life's travels, so this plane ride would be my first, and I was a little nervous. Okay, a lot nervous. Weird mechanical sounds came from everywhere as we settled on the edge of the runway, waiting for our turn to take-off.

I was torn between wishing the moment would never come and the urge to get it over with. My mouth was awfully dry.

Liam eyed me humorously for a few minutes until I couldn't take it anymore.

I grasped the armrest. "Shut up, I'm not used to this."

"I didn't say anything."

"You were 'not saying anything' very loudly."

"Here, that'll help." He handed me his drink, and I didn't bother refusing. I emptied it in one gulp and hoped the liquid heat would melt my fears.

Liam leaned in and whispered, "What are you so afraid of? You know I'd never let anything bad happen." It was unusually nice of him to say that, and I relaxed. "Besides, if you were to die today, it wouldn't be because the plane crashed."

I tensed up again, and the pilot chose this moment to initiate lift-off. I held my breath as we rose into the air and concentrated hard not to vomit. At some point between two gulps of air, we reached cruising altitude.

THERE WAS no safe house in the golden state, so it meant Liam had to stay with me 24/7. That rule also included the nighttime hunt for the seer.

After we *borrowed* a rental Jeep from the airport, I was antsy to see Thom, but Liam insisted we go for the kill first, pun intended.

The suburban neighborhood was dark at this hour. Street lamps were the only source of light. The manicured yards had a set of sprinklers each, the waste of good water no obstacle for the eternal quest of a perfectly green lawn. American flags floated in the chilly wind of the warm-by-day cold-by-night desert climate.

Thank God, I'd brought a coat with me and tightened it around my shoulders.

The Jeep stopped in front of a big ranch style home. The graystone facade was impressive. The business of seer-ing was either booming or this one had a lucrative day job.

Liam turned the engine off and reached for something on the back seat. He pried a black-hooded robe from his bag and dropped the lump of cloth into my lap.

I flattened my body against the seat. "Why am I here?" The question was mostly addressed to myself.

He unfolded a thick leather wrap on his thighs and perused an assortment of knives. A triangular dirk was the lucky winner, and he folded the weapon stash shut before putting it back. "Because Thom begged me."

The information made me feel all warm. "He did?"

"Oh, for fuck's sake! Will you guys do it already?"

Brushing aside his comment, as always, I asked, "What do I do?"

"You stay put. I can manage your beacon from inside, but do *not* move."

"You're really going to kill that guy?"

He rolled his eyes. "No, I'll make him some tea, he'll realize the errors of his ways and you'll join us for some bonding activity, probably paper mâché."

Being a man of few words, he sure saved them for sarcasm.

"You're so annoying when you do that," I said.

"You're annoying all the time."

"Am not."

"Are too."

"Oh, just go," I waved dismissively.

He stepped out of the car, put the cloak on and yanked the hood over his head.

I turned on the radio but promptly switched it off a moment later, thinking the noise might attract unwanted attention. Instead, I pried my iPod out of my purse. Would music be enough of a distraction to keep me from processing the fact that a guy was being murdered a few yards away? Doubtful, but I tried anyway. Once my ear-buds were in place, I eyed Liam's portable weapon stash. It lay on top of his unzipped bag, and I grabbed it, curious. I tugged on the safety thread and unfolded them again.

My vision blurred to anything but a vintage zigzag dagger. The intricate patterns decorating its hilt were so familiar, I could have drawn them by heart. My shaky fingers ran along the gold lines, my eyes unable to believe the sight. It was the blade Liam carved me with almost every night.

Sweat gathered on the nape of my neck, goosebumps running wild, and queasiness climbed up my stomach like a zombie clawing out of its grave.

I fisted the leather with everything in it and crammed it back in Liam's bag. I didn't want to see or touch this damn blade ever again. I opened the door and descended on the curb. The dry air acted as a salve to my fevered skin. This meant nothing. *Nothing!* I refused to believe my dreams were premonitions.

Maybe I'd seen this dagger before? I negotiated, but I knew damn well I hadn't.

It can't be. Liam wouldn't go through all this trouble to kill me.

But what if he went all demon-y again? He had one weakness in the whole wide world, and it happened to be witch blood. It wasn't too much of a stretch to imagine he could go off the deep end again. I'd feel stupid if I ended up bound to a bed beneath him and did nothing to stop it.

A street light clicked and died, and I squinted at the darkness. A man stood under the burnt bulb, his short blond hair catching the rays of the moon.

I held my breath as he took a few steps in my direction. His cowboy boots clanked against the pavement, and something in the way he moved reminded me of Liam. I backed away, ready to spin and run, before a small dog's silhouette appeared at his side. The tension in my body melted. False alarm.

From this angle, a small pink bicycle lying on its side next to the seer's house caught my attention.

Dread and disgust spread to the pit of my stomach. How naïve was I? This seer wouldn't live all alone in such a big house. He had a family. A daughter! I was the lookout, the getaway car passenger, and an accomplice in the murder of a young girl's dad.

My throat tightened as I got back in the car and dried my sweaty palms on my pants. I noticed a trail of blood originating from a small cut on my thumb. I must have nicked it with one of the blades.

As I put my seat belt back on, a faint sound attracted my attention to the passenger window. Two cloaked figures towered next to my door. I jerked away from the glass violently. My arm bumped against flesh, and I jolted upwards as a high-pitched wail ripped my vocal cords.

"Boo," Liam breathed from his seat. His mischievous grin spoke for itself.

I groaned out loud and sunk back into my seat. The bastard was toying with me. "You're mean."

"I'm trying to teach you how to fight me."

"You're trying to freak me out."

"That's a perk of the job." He grabbed the steering wheel, and a splash of red on his wrist caught my eyes.

How did he do it? Banter. Murder. Banter. He didn't appear fazed or bothered. Just another day on the job. I felt sick. Who were we to decide who lived and who died? Whatever this seer had done or planned to do, this little girl would be devastated.

"Do you realize what you did?"

Liam's eyes darkened. "Killed a bad man."

"That's just it. You killed a human less than five minutes ago, and you're already playing pranks on me."

"We can't all be doe-eyed damsels in distress."

"I'm not a damsel in distress, I just—I have a heart." I regretted the words as soon as they flew out of my mouth. I was implying I thought he didn't, and that was harsh.

He clicked his tongue. "You act all mighty with your principles, but you wouldn't survive a day in my world."

The condescension in his voice got my blood boiling. "I don't want to live in your world."

A hard line stretched his lips. "Cry me a river, we don't always get what we want."

"Can't you open your mind for a second and—"

"This conversation is over."

The nerve! I didn't regret my jab anymore. In fact, I had to cross my arms and bite my tongue not to tell him he sounded like a closed-minded misogynistic sociopath.

THOM JUMPED to his feet when Liam and I entered the brightly lit condo. I let my bag fall at my feet and scurried over to him, walking right into his outstretched arms.

He hugged me tight. "Is it done?" He asked Liam.

"Yeah."

My heart fell. I'd had no intention of rekindling the fight between Liam and I, but I had to get this off my chest. Maybe now that Thom was present, Liam wouldn't be such an ass. "Why do you kill the seers, exactly?"

Liam huffed. "Because they deserve it."

"Says who?"

He notched his chin up. "Me."

I left Thom's embrace and mirrored Liam's glare. "And that's enough for you, isn't it?"

Thom stepped between us. "Time out, guys. What's this about?"

"Your girl is a judgmental pain in the ass."

Why did he always do that? Talk to Thom like I wasn't there. "Your brother is a jerk."

Thom's eyes flicked between the two of us. A weird expression shrouded his face, his eyebrows creased in confusion, his fingers in front of his mouth.

"What?" Liam and I asked at the same time.

"Liam, a word?" Thom motioned for Liam to follow him outside.

They slid the big glass double door shut behind them. Thom's lips moved, and Liam tensed. Thom spoke again.

Liam's sneer melted, and he nodded in approval at whatever Thom had said. In perfect sync, they ran a hand through their respective hair. The gesture always appeared when Thom felt awkward, and I guessed it applied to Liam too. If only I could hear their conversation.

I looked around. The two-story open-concept condo was white from floor to ceiling. Yellow and orange pillows decorated the white furniture, matching the table runner, giving a sunny citrus vibe to the place. The joyful atmosphere was a welcome change from the gloomy dark wood back home.

The boys came back inside.

"Where are we? A random rental?" Another rental we hadn't paid for.

"We own this place. Southern California is big on the demon scene." Thom grabbed my bag and led me to the bedroom on the first floor. He laid on the bed while I went to the bathroom to change and brush my teeth.

His arm braced beneath the pillow, he looked both delighted and contrite. "I hope you're not angry about the seer thing, but I agree with Liam. It's better if they're dead."

I disagreed, but I'd had enough arguing for one night. "Not at all," I lowered my voice, "I've missed you."

"Me too. Liam wasn't too much to handle?"

My lips curled up as I lay next to Thom. "Oh, he's a handful, but I'm okay."

"Lilah doing fine?" His fingers played with mine, each soft brush tugging on my heart's strings.

"Yeah..."

We stared deep into each other's eyes, and he leaned in. I'd not only missed him, but our connection.

I was ready to... explore it further, but loud music boomed from the loft and startled us. We giggled nervously, and the moment was over.

"I should go to bed," Thom said.

I drew my bottom lip into my mouth and nodded. Yes, I'd been fighting the crush, but I was at a point where I wanted it to happen already, for better or worse. I could handle a simple kiss. It didn't have to shatter my world and redefine the rest of my life. Maybe it didn't have to be awkward. It was a bad idea to date a roommate, especially a roommate I had to depend on for the foreseeable future, but I didn't care anymore.

Arms stretched on both sides, I sprawled on the mattress and stared at the ceiling. The music stopped, but I couldn't hear any voices, so I clicked my lamp off and waited for my heartbeat to slow down.

I WOKE up screaming at the top of my lungs.

Another nightmare, another round of tattoos carved into my skin.

Only this time, I'd grabbed the dagger and helped. Maybe my subconscious was saying I was as much to blame for the seer's death as Liam. I checked my body for actual wounds but found none.

A quick movement captured my attention. Liam glowered next to my bed, and I shrieked even louder. Was this a dream within a dream again? Every time I woke up to find Liam in my bedroom, he killed me. Adrenaline and sleepiness dizzied me. I jumped to my feet on the mattress, almost toppled over and grabbed the wall with both hands.

"Whoa, calm down." Liam placed his palms up in front of him and inched forward.

"STAY BACK!"

"What's wrong?" He canvassed the room for the source of my hysteria and found squat. He should have looked in the mirror. "Thom!"

He never called for Thom in my dreams, so maybe this was real.

A groggy Thom stumbled through the doorway, rubbing his eyes. "What's going on?"

Tight-lipped, Liam said, "I don't know."

"What are you doing in my room?" I asked.

His eyes hardened. "You were screaming bloody murder."

"I had a nightmare."

"About what?" Thom asked.

My gaze flicked over to Liam a second too long, and I didn't know what to make of the grim line that twisted his face. I expected him to be proud his intimidation techniques were working.

Thom offered a hand to help me get down. He pulled me to him, and I melted against his chest, burrowing myself in his heat. A sigh of relief escaped me as the woodsy scent of his aftershave caressed my nostrils.

Liam shook his head in aggravation, eyes in the air, and walked out.

I waited until he was out of earshot and whispered as an extra precaution. "Can a witch have... clairvoyant dreams?" The ordeal freaked me out. I could taste blood on my tongue.

"It's not unheard of. Why?"

Major jitters followed his answer. "Do they always come true?"

"No. Foretelling the future is like making your way through quick-sand. Take for example how the Collective learns where to hunt for randoms. One good lead among a dozen false ones. Liam wades through the slush pile, but we don't always select the right people. Your dream might come true, or it might just be a remnant of what might have happened. Or it could be just a dream."

I was sure the last choice was a no-go, so I was left with *might happen* and *might have happened*. It didn't help much. A chilly tremor went up my spine.

Thom tilted my chin up and searched for my gaze. "What's this nightmare about?"

"Don't worry, it's nothing," I lied. Thom trusted Liam with his life, so he wouldn't believe me. Or worse, he'd tell Liam about it.

"Hey, you can tell me."

There is no good way to say "your brother carves and kisses about every inch of my skin—while I'm naked, by the way—before he kills me," so I kept my mouth shut.

Divination. *Divination is the ability to see the future. Some druids are known for a highly accurate recounting of future events. Witches are also suspected to possess this ability through spells and potions. A famous random witch at the turn of the first millennium was sold to a sultan and described his death and the fall of his empire in detail decades before it happened.*

Seers. *Humans attuned to the supernatural. They can see auras and sense magical flares. The gift is genetic and passed down generation to generation. A few families have been associated with demons for centuries, and those without loyalties are for hire.*

16

ITSY. BITSY. TEENIE.

Alana

After breakfast the next day, I accessorized my red bikini with a pair of white superstar-sized sunglasses and walked past the boys working at the dining table. The eat-in kitchen offered an unobstructed view of the backyard, and I slid the large glass patio door open. I needed a vacation from all the supernatural talk. The boys had been all work and no play all morning.

As I stepped out, Liam said, "Don't go beyond those purple flowers." He pointed to the flower pot bursting with violet gerberas multiple times like I was too dense to grasp the concept.

The condo complex had a pool area in the center of the shared yard, and I swayed my hips to a lounge chair, determined to stay there until I had a noticeable tan.

Scornful of Liam's abrasive tone, I lined the chaise longue next to the *oh-so-important* planter, at the edge of the twenty feet of free space between our condo and the flowers.

I laid on my back, and my face tingled under the powerful rays of the California sun. The drapes from our unit moved, and Liam's scowl burned holes in my bared skin. I smiled at him and waved. If the distance made it harder for him to block my beacon, good. Had he been nicer, I would have been more inclined to play by his rules.

Thom and Liam had discussed various scenarios that morning, in case the new potential needed to be brought back to Virginia. The mileage was a complication. To fly with an unwilling guest in tow was impractical, so we might have to drive back.

From their discussion, I understood better the inner workings of what they called my demon beacon. There were two separate issues, the beacon itself and the aura.

The beacon, a flare of sorts, worked as a series of breadcrumbs dropped wherever I went. Demons possessed the ability to spot the trail and follow it to its source. Liam muddied the path by leaving a stronger trail, so an unsuspecting demon wouldn't think that a witch had passed by but another demon.

The aura was a different matter. It was a bright halo around me, visible only to seers and the like. If I stayed home and bolted the doors, nobody could sense it from a distance, so it wasn't as much a nuisance.

I'd taken advantage of Thom's presence to ask a lot more questions about our goals here in California. The new potential warlock, Duncan, was a waiter at a restaurant, and Thom had been working there as a bartender since he'd left Virginia. It had allowed him to identify the seer and keep an eye on the nineteen-year-old waiter. Now that the seer was dead, Thom's surveillance schedule could ease up a little, but the boys were wary of a possible back-up seer.

Duncan's birthday was coming up in two weeks, so the odds of him *activating* were increasing every day.

I wondered how life might work at the house if a warlock were to join us. Would he freak out? Would he want to be saved?

If he hadn't *activated* by midnight on his twentieth birthday, he never would. Not if he was truly a random witch.

My birthday party had taken place on my actual birth date, so Thom had waited on midnight to say goodbye. It also explained why Liam had been in such a hurry to leave at 12:01 am. My survival had hinged on Liam getting a random vision of me while he meditated the night after. He'd reached my parent's street in time to see the van drive off and followed. If he'd arrived thirty seconds later, I'd have been dead.

It's weird to owe your entire existence to a crazy random happenstance, but I guess it's the point of life. Either you believe that nothing happens by chance, that there's a grander design beneath it all, a destiny that awaits you, or you contemplate the terrifying alternative. Everything happens by chance. Staying alive depends on dumb luck. The universe doesn't care.

But Thom did. Thom cared *a lot*. He was enthralled by his mission to save a guy he barely knew, even though Duncan's chances of becoming a warlock were slim. I was in awe of his passion and commitment. The way he talked about Duncan, I could have sworn they were best buddies. Maybe he felt he had to care for two since Liam wasn't in this crusade because of compassion.

Despite his efforts to secure the life of Duncan, Thom hadn't kindled a relationship with him. He hadn't disclosed his identity, either. I suspected he'd only broken that rule with one person. Me.

Had he approached me because he'd found me attractive? I couldn't believe it was that simple.

THE CROWD around the pool quickly thickened, the temperature rising. As I devoured my book, a few twenty-something guys shot appreciative glances in my direction. I caught one staring from across the pool several times. With long blond hair set behind his ears, he had a surfer look about him and the body to go with it. If Ken had a real-life counterpart, this guy would have given him a run for his money. After so many months of cabin fever, the attention was thrilling, and I might have encouraged him by flapping my high ponytail behind my shoulders and tucking my stomach in.

I painted my toenails blood red. Blondy McSurf approached me as I was twisting the nail polish cap shut. He'd seemed cute from afar but looked full of himself up-close. He passed a hand through his greasy hair and puffed out his chest.

Even his voice was disappointing when he said, "Can you touch my hand? I wanna tell my friends I've been touched by an angel."

Lamest line ever. I gave him a tense smile. "Mm, no."

"Why not?"

Buddy, a girl knows when you're looking at her breasts instead of her face. "I have a boyfriend," I lied.

Disgruntled that my prince had turned out to be a frog, I gathered my things and made my way inside. My white pareo flowed around my waist as I walked away, and I could practically feel the guy's sleazy gaze lingering on my butt. *Ugh.*

Liam and Thom were surfing on their laptops at the dining table, and I sat on a stool next to them as I drank iced tea from a fun loopy straw, waiting to see if Froggy McSurf would leave. Liam's contemptuous glare skimmed me from the tip of my painted toenails to the highest hair of my ponytail. If he had his way, I would stay cooped up inside for the rest of my adult life. His darkened eyes shot up from his computer's screen a few times, enough to make me feel on edge.

Thom looked like he needed an escape, too. He passed a tired hand over his face, his shoulders sagging.

An idea struck me. "Let's go see the Pacific."

Liam shut me down. "We're not tourists."

The fight from the night before had made him even more sullen than usual. *Who wears long sleeves when it's 90 degrees outside?* Liam leeched the fun out of everything.

"We have nothing left to do until tomorrow," Thom said, the light in his eyes telling me he loved my idea.

Liam slammed his laptop shut. "Fine." In Liam's dictionary, *Fine* must be listed under synonyms for *you piss me off.*

THE COASTAL TOWN we drove to was charming. We walked along the pier and admired the sea on one side and the colorful houses perched on the hills on the other. I grabbed a few items from the outdoor shops, adding to my summer collection. Thom paid for them with actual money, his tips from the week, to ease my guilt. It was one thing to get a stack of cash from a bank or take an iPod from an Apple store, but to steal from these small boutiques along the beach was another.

I might do an essay one day about the various degrees of stealing. It'll be utter crap because stealing is stealing, but it'll show the lengths we take to justify ourselves. Truth is, as time went on, I felt more and more disconnected with the *real* world, but I still had a few scruples.

The sun lowered in the sky, the bright orange disk blanketed by streaks of pink woolly clouds. Beginner surfers were taking advantage of the small waves to practice before twilight. Seagulls chirped overhead, and the salty air was sweet. A sense of peace engulfed me. I kicked my sandals off and picked them up.

"Last one to touch the water loses," I said before sprinting towards the striking blue waters.

Thom was quickly on my heels, and I squealed. We ran.

He let me win, and I jumped with both feet to the junction between sea and land first, my toes licked by the cold water.

I turned, arms raised over my head in victory, and my long hair flowed in my eyes because of the wind. A big goofy grin brightened Thom's face. I brushed my hair behind my ears in vain and looked beyond Thom to Liam.

He had an "I hate the beach, I hate the world, why the fuck am I here" kind of look.

Thom had bought a small football, so we played in the soaked sand, throwing it back and forth. Just the two of us. I didn't suck as much as I expected.

I noticed from the corner of my eyes Liam had removed his black Nikes and socks, his toes in the sand. He was keeping a watchful eye on every pedestrian that wandered in a certain radius of us.

Liam, our enslaved chaperone... A pang of guilt itched in my chest, so I gripped the ball and aimed at him. Despite the surprise and the fact that I'd missed my mark by about a foot, his hand shot up over his head and caught the ball, his reflexes sharp. He considered the peace offering, his head tilting to one side. At first, I thought he'd just toss it back with a tired look, but his demeanor changed as he looked up at me.

"You were picked last in gym, weren't you?" He said the words as a playful quip, not as a derisive remark. On Liam's scale, this meant he was ready to bury the hatchet.

He stood up and threw the ball to Thom. We passed it around until the sun sank behind the horizon.

"It's getting dark," Liam said.

"Yes, we should go," Thom agreed.

"Give me a minute." I stripped from my high waisted shorts and white tank top to my bikini.

Sooner or later, I would head back to my cage, and I wanted to spread my wings if only for a short while. The boys gawked at me as I sank waist-deep in the ocean. My skin tingled at the cold caress. Goosebumps branded the upper half of my body, and I leaped head first in the gentle waves. One thing I could check off the bucket list.

The playful breeze turned into icy gusts when I got out. I slipped my feet into my sandals, sand scratching at my soles. The walk to the car wouldn't be comfortable, and we had parked far away.

Shivers coursed up and down my wet body, but I didn't regret a thing. I walked beside Thom, Liam trailing a few steps behind us. My wet hair clung against my neck and created a constant drip of cold water along my back.

Thom glanced at me sideways every few seconds. "You're cold."

"I'm fine," I lied, teeth clanking together.

"I'm sorry I didn't take my coat, maybe—"

"Oh, for God's sake, take mine," Liam said as he removed his jacket and flung it over my shoulders. He strode past us, "If you offer to hug her to warm her up, I'll die in a fit of laughter."

For the first time ever, I saw Thom blush.

It was my turn to be gracious and change the subject. "I call dibs on the shower."

AFTER I'D WARMED up and removed the salt from my hair in the shower, I nestled in a comfortable pair of shorts and a long-sleeved shirt. I opened the refrigerator to get a drink, but we were out of iced tea. I needed a quick fix of sugar, so I juiced three lemons, threw a spoonful of iced tea mix in the empty pitcher and filled it with water.

All I was missing was ice. "Liam, I'm going to get ice," I shouted.

The condo was quaint, and Liam was always in earshot when I spoke loudly. It was a pain to warn him before I did something as simple as get ice—too much like asking for permission—but the ice machine was in the corner of the building outside, coupled with a few vending machines.

As I reached my destination, the creep from the pool stumbled to his door. I froze when he spotted me. He leered in my direction, a smirk on his face, clearly inebriated. "Hey gorgeous, how are you?"

I concentrated on my task and filled the tray to the brim.

"Your hot bod is about to give me a heart attack. I might need resuscitation." The line was slurred.

Ice in hand, I ignored him.

"Come on. Be nice."

I shrugged, giving him a frosty *get back* stare as he closed in on me. He placed himself so I either had to stay and talk or walk right by him to leave. Even from a couple feet, he reeked of weed and alcohol.

"Step aside."

"It's a free country." He laughed like he was the funniest, most charming guy in the world.

I was not in the mood to argue with a disgusting drunk, so I hugged the tray to my chest and marched around him. Up to this point, I hadn't expected him to touch me, thinking he was a harmless nuisance. I was wrong.

The jackass squeezed my butt as I passed, and I froze. Taking it as a good sign, he palmed me once again. His slimy hand made my entire being shudder in revulsion, and I saw red.

The tray fell from my hands, ice cubes scattering on the stones as I punched him straight in the face. The sleaze-bag's eyes widened in disbelief as blood spurted out of his nose. My knuckles whined in pain, but I was fucking proud.

"Bitch!" His groping hand flew to stop the hemorrhage.

I strutted back to the condo without looking back. "Watch your language, or you'll get a black eye too." To hell with ice, I was afraid of what I might do if I stayed a second longer.

Liam was leaning against the opened patio door, arms crossed. He hadn't missed a lick of what had transpired. His signature smirk greeted me, "Summer love?"

"Oh, shut up!" But I could tell from his bright eyes that he was impressed.

I headed straight to the sink to wash my hands, not wanting a single cell of that guy to remain on me. I could still feel his repugnant grip on my butt cheek and dried my hands hard enough to scrape skin off. The pain radiating from my knuckles made me wince. Punching bags were soft compared to facial bones, but I would have beaten the bastard's face down to a pulp if I thought it might teach him a more valuable lesson.

"Here," Liam handed me a few ice cubes wrapped in a rag. The ice tray lay on the counter, full. "I guess I should be more careful about getting you angry, huh?"

I grinned, applying the ice to my injured hand. "You certainly should."

PALM TREES SWAYED in the late afternoon wind as I stared outside the bedroom window. My skin itched from a light sunburn, and I doused it with lotion. The day had been another scorching one, and I'd been pleased not to see an inch of my frog by the pool. He was probably too busy sticking tampons up his nose.

Thom had gone to work, and Liam was upstairs. The only noise audible was the air-conditioner working overtime, the low grumbles of its fans making it seem like the whole house was snoring.

The ticklish sensation of a feather-like object being dragged across my arm coaxed me out of my unplanned nap, and I blinked.

My stomach did a somersault, and my entrails tightened at the sight of a throng of huge spiders crawling in bed with me, on me, all around me. I yelled and shot out of bed. The disgusting creatures scattered at my feet, scampering to find a crack to crawl into.

My blood was racing. I almost retched, but, as my mind caught up with my body, I knew this was another one of Liam's tests. I tried to slow my breathing and concentrated on the horrible bugs to make them disappear and cringed when they didn't.

One was perched on my shoulder, and I struggled to wipe it away without touching it. It wouldn't budge, and its hairy legs brushed my neck, making me want to crawl out of my skin.

"Liam, enough!" I screamed. My lifespan would be cut in half by all the stress.

He appeared with a chuckle on the bed, and I gasped. How long had he been there, exactly? "God, stalk much?"

My comment rolled over him like oil on water. "Emotions get in the way. To counter me, you must be calm and centered."

"Make them go away."

"You do it." His lips were curved upwards, his eyes—silver, I noticed—were cheerful, and the disapproving scowl was nowhere to be found.

"You're enjoying this too much."

"Maybe the spiders are not scary enough?"

The eight-legged abominations were replaced by long, undulating snakes of assorted colors. Stacked on top of one another, they formed a swelling circle around my ankles. The bright red one wrapped around my neck stuck his tongue out, tasting the air. I gritted my teeth together as its scales rubbed against my skin. The only snakes I liked were the ones shaped like handbags.

It's not real, it's not real, it's not real, I repeated like a prayer. I forced myself to stare at the snake, and its sparkling green eyes stared back.

A tingle at the back of my skull pulsated, and, at last, the only creature left in my room was Liam, sprawled on my comforter.

I did it! I won! I beamed, thinking he might not be such a bad teacher, skipped over to him, and held my hand out for a high five. I think I deserved one.

The smile on his lips fell like I'd slapped him. Wondering where the strange undercurrent of tension came from, I frowned.

A loud ring coming from Liam's phone startled us both.

I sat down close to Liam to try and make out Thom's fast-paced words. The demon bounced off the bed in a flash, and his body stiffened as he spoke in quick, harsh whispers, denying my curiosity.

He shoved the phone back into his pocket. "Thom needs back up. We need to leave."

I was tempted to do a military salute and answer 'Sir, yes Sir!' but slipped my knitted summer boots on instead. I grabbed my long-sleeved jacket and ran after him to the car.

My seat belt clicked, and I shifted in my seat, nervous. "Please explain."

"He ran into trouble."

"What kind of trouble?"

The silence stretched on, and my patience grew thin. "Liam," I insisted, annoyed at his tendency to keep me in the dark.

"The potential is a bounty hunter."

"A what?"

"He hunts demons and witches for money. It's funny, actually."

Liam and I often had different views on humor. "Funny how?"

"Well, considering he could become one of the most wanted men alive, it's ironic." He turned towards me, a sleek dagger in his hand. I flinched, and a deep sigh heaved his chest, "Relax, it's for you."

"For me?"

"All this talk about self-defense, and you squeak in terror at the prospect of carrying a knife?" I snagged the blade from his hand. "Put it in your nonsensical shoes, and don't use it unless you absolutely have to. Wouldn't want you to kill yourself by accident."

I bit my tongue hard not to grimace. *What nonsensical shoes?*

17

I NEVER MET A GIRL LIKE YOU BEFORE

Alana

Broken glass creaked under the tires as we parked in front of Thom's workplace. The restaurant's facade was shattered, and it looked as if a bomb had gone off inside. I trailed Liam as he raced across the curb and stepped through the broken window. Tables and chairs were in pieces across the floor.

Worry flooded my veins at the sight of blood tainting the white tablecloths. The place was silent as a tomb.

Liam dialed Thom's number, and I swallowed hard when he didn't get an answer.

"Fuck!" Liam cursed. He closed his eyes in concentration. When his eyes snapped back open, his gaze zeroed in on the wet bar.

Quick as lightning, he reached behind it and retrieved a small lanky man. The shaking figure yelped like a girl and tried to run.

Liam pinned him to the counter with one hand. "What happened here?"

The man held both his hands up in surrender. "I don't want any trouble. Please don't hurt me."

The muscles in Liam's body moved with precise purpose as he

tightened his hold around the man's neck, and a low grunt rumbled between his teeth. If I had been the one pinned down, I would have pissed my pants.

The guy's lips loosened. "A freak came dressed in an expensive tux. His face was wrong, man, like a dog or some shit. He forced everyone else into a van, but I hid."

"Who's everyone?"

"The waiter, the three patrons, and the bartender."

Thom.

Liam cursed again and freed the witness who took one last terrified look at us before scampering off.

"What now?" I asked.

"I heard of this guy before, but I don't know where he lives."

We hurried back to the car, and Liam sped up. I braced myself for a wild ride. He clearly had an idea on what to do, and I didn't complain. Thom was in danger.

We parked next to a large, disaffected pub. Did Liam think the beast the guy had described lived here, or was he hoping to find answers nearby? He didn't say. We skirted around the building towards a badly-lit and secluded alley. Why did it always have to be dark and filthy alleys? Why couldn't demons hang out at the beach?

There were dumpsters crammed in a corner, and we used them as cover. From this angle, we had a good view of the back door of the building.

The smell of rotten fruit and the buzzing of the flies made my throat itch. "What are we waiting for?" I asked in a whisper.

"Shh."

I rolled my eyes.

The back door opened. Two huge security guys threw a tall dude out, and he collided with the asphalt. His left eye was swollen shut.

"Humans are not allowed." One guard spat on the ground before shutting the door.

Humans not allowed? I put two and two together. This had to be a meeting place for the supernatural. I was baffled that such a place existed, and my curiosity spiked.

A bunch of *not-human* people walked past us in the next few minutes. One had horns, one had a tail, one had a rod embedded in his neck—!?—and a few had blue or red skin, but most *looked* human. Those crept me out the most.

None of them made Liam move.

He was on high alert, his body exuding a barely-tamed rage, and the shimmer was back. Tiny black flames sucked the light away from his skin as they licked it. Their patterns were mesmerizing, and I was tempted to drag my fingers across the dark fire to see if it burned.

Liam didn't utter a single word or glance in my direction, and I was getting antsy when another silhouette came into view.

A woman dressed in an Asian-inspired school girl uniform strutted in our direction. The whiteness of her skin reflected the moonlight and contrasted with the black skirt that barely covered her butt. The buttons of her white blouse were undone to emphasize her pushed up cleavage, and a small black tie fell between her breasts. Long, almost translucent hair was tied in two low ponytails falling on either side of her face, and blood-red, heart-shaped lips completed the look. Despite the slutty outfit, she was without a doubt the most beautiful woman I had ever seen.

A certain *je ne sais quoi* in the way she moved commanded attention. *Look at me, worship me,* it murmured. A golden glimmer rose from her smooth skin.

Liam sucked in an audible breath. "I'll be damned... do not move," he said before shooting out of our hiding spot.

The goddess stopped her stride when he emerged from the dark and crouched into a defensive stance. A snarl bared her teeth and left me no doubt this woman had claws and knew how to use them.

She opened her mouth to speak before recognition painted her features. Her body relaxed, and she crossed her arms around her breasts. The old trick emphasized them, and she pursed her lips in a sullen pout while somehow remaining drop-dead gorgeous. *Not human, indeed.*

Liam took three confident steps to close the distance between them. Was he going to strangle her like the guy from before? I gaped as he grabbed her neck and planted an unbridled kiss on her lips.

I couldn't have been more surprised if he'd gotten on one knee to serenade her.

She resisted half-heartedly before melting into him, meeting his assault with passion. Liam's skin began to cast a similar golden glow, as if he'd absorbed a bit of the woman's power. The surrounding air thickened. Raw sexuality exuded at their every shift, and I had to tear my gaze away.

Out of breath, she said, "I'm still angry."

I peeked at them again.

Liam leaned to her height, eyes closed, and rested his forehead on hers. "I know."

She chuckled, and his eyes snapped open at the hypnotic sound. Lost in each other's intense gaze, they kissed again, long and hard. I clicked my tongue in anger. Were we here to save Thom or get Liam laid?

Finally, he went up for air. Thank God.

"I need something, Vicky," he said with a sheepish grin.

Who knew Liam could do meek?

"Of course." She broke from his embrace.

"I need a name and address. I'm looking for a Cerberus who runs around in a fancy tux."

Both hands on her hips, she gritted her teeth together. "I'm not a phone book."

"He's got Thom."

She glanced up at the sky and shook her head like Liam was the biggest ass on the planet. I tended to agree. She reached into her knee-high boots for her phone, pressed a couple buttons, and showed him the screen. "There, you happy?"

He bent to kiss her again, and I fumed. Weren't we in a hurry? "V, I owe you one."

"More like four, but who's counting?" She rolled her eyes again, but I could tell she wasn't angry anymore. In fact, she pressed her hips into him, her leg stepping in between his. Her fingers grazed Liam's stomach over his shirt, and she licked her lips. "After you settle this, come and see me. You can even bring your friend..."

Her piercing eyes narrowed in my direction, and I jumped. She knew I was there. The ardent gaze made my pulse chant.

"Nah, she's a bit of a prude."

Bastard. "Hey!" I came out of the shadows. It was pointless to hide if she'd spotted me. I was being silly. Who cared if this girl thought I wasn't interested in a threesome? But weirdly, I did care.

One dark glare from Liam made me regret my decision to come out.

"My, my, I understand why I haven't heard from you since Valentine's Day." Her voice was liquid honey to my ears.

Liam scratched his head, "I meant to call."

"Don't bullshit me, Liam. It's not your style." She glided forward, skin sparkling as if a million diamonds were hiding beneath the surface.

A rich shade of purple colored her irises, and I wondered if she wore contacts. Probably not. Everything about her beckoned, and my insides felt all funny under her scrutiny. My sight fixated on her long golden lashes, heat spread from my chest to my thighs as a wave of undiluted lust softened my knees.

She tilted her head to the side, sizing up the competition, and purred. "Let's see what we have here."

Spellbound, I didn't pull away when she planted a sensual kiss on my lips. I'd never been attracted to a girl before, but I moaned as her hot tongue danced against mine, my entire body ablaze with arousal. I'd let this woman do anything and everything to me for the longest time possible.

She squealed, her mouth leaving mine too soon. "Li, you've been a bad, bad demon." She examined me with a newfound interest. Her soft fingers stroked my neck, and I exhaled with difficulty. My breasts were so heavy and full inside my bra they hurt.

There were promises in her eyes of feelings beyond my understanding, and I reached up to run my fingers through her soft hair. The strands were like liquid silk, and I moaned.

I needed to drag them across my skin. I needed to feel her lips on my body. I needed...

Liam clasped her wrist and yanked her away from me. My control over my limbs returned, but I'm ashamed to say I almost reached out for her again, grieving the loss. The haze lifted, too, a second after.

Cheeks burning in humiliation, I buttoned my shirt back up. I'd started to undress in front of them. *Oh, God!*

Liam's eyes were murderous, his fingers digging into her arms. I couldn't tell if he would punch her, fuck her, or both. His gaze dropped to her lips a few times.

She dragged her nails from his chest to his crotch. "You should share."

Their mouths inched close to one another. They were engaged in a battle of will, his powers against hers, and I had a too clear picture of what would happen if she won.

A roar tore Liam's throat, and he grabbed a fist of her hair to hold her back. "I don't like to share."

"Fine!" The golden aura vanished. She certainly shared Liam's cynical use of the word *fine*.

Liam gripped my shoulders and pushed me towards the car. The sharp touch blistered my cold skin through the thick fabric of my jacket, the pulse of his anger tangible.

"Liam!" she called after us, her voice cracking a little. He didn't even slow down until she added, "Frank Hale is in town."

That got his attention. Big time. In a blur, he was back next to her. "Frank is *here*?"

"He came around the club two nights ago. I avoided him, but I talked to a few patrons, and he was definitely trying to pick up your trail."

"How does he know I'm here?"

"Don't take that accusatory tone with me. You know I can't stand him since he killed two of my girls. I would have warned you... if I'd known you were on this side of the continent." The reproach was crystal clear. She was pissed he hadn't told her about his trip. What kind of relationship could they have if he had not even texted her?

He kissed her again, and I shifted my gait from one leg to the other, trying to extinguish the fiery lust still raging. My underwear was soaked. *What a nightmare.* I'd have to brush my teeth for days to erase her sweet taste from my mouth. Whatever this girl was, she was powerful and dangerous.

A good match.

THE DRIVE through the city was strained. Liam's jaw was tight, and his fingers tapped furiously on the wheel. His I-know-better attitude was infuriating, especially considering his lack of openness about things I had no way to know. If he'd explained the rules better instead of locking himself up in his broody world, I might not have betrayed my witch-y-ness to his *girlfriend.*

Not able to suffer the weight of his outraged silence for a second longer, I said, "She knew I was there."

"She knew nothing."

"It's all your fault anyway for not explaining this beforehand."

"I told you not to move."

"She's your *friend,* isn't she?" The word friend sounded as insincere as it was inaccurate.

"Vicky's a Vandella. She can't keep her mouth shut by default. That's why she's so helpful. She'll run her mouth off to every demon on the west coast that she kissed a full-blooded witch."

Helpful was a bad word to describe your girlfriend. No wonder she felt used. "But you dated her!?"

A dark chuckle rasped his throat. "You don't *date* Vicky. You fuck her until you pass out."

I could picture that really well. Too well. "Please stop talking."

"You asked."

"Who's Frank Hale?"

He looked pained. "Frank is a problem. We need to leave town *tonight.*"

Again, he hadn't answered my question. Whoever Frank Hale was, he rattled Liam to a whole new degree. Frustrated, I used my hair as a screen to erase Liam from my peripheral vision, desperate for a break from his constant resentment. My existence pissed him off.

"Shut up!" he roared.

"I didn't say anything," I said, taking offense in his rudeness.

"I'm not talking to you."

My forehead crunched in question. *What?*

He tapped his temple with his palm as if he was trying to shake something out of his head. "Shut up. You're wrong. You're fucking wrong." Eyes closed, he dragged his jaw against his hiked-up shoulder.

The demons were talking to him? *Now?* They had seriously bad timing.

Liam slammed on the brakes. The car stopped in the middle of the road, and the seatbelt prevented me from flying through the windshield. It was late, and the sketchy neighborhood was silent. Thank God we weren't on the highway.

Liam opened the door and lurched out of his seat. Out of breath, he glanced in circles around him like he didn't see the car or the road, but something else. And whatever he was seeing wasn't good. A sick glow leaked from his skin, his face pale and ghastly.

In apparent pain, he grabbed his head with both hands and fell to his knees on the asphalt. "I'd rather die."

I walked to him. "Liam?"

He looked right through me without seeing me. "I was never yours."

Who is he talking to?

His fingernails scraped skin off his face and left a trail of blood in their wake. The invisible force haunting him had serious mojo.

"Liam, stop." Freaked out, I leaned to his level and gripped both his hands. He had to stop before he gouged his eyes out. I squeezed hard, my nails burying deep in his palms.

He paused.

Yes! "Liam, it's Alana. Can you hear me?"

He lowered his hands so they no longer obstructed his face. I wrapped my fingers over his. The glaze over his eyes lifted, and his stare met mine. "Alana?" The low baritone of his voice trembled like he'd woken up from a deep slumber.

"Are you okay?"

"No, I'm not."

The sight of his obvious despair was jarring, and I squeezed his hands tighter.

A loud cacophony of honks made me jump, and Liam stood. A car had stopped behind us and was waiting impatiently for us to move out of the way. The driver cursed from an open window, his language foul and uncalled for.

Not a good time, buddy.

One glare from Liam, and the man shut the fuck up. Moving deliberately slow, Liam leaned over the hood of the impatient motorist and flicked the windshield with his middle finger and thumb.

A crack appeared in the glass, running from right to left, before the windshield disintegrated like sand. The driver's eyes opened as wide as saucers, and he rolled his window back up.

I smirked. *Good luck with your therapist.*

Liam motioned to the car with a quick tilt of the head, and I got back in my seat. What had the demons shown him? He didn't say anything, and I held my tongue not to aggravate him, knowing it wouldn't help. If only that stupid driver hadn't come, he might have told me.

18

KRYPTONITE

Alana

Strobe lights pulsed in the busy nightclub as Liam and I stepped inside. Red, green, and blue lasers swirled in fabricated smoke, and the synthetic noise rising from the speakers numbed my eardrums. Musk and desire clogged the air. A sea of human forms rippled against the dance floor, bodies moving in synchrony, indistinguishable from one another.

I tried to follow Liam's lead and wade through the crowd, but, after a few paces, I lost sight of him. Skin, arms, and chests brushed against me from all sides.

A tall, muscular guy bumped into me as his partner, a blond girl about my age, pressed flush against him. They writhed against one another, the movements leaving nothing to the imagination.

The more I tried to push through, the more the dancers closed in, and sweat dripped down my back from the heat. My mouth dried up and my vision fizzed.

Liam's arm wrapped around my shoulders and rescued me from the mayhem. I cowered against him, and we moved as one to the back of the club. From the appreciative leers I received, I suspected I had a slutty glamor around me. The best way to blend in.

Two bouncers guarding the VIP section blocked our path.

"I need to see your boss," Liam said, and it wasn't a request.

They snorted and motioned to the exit, but the humor died in their throats when Liam flashed them his all-black demonic eyes.

They exchanged a serious look and marched us to a back room. One of them made a quick call on his cell phone, but I didn't understand a word of the hushed conversation. Still reeling from my encounter with the Vandella, I'd seen enough demons for the night, but this was the only way to save Thom.

After a few minutes, the leader arrived. I'd been preparing myself for a dogman, and a dogman I got.

The demon's snout was adorned with thick whiskers, and his lower mandible protruded forward. He was large at the shoulders, but leaner at the waist, and about my height. His arms were terribly muscular and three-times the size of his legs. With all of that added to his bald head and irritated expression, he looked like a botched genetic experiment between a bulldog and a wrestling champion.

He took a few steps forward and sniffed the air around Liam. His speech was gruff as he said, "Yes, a Shadow Walker, been awhile since I've seen one of you disgusting half-breeds."

Liam disentangled himself from me. "We don't exactly run in the same circles."

"No, you guys think yourselves superior because you can put on a good show and wave your fingers around to make people obey you. But your little magic tricks won't work on me, little boy."

Liam clicked his tongue. "Where are the hostages you picked up earlier tonight?"

"How is it your business?"

"My brother was among them."

A flash of recognition passed in the beast's eyes. "Ah, yes, the blond one put up a hell of a fight. Your brother put his nose where it didn't belong, but he's alive. That can change. Depends on what you have to offer."

"You won't get anything from me," Liam said through his teeth.

The dogman ignored his answer, and his vile stare zeroed-in on my breasts. "You've got quite a date. I'm sure she can show me a good time."

To my knowledge, demons saw through any glamor, so this one was interested in the actual me. *Ugh.*

The creature lifted a claw in my direction.

Liam growled. "Don't touch her."

"Don't get rude, little boy, or I'll get angry."

"Let me see my brother," the menace in Liam's voice was thick. "You might enjoy taking humans prisoner, but you don't want trouble with me. You're big, but I'm fast… could get bloody."

The demon's gaze appraised Liam like he was trying to decide if he was bluffing. Liam glared back without blinking. The dogman finally rolled his eyes and turned up his nose in disgust. "I'll give you back your brother, but I better not see him, or you, ever again."

Liam responded to the offer with a curt nod. "No problem."

The armed men in tow, the dogman escorted us outside.

My pulse was racing. The knife Liam had given me burned against my leg. What if I needed to use it? My breath quickened.

I wasn't equipped to fight any of those men; they were insanely buff. Panic surged, and my throat constricted.

Suddenly, Liam's voice boomed in my mind. *"Don't worry, stay close, and do not say a word."*

I nodded and stepped closer to him. If he could sound cocky telepathically, he must not have been worried.

They led us across the street to a gigantic three-story warehouse. A murky scent floated in the moist atmosphere, and the entire place reeked of fungi and misery. We climbed three dingy flights of stairs and walked down a long, narrow corridor before emerging into the main room.

We were standing three stories up on a see-through metal ramp that squared along the walls of the building and towered above a barren, cement first level. I gasped as I spotted Thom in a human-sized cage on the ground floor. He was sitting in the middle of the cage, but we were too far to see if he was hurt. I wanted to call out to him but remembered Liam's advice.

There was no other dogman in sight.

Six men with rifles guarded the cage next to Thom. The young man occupying it was laying on his back, and his white shirt had a huge blood stain on the front.

Duncan, I assumed.

There was a stairway in each corner of the ramp.

The beast pointed to the closest one. "Here's your brother. You can free him. But you leave the other where he is, or we're going to have a problem." Liam's eyes flicked from me to the creature. It sure sounded like a trap. "The girl stays here, so I know you won't double-cross me."

A long, full-bodied shiver struck me at the prospect of being alone with that thing, even for a second.

"It's not that far. It's like I'm right next to you," Liam said in my head.

Our eyes met, and I tried to convey determination and understanding. *I trust you.*

Like he'd spied on our silent conversation, the beast added, "Oh, and mister Shadow Walker, slowly, so I can see you. No tricks."

Liam descended the stairwell at human speed, and my heart pounded faster at every step. Twenty steps a floor, three floors, that was about sixty steps down. It was far, even for him.

In a loud crash, everything went wrong. Three men erupted commando-style from the windows next to the cages, a wave of broken glass storming across the floor. Gunshots tore the air.

"Let's go, sweetheart," the dogman slurred as he grabbed my arm.

I resisted, but the claws broke through the skin.

"Let me go." My yelp only made the clammy hold stronger, and I winced at the pain.

"You come with me or you die. Your choice."

Liam materialized next to us and plunged his dagger into the demon's heart. "I warned you not to touch her."

The sharp talons set me free, rose to stop Liam's attack, and tore the flesh of his lower arm. Liam's jaw tensed, pain visible on his hardened features, but he kept the blade in place. After a few long seconds, the robust carcass slumped down to the floor, and Liam decapitated it under my frozen, horrified stare.

A series of shots blasted in our direction. Liam pushed me against the wall, shielding me with his body. Bullets ricocheted off the concrete next to us.

"What happened?" I couldn't see anything sandwiched as I was between Liam's body and the wall.

"I opened the cage, but Thom—" his voice melted into a soft whisper, "you're bleeding."

I looked down. A small trickle of blood flowed down my arm, but it wasn't so bad.

Liam's injuries ran way deeper than mine. He was bleeding all over my jacket. "It's just a couple scratches." A hot pant brushed my ear, and I gasped. *Blood. Fuck!*

His body pressed close, too close.

A fierce blush crept up my chest as Liam's large hands encircled my waist, dipped under my shirt and dug into my sides. He held on tight as if he was about to plummet down a cliff and my hips were his last lifeline. Nuzzling my hair, he breathed deep.

What could I do? Heal myself? I had no idea how. Instead, I used what little wiggle room I had to wipe the blood away with the opposite sleeve. Would it make a difference?

Before I got an answer, Liam was ripped off me. A new dogman had crashed the party.

Growls and barks resonated as Liam and the beast walked in circles around one another. I drew quick short breaths. The stilted air rasped at my lungs, my chest heavy and my underarms wet.

If only I could melt into the background and leave this terrible place. Why didn't my powers involve walking through walls?

The beast lunged forward. Everything blurred, and I struggled to focus on the pair as they fought. My guts were in tight knots, praying the lion would win over the wolf. I'd take a blood-crazed Liam over the alternative.

When the noises stopped, and the ball of limbs stilled, the

dogman's head rolled at my feet. I met Liam's stare. He looked mightily embarrassed. The fight had sobered him up.

Loud steps echoed over the chaos taking place three stories below and shook the metal floor beneath our feet.

In horror, I spotted that more demons were coming from the way we'd arrived. Liam and I hurried across the ramp to what appeared to be another exit. We made it through a first door to another squared staircase. Liam grabbed me by the waist and jumped over the rail.

I held my breath.

We crashed on the ground floor a second later, his legs absorbing the impact.

He put me back on my feet. "Come on."

I almost toppled over about a dozen times as we ran through two sets of doors and a narrow corridor. "Wait, what about Thom?" We were going too fast for him to catch up. What if more demons arrived? What if they captured him again? What if they killed him?

"He can handle himself, unlike you. We need to leave."

"No!"

"Come on, Alana, you can't possibly fight these things, and I can't help Thom while I'm babysitting you."

It was not the time to argue about my self-defense skills. "Stop treating me like a child."

He dragged me forward and pushed me through a door into the street, but I battled against him. He couldn't use his super speed with me playing dead weight, and I wouldn't go a step further.

When he grabbed my waist again and threw me over his shoulder, I growled and bit him hard. His swift response had me flying to the ground. A dangerous glint in his eyes mingled with plain disbelief as he brought a hand to his neck. In my mouth, a metallic taste. I'd drawn blood.

"I won't leave without Thom," I repeated. How could he leave his brother stranded with these monsters? Who cared if my beacon activated? Thom's life was at risk, and this place was crawling with demons. "What kind of brother are you?"

"Fine." He disappeared, his blurry trail headed back inside the warehouse.

A crow snickered overhead, and I scattered to my feet. The sudden silence of the empty street was in stark contrast to the raging violence inside the building, and I felt like I was going to implode.

If something happened to Thom... I couldn't tolerate the thought.

I got the dagger out of my boot in case another villain appeared. The heavy metal door crashed open, and I gripped the hilt, fear grating my insides. Relief washed through me as I recognized Thom. He sprinted in my direction, a semi-automatic in one hand.

He was alive.

Fingers entwining with mine, he said, "Liam's got them. Let's go."

The whole point of my tantrum had been to leave no one behind, but Thom was tugging on my arm, and Liam was invincible. With a pang of regret tightening my stomach, I let Thom lead me away.

We bolted as if the hounds of hell were after us around the large building. Voices and loud music were audible in the distance. If we made it far enough beyond the crowd, we might be okay.

The jog was arduous in my ill-advised girly shoes, and I was soon out of breath, lungs burning as if my bronchioles were having a bonfire. Thom noticed my struggle and slowed down.

The emotions bouncing around inside my pinball-machine heart came to a standstill. I threw my arms around him and squeezed. Rock-hard muscles embraced me, and my insides tightened.

I backed up to stare deep into his eyes. "I was so scared."

"I'm okay."

I wet my lips. Electricity arched from my fingers as I laid my palm on his chest. My gaze flicked to his mouth and back. I stood on my tiptoes and leaned closer.

And closer...

I closed my eyes.

Just as ours lips brushed, he spun around and took three deliberate steps to put some distance between us. "Let's get the car."

What. the. hell.

Ouch. My pride had just been thoroughly trampled. No misunderstanding here, no interruption. He'd pulled away deliberately, almost tearing himself away from my grasp. The frown on my face must have been worth a thousand words.

The timing sucked, I admit, but the rejection stung all the same. Waiting for an apology or at the very least an explanation, I stared blankly at Thom as he canvassed the parking lot. He acted oblivious, but I wasn't stupid, and the way he was thoroughly avoiding eye contact made it clear how aware of the situation he was.

A splash of red on the hem of his jeans caught my eye, and an icy feeling slithered into my chest. Blood was oozing out of his lower back, his shirt punctured in a perfect circle. The bullet wound dug right beside his spine, and my stomach churned.

I couldn't process it; it didn't feel real. More blood dripped and stained the denim, making my heart rate go wild. *No, no, no, NO!*

He turned back towards me. "Let's go this way."

I gawked at him. "You're hurt."

He didn't know he had a bullet embedded in his back. It didn't make sense. Not a lick of sense. Maybe he was high on adrenaline?

Maybe... bile rose into my mouth.

I'm a fool.

Such. a. fool.

Thom wouldn't be able to ignore a gunshot. Liam would. I recognized the lie.

Angry tears spilled over on my cheeks. "You tricked me!"

Thom's open features melted into Liam's tight jaw. "I saved your life."

I pushed into his chest with all the strength I had. "You tricked me."

Sobs flowed through my lips, my stomach in knots as if I'd been served a burger made from the blended pieces of my heart.

"Gee, Alana, what about thanking me for the bullets I took for you?"

"I hate you!"

He stepped forward. "God woman, if I have to knock you unconscious to get you out of here alive, I'll do it."

"Charming. Hitting women over the head must be on your list of favorite things to do."

"Do you want to die? Because if that's what you want—"

"You are the most condescending, insufferable *thing*." I refused to call him a man.

"And you're a stubborn, stuck up, ungrateful *child*."

Liquid rage scorched my veins, and I raised my hand to slap his face. A few inches from my mark, he gripped my wrist and held it in mid-air.

The fingers cuffing my wrist dug deep and would leave a mark. His control over the super-strength was either slipping, or he meant to hurt me.

I swallowed hard and breathed, "You're hurting me."

One after the other, his fingers loosened their hold as the rest of Liam went completely still in a way that reminded me how un-human he was.

I should have noticed it was Liam sooner. Thom would have kissed me.

Oh, get over it!

Thom's voice reached my ears, and I broke the staring contest.

"Liam, I could use some help." Thom yelled from about fifty feet away. Arm bleeding and face bruised, he was half carrying a beat-up Duncan.

Liam picked the potential warlock up in a blur. "Where are the three other men?"

Thom's jaw tensed. "Dead." He stretched his shoulder with a painful grimace before taking my hand. "Let's go."

A minute later, Liam dumped Duncan in the trunk, face first. I arched my eyebrows at him, but he ignored me and climbed in the driver seat while I crashed in the backseat.

Blood was flowing down Thom's right arm, and I bit my lips. "You're hurt."

"A bullet went straight through."

Liam cut the driver's side seat belt and tied it higher than the bullet wound. "We'll have to stitch that up ASAP."

Thom inspected the gash and nodded. "Do we have something for the pain?"

"There must be some oxycodone in my bag. Side pocket."

The motor roared to life, all road markings ignored, and we were soon far enough away for me to breathe again. I unzipped the bag laying at my feet and rummaged through the various pills until I found the right ones and handed the bottle to Thom. He popped two of them into his mouth and swallowed before he relaxed, too. Or maybe he was getting woozy.

"What are we going to do with Duncan?" I asked. He was badly battered, and I glanced behind my seat to check if he was still breathing. His chest rose and fell at regular intervals, so he was alive.

"We're going to dump him at the nearest hospital and get the fuck out of here." Liam answered.

"Dump him? You mean we're not going to wait to see if he activates?"

"Nope. He's a bounty hunter. He can deal with his own crap."

Thom nodded weakly in agreement.

Liam gave his brother a dirty look. "I don't care what you say. I am *never* bringing your girlfriend *anywhere* again."

"I was stupid to ask you to take her."

"Very stupid."

Argh. Here they were again ignoring my presence. "Um, hello? I'm right here!"

"You could have been hurt tonight, Lana," Thom said.

I pointed to his injuries. "You're the one that's hurt."

"But it could have been you, you'd be safer at home."

Safer at home? Didn't that also apply to him? We would all be *safer at home*. Hell, if we never stepped outside, we might live to be ninety. His logic was aggravating, and I wished he'd only try to live the way he wanted me to live.

I crossed my arms. "Home? In prison, you mean?"

He passed a hand over his face. "Let's take a deep breath. We had a rough day. We'll talk about this later."

I reclined against my seat. "Fine." Apparently, I had adopted Liam's dictionary, too.

19

STICHES

Liam

The curb is silent, but my head is filled with noises. The condo's lights are on, and my eyes scan the street for any sign of Frank or any other shit he might send our way.

"What now?" Alana asks with her arms crossed.

"Now we pack our things."

Thom is as white as a porcelain toilet as he staggers out of the passenger seat. As much as I want us to hurry, I know I need to stitch him up first. I guide him inside, sit him at the kitchen table and run to get the first-aid kit. Alana is stroking his neck when I come back, her face twisted in worry over his wound.

I grit my teeth together. "I said you should pack."

"I heard you." She doesn't move an inch.

There are so many things I want to say, but the grievances get stuck in my throat. I focus on Thom's injury instead. Luckily, the bullet passed right through his arm, and didn't sever any major arteries. I grab a surgical needle and thread and get to work. I'm no stranger to stiches, and the familiar task calms me down a bit.

Alana finally goes to her room, and I decide to break the news to Thom. I can't keep it secret, even if he's hurt. "Frank is here."

Thom's entire body tenses and his mouth twists downward in a mix of anger and disgust. "Fuck."

"Fuck, indeed."

"We need to hurry. We can't have a big revenge showdown with her around. We need to protect her from him."

It's so typical of my dear brother to worry about her with a hole in his arm. He cares for her something fierce, and I nod in agreement. "Yes."

Alana emerges a few minutes later with her bag in tow. Her arms are tensed at her sides, and her neck is stiff from all the efforts she's putting into *not* looking at me. She thinks I'm the one in the wrong. She's infuriating. A child, a stubborn, stuck up, judgmental, dangerous wild card.

Can't leave without Thom, she said, *can't leave him behind.* Well, she had no problem leaving *me* behind, so I know where I stand on her totem pole. Rock bottom. And, in the middle of the damn run for our lives, which had to be made at human speed to accommodate her, she tried to fucking kiss him. To. Kiss. Him.

We were in mortal danger, and yet, she wanted to smooch with my brother bad enough to put our lives in danger. One or two of those dogs, I can handle, but dogs live in packs, and the pack is deadly. We would have died if I hadn't tricked her out of there.

She's pushing her obnoxiousness to the limit by acting like she's the wronged party. Her precious little pride was hurt by the mix up, while I was only trying to get us out alive.

My hands tense around the needle, and Thom flinches away from me. "Careful."

I bite the inside of my cheeks hard to regain focus. Can't lose my shit now that Frank's in play. I remove the tourniquet and check for blood before applying a bandage to what's left of the gash.

Thom points to a small vial of antibiotic at the bottom of the kit. "Better not take any chances."

I nod and inject him with a nice dose of penicillin.

His pained grimace as he moves the arm pinches my heart. I hate when he gets hurt. Alana obviously thinks I don't give a damn about him. I was worried sick about Thom earlier, but I couldn't go back for him. Not until I got her out of danger. If I'd let the Cerberuses get a whiff of her true nature, they would have hunted us to the ends of the earth. They still might, but I suspect the bounty hunters will be blamed for what happened.

I need a break. I need a fucking vacation from her, but noooooooooo. Instead, I'll have to drive in the same car with her for a few days. Close enough to reach for her, forced to smell her day in and day out, forced to endure her tantrums. The prospect is nearly making me gag.

Alana plays with the hem of her shirt. "So... who's Frank?"

I congratulate myself on filling Thom in, and our eyes meet as we both silently agree to ignore her question for now.

Thom clenches his jaw, resolute to work through the pain. "Pack up my stuff. I'm going to get us a new ride and meet you outside in ten minutes."

I know better than to tell him to take it easy. Thom can be more stubborn than I when he puts his mind to it, and he needs a second alone to process Frank's sudden reappearance into our lives. Commando-Thom is not to be messed with.

"I can help," Alana offers.

"Help Liam."

Surprise registers on her face at the brush-off.

I'm left alone with the annoyed witch and sigh. "Let's do this quickly. You get Thom's things, I'll get mine."

She nods, and her ice-princess scowl makes my skin boil. I think back to the look she gave me while she thought I was my brother. For a moment, I gazed into her green eyes and forgot I had a glamor on.

She likes him too much. I'd love to know what he's done to deserve that look while she treats me like trash. He's killed, too, and he agrees with me on about everything. I shouldn't care that they like each other.

A snide voice in my head says, *"but you do."* The damn Collective latches on to my frustrations and gets louder every time Alana and I fight.

I need a time out. I need space. When we get home, I'll double back and find Vicky. Let her fuck my brains out. *Fuck! Vicky...*

The mental picture of Alana and her kissing is seared into my mind forever. I can't shake that witch, and the voices are taking advantage of my frazzled state. They are whispering lies, making suggestions. I don't know if I can trust my own thoughts anymore, but I must rise above the restlessness and rage.

Frank is on the prowl, and I won't let him catch up. His voice high-jacks the Collective as he slurs *"Liam and Alana sitting in a tree."* He's always been jealous of my relationship with Thom, always blamed him for my reformed ethics. After all this time, there's only one reason why he'd show his face. It's because of *her.* Everything is *her* fault.

Starting right now, I don't care anymore. I won't let her get a rise out of me. I'm over her petty grievances, over her damn pouts. She can hate me for all I care. In fact, it's better this way.

Way better.

20

HIGHWAY TO HELL

Alana

My travel bag tucked at my side, I waited under the cold glow of a lonely street light while Thom retrieved our new ride from the parking lot. Liam was fuming behind me, fists balled at his sides, like I was the one who'd done wrong. His intense stare prickled the skin at the back of my neck without mercy. I would have killed to read the thoughts hiding behind his dark eyes and clenched jaw.

I was waiting on an apology that would never come. He'd had no right to pass as Thom. No right! The heat-of-the-moment attempt to kiss Thom/Liam haunted me, and, thinking back, I was sure Liam could have averted the situation. It had taken him a *really* long time to react, our lips a hair apart like he wanted to humiliate me.

He'd abused his powers to manipulate me outside the sphere of training, and I wouldn't stand for it. He could go to hell.

Arms crossed, I chewed on my bottom lip to keep from telling him so. "Why are we driving home again?" I asked.

Liam's teeth gritted together. "Because Frank will be watching the airports, and he might not be alone since you messed up and betrayed your identity to a Vandella. I still can't believe you let her kiss you."

"I had no choice," I said.

He raised both brows, an evil glint in his eyes. "Are you so sure about that?"

The question nagged me, even if I suspected it was just Liam being Liam, always daring me to reconsider my assumptions and beliefs.

Could I have resisted Vicky? Did demons rule the world from the shadows? Did the saving of innocent lives make up for extinguishing morally-dubious ones? Did we exist outside the rules of the normals' world? Outside of traditional justice and laws?

Better yet, should we? Did the end justify the mean in all things?

Good questions. No answers. Born in a clear moral pond, this murky sea of gray ethics was disorienting.

THOM PULLED up in a large van and climbed out of the driver's seat.

"Are we going on tour?" I joked, trying to shelf my anger. I wouldn't waste another minute focusing on Mr. Cranky Black Pants. I had to concentrate on the fairer brother.

"I love this model. It's comfortable," Thom said, massaging his lower arm.

I peered inside. There was a generous gap between the two front seats, and the back-row seat was wide. The huge space in the back was overkill for our three reasonably-sized pieces of luggage.

I hated large vehicles. They made it harder for me to keep my stomach in check. "Isn't it a little big?"

Liam stowed our bags and strolled past me. "Always complaining. Don't forget why we have to drive."

I glowered at his barb. "It's all my fault. You've said so about a thousand times."

And I wasn't exaggerating... much.

The driver's side door slammed shut.

"Want to ride shotgun?" Thom offered.

As much as I hated the thought of riding in the front with Liam, I wouldn't fare well in the backseat. "Front is better for motion-sickness."

"Brace yourself. We're going the long way around to be safe. It's a 70-hour drive."

Oh God! "Damn, I'm sorry."

Liam rolled down the electric window. "Can you say that a little louder? Didn't quite hear you."

"Go to hell." Heated, I bit the insides of my cheeks. I wouldn't let him affect me anymore. I was done with him and his rants. One of us had to act like an adult, and it clearly wasn't going to be him. I sat beside him and ignored his glare.

Thom sprawled out on the back seat, exhausted. He'd lost a lot of blood, and the pale, joyless expression looked bizarre on him. I'd thought about trying to heal him, but things had been too hectic; I hadn't had the time.

I angled myself towards the backseat and entwined our fingers. "I want to heal you."

Liam's nails tapped on the gearshift. "Won't work."

My teeth gritted together. "Why not?"

"You're not ready."

Eyes closed, I concentrated hard. I needed to prove Liam wrong. Nothing happened, but I kept searching for the special sixth sense. After a few minutes, I huffed in frustration.

Thom squeezed my hand. "Hey, don't worry about it. I'll be fine."

A sad smile stretched my lips. What if I never succeeded? What if I had to live at the house for the rest of my life? What if I had to negotiate with Liam for every outing until the edge of forever?

I propped my left foot up over the glove compartment, removed my boot, and winced at the sight of the blisters I found. Liam's sideway glance said, *I warned you about those shoes.*

Rolling my eyes, I reached into my right boot to retrieve the dagger. They were not run-for-your-life shoes, but I hadn't known beforehand I'd have to perform such a feat. I wouldn't make this rookie mistake again. From now on, if I went out for demon-related issues, I'd always wear sneakers, and I'd always have them on hand otherwise. Boots and boys were too touchy.

***BOUNTY HUNTERS.** Human scum. They hunt the supernatural for money. Kill on sight.*

***VANDELLAS.** Powerful half-breed demons sometimes confused with the deadlier succubus. Highly sexual, they feed on the desire they incite in their prey. Highly social, they get along with many species and are sought-after mates. They are born human. The change usually happens around puberty, a process that's as mysterious as the creatures themselves.*

***CERBERUSES.** What they lack in brains, they make up for in brute strength. They live in packs and are highly loyal allies. Their sense of smell is unparalleled.*

THE FIRST FIVE hours of the trip were pure torture, each minute more bothersome than the last. Thom napped to gather strength to drive the next shift, so Liam and I were left to our own devices. I hadn't uncrossed my arms, and my neck hurt from constantly looking out the window and away from the driver's seat.

Liam's hands cramped around the wheel whenever I spoke, and I couldn't wait for the boys to switch places. An atrocious heavy metal song played on the radio, indistinguishable from the others that had scratched at my eardrums for the last few hours, and I reached to change the station.

Liam slapped my hand away from the console. "The driver gets to choose the music."

What a baby. "I'll take the wheel, then."

"Oh no. You're not driving."

"Why not? Because I'm a girl?"

His biceps flexed, straining against his shirt. "Now I'm sexist? Please, if anyone here has prejudice, it's you."

"What?" What the hell was he alluding to? *What prejudice?*

"You want to drive, fine."

The brakes screeched, and the car slid to a stop on the side of the road.

Both our doors swung open before the engine died. I started to walk around the back, but changed my mind and spun around, meeting Liam in front of the bumper.

"What do you think me prejudiced against, pray tell?"

He puffed his chest. "Me."

My teeth gritted together. "You fucked with my brain. Can't you apologize?"

"Never. I did what I had to do."

"But Thom—"

"Thom is a grown man."

"And I'm a child, right?"

He tipped his chin up. "You're a newbie. I know better."

The more he treated me as a child, the more I wanted to throw a fit and scream. So much for not letting him under my skin.

A loud honk stopped our bickering.

Thom was awake, leaning over the driver's seat, a hand on the steering wheel. "Both of you are acting like children right now. In the car!" A disapproving glower twisted his face. I don't think I'd ever seen him this grumpy. The resemblance to his older brother was disturbing. "You guys have been at each other's throats like toddlers since the day you arrived in California. Why—no, wait. Don't answer that. You'll just fight again. Can't we have peace? I'm the one with a hole in the arm, and I'm begging you to *calm. the. fuck. down.*"

Guilt pinched my gut. I'd come to the same conclusion, but my temper was too hot to obey. With a deep breath, I put the vehicle in gear and chose the cheesiest pop radio station to aggravate Liam.

Thom didn't complain but put his headphones on. Liam's words had struck a chord. Why would he say I was prejudiced against him?

Sure, I'd been afraid at first, but not anymore, and he couldn't hold a grudge about that.

I thought and thought without finding one logical explanation for his anger and biting comment, and it gnawed at me. I wanted to understand. I needed to figure out this puzzle before letting it rest.

Not wanting Thom to scold me again, I whispered, "Why did you say I'm prejudiced?"

Liam answered in the same hushed tone, "Let it go."

"I want to know."

A loose strand from his jeans captured his attention, his fingers picking at it. "I don't know why I said that."

Liar. "Tell me."

"Will you stop?!"

I pressed on, hoping he'd crack. "Tell me."

His discreet nod pointed to the back seat. "You'll get us into trouble again."

"Tell me."

Stormy, silver eyes shot daggers as he met my stare. "You left *me* behind!"

I paused. Left him behind? At the warehouse? That was the source of his anger? I'd meant nothing bad by it. I knew Liam would prevail over anything. It was a compliment, really.

"It's not the same," I explained, but my voice was on the defensive. "Thom's human," I added, trying to clarify.

Liam's eyes scrunched, arms crossed, and his body flattened against the seat. He put as much distance between us as possible, and I realized that was not a good thing to say. It sounded... racist. *Say something else, say something better.*

"You— you're strong, you're used to all the violence, you can heal... and stuff."

He retreated even further into his seat, fists clenched against his thighs.

Shit. I shouldn't have said anything.

∞

NO MATTER how famished I was, I couldn't eat in the car. Women are known for multitasking, but I spat bile in a paper bag when Thom and Liam got burgers at McDonald's. The odor of greasy French fries turned my empty stomach faster than a day's worth of driving. We stopped along the highway for me to vomit into the dirt, and Thom's hands came around my neck to hold my hair as I retched.

Not my best look.

I bought Listerine at the next gas station and relied entirely on water to sustain me.

After 25 hours of driving, Thom and I voted for a night at a motel. Liam would have preferred not to stop, but he had supernatural stamina, so we overruled him. A shower would be heaven, and I couldn't wait to dig my teeth into something of substance.

A gigantic oatmeal cookie was my reward after which I showered and crashed into bed.

The two adjacent rooms we squatted in had no style. The motel was one of those truckers' stops indistinguishable from another. It wasn't dirty, per se, but it wasn't clean. The smell of diesel and mildew reminded me of my grandpa, and I couldn't have been happier to have a few hours of privacy if we'd stopped at the Ritz.

I WOKE up early the next day. The mattress was stiff and creaked at my every move, and my body had been idle for so long that it couldn't stand to lie down anymore.

A knock on the door echoed as soon as I was done changing. I expected Thom but found Liam on the other side.

"What," I said, a hand on my hip, my voice drier than the Sahara.

"Come with me." He spun around, hands shoved into his jean's pockets.

I dragged my feet and followed him to the empty parking lot. Silent, he got a dagger from the car.

"What are we doing?" I was not in the mood for games.

"Training. Thom can use another hour of sleep."

"What? Why?"

He wanted us to work out? Together? Now?

"You almost squealed in terror when you saw the knife the other day," he explained matter-of-factly.

"I did not!"

I had, but hell if I would admit it. Maybe a week ago, I would have been eager to learn how to hold a knife properly but not anymore. Any situations in which Liam acted as a teacher stressed me out. Wasn't there a witchcraft for dummies? Some explanatory website? A funny YouTube video?

"Why can't *I* sleep another hour?" I asked.

"You were up."

I arched a suspicious brow. "How would you know?"

"I have to know. Part of my job description." From his curt tone, I gathered it was a great inconvenience to be aware of me at all times. He held the blade out in his palms.

A demonstration was coming my way, and I scratched the tip of my flats on the asphalt. How could I get out of this?

"Daggers pierce lungs, hearts, stomachs. There are two ways to hold them. The forward grip has easier thrusts. The reverse grip excels at directional attacks and has faster recovery. Mostly you want to use the forward grip." He showed me how to hold it. "Never switch your grip. You'll drop your blade. When you have a weapon, it becomes your shield. Point it at your opponent, always. But remember, you'll never have the upper hand. If they have a gun, run and hide; if they have claws, run and hide. Running and hiding should always be your number one option. This lesson is meant only to make it seem that you know what you're doing enough to discourage your attacker in case you can't avoid a fight."

Holy crap! That had to be the longest speech he'd ever made. He wasn't looking to put fuel on the fire but actually wanted to teach. And it didn't involve tricking me into seeing gross stuff. I swallowed my grievances and paid attention.

"Put one foot in front of the other and pull one shoulder back. You'll present a smaller target." He mimicked the correct position.

I copied him.

"When you face your opponent, always hold the blade at eye level. Their first instinct will be to secure your hand. If you hold it too low, it will be easier to grab your arm." He reached in the car again and passed me a long-bladed knife.

I grabbed it and got a feel for its weight as I passed it from one hand to the other. "What else?"

"Don't cut yourself."

What about him? The edge was shiny and deadly. It wasn't wise to train with the real thing. "Don't you have a plastic one for practice?"

"You won't touch me."

His assurance annoyed me, and my eyes narrowed.

"Keep your elbows in like a boxer. Keep your hands and feet moving. Cut with small circles. I'll only be trying to disarm you at human speed."

We circled around each other.

The knife fell to the ground with a clank as he grabbed my wrist. *Whoops.*

Damn!

Again?

Ow!

That last arm twist was a little harsh.

After four epic fails, Liam paused. "You're somewhere else. Focus."

I massaged my sore elbow. "Why do we always have to do things on your time? Maybe I didn't feel like training this morning. Ever thought of that?"

"Will you get over it already?" The anger mingled with impatience on his features, but with a touch of… disappointment?

"Will you say you're sorry?"

"You're just pissed you tried to kiss me."

The blood drained from my face. "I tried to kiss *Thom*."

"I KNOW THAT."

Why did he act like he was the wronged party? Fingers clenched around the hilt, I lunged at him, blade held high.

I missed my mark, but he'd used his super-speed to step aside. *Ah-ah!*

This was the better way to work out our issues, and I didn't give a damn that he was better and faster. I needed to draw blood.

Something wicked simmered inside, and I drew a fast circle with the dagger, the edge forming a perfect arch towards Liam. He moved out of the way again, but, as he twisted his elbow to look at the back of his lower arm, I saw a tinge of blood.

A shallow cut, barely a scratch but... *Victory!*

He stared as if I'd grown two extra heads.

"What?"

"You moved really fast, how?"

"I moved like I always do."

He pinched the bridge of his nose. "Yeah, I guess."

I looked at the blade again, this time with enthusiasm. Maybe I could learn after all.

All the anger evaporated like snow in July. *Well, that fight was therapeutic.*

I stretched my arms to ease the stiffness in my muscles. I needed a good run to erase the languid ache that resulted from sitting down for hours and sleeping on a bad mattress.

Since leaving Virginia, I'd treated the time outside the house as a vacation and hadn't jogged at all. It would be a real treat to run outside instead of on the boring treadmill.

I bit my bottom lip. "Can we go for a run?"

Surprise registered on Liam's face. "I thought you didn't want to train."

"I changed my mind."

He looked about to refuse, so his soft, "okay," baffled me.

Liam had to follow my slow strides, but he didn't complain once. I wondered how fast he could run and how amazing it must feel to have such strength and energy. I was pushing myself beyond my limits, and he wasn't even breaking a sweat.

A few people shot glances in our direction. My hair was damp and in knots. Sweat had run down my skin and pooled in unflattering areas, mainly under my breasts and armpits while Liam looked ready to step onto a *Vogue* cover with his fitted dark blue jeans and black designer button-down shirt, hair styled to perfection.

So unfair!

THOM WAS STILL SNORING when we came back. His injury had drained him good.

A quick shower washed the grueling workout off my skin, and I inventoried my clean clothes. I'd have to do laundry soon if I didn't want to be stuck in smelly underpants. I set aside one shirt to change into during a bathroom break and tucked it into my purse before zipping everything up. As I stowed the bag beneath my arm and stepped into my flats, a wince of pain panged my side.

I inched my tank top high over my stomach, stood sideways, and faced the mirror to look at the bruises on my waist. Liam's fingers had branded five distinctive marks on both sides, nasty leftovers from his blood mania at the warehouse. I bruised like a peach.

The door opened behind me, and I let the fabric fall.

"You ready?" Liam asked in a low voice.

"Yeah."

His silhouette disappeared from the doorway, and I gathered my stuff in my arms again.

Liam re-appeared. His forearm leaned against the door frame, his fist balled. He was shaking, unmistakable fury deforming his mouth.

What now?

In a very un-Liam way, he stared at the floor instead of meeting my gaze. Lower lip drawn between his teeth and jaw clenched, he sighed. "I'm not sorry I tricked you, but I'm fucking sorry about those bruises." He tapped the frame with his fist before walking away.

The shame-laced words hung in the air and melted my heart. It might not be the apology I had been waiting for, but it would do.

THE ROAD-TRIP STRETCHED ON. Thom's mood had improved since Montana, and Liam and I were no longer fighting. Thom and I sung at the top of our lungs while he drove, but, after a few short hours, he had to switch with Liam again because he was still reeling from his injury.

About twenty hours from home, we stopped at another motel.

Instead of going straight to bed, Thom asked if I wanted to watch *The Sound of Music* with him on his laptop, and I wholeheartedly agreed. I snuggled against him, resting my head against his chest. He propped up the computer on his thighs, and I played with the zipper on his hoodie, grateful for our first alone-time in days.

"We need a safe word," I said.

"What kind of night are you planning?" A mischievous glint brightened Thom's blue eyes.

Safe word...

I slapped his sound shoulder. He was messing with me for putting my foot in my mouth, but he knew what I meant. "A secret code. Something just you and I know, so Liam can't pull another body switch."

Thom grinned. "What about Edelweiss?"

"I like that."

He started the movie, and I buried my knuckles in his shirt, secretly trying to heal him. Trying to find the secret path to success. I thought about the circumstances surrounding the healing of my dad. I'd wanted to heal him. *Check.* I cared for him. *Check.* The do-or-die situation might be the missing link, but I couldn't replicate that.

Oh, Thom can you stand in front of a moving car, so I can try to heal you afterward?

Bad plan all around.

ABOUT HALF AN HOUR LATER, a soft and regular drumming noise distracted me for the screen. At first, I thought I was hearing Thom's heartbeat through the fabric of his shirt, but the eerie sound got louder. It wasn't his pulse, but mine. Loud as a moving train, it echoed at my temples.

I grabbed my forehead. "Pause the movie for a sec. I feel weird."

Sweat gathered on my palms, and the over-shirt I was wearing turned into a sauna in a matter of seconds. I passed it over my shoulders and used it as a fan. The heatwave scorched my skin from chin to navel, and a ball of sour saliva pooled in my mouth.

This is what menopause must feel like. Maybe I'm 20 going on 50? I marched to the bathroom and splashed cold water on my face.

A faint and dull buzz vibrated in the air around me, and I closed my eyes, trying to pinpoint its origin. I tilted my head up to inspect the ceiling. Maybe there was a bunch of flies around? The low-grade motel bordered on inhabitable.

Thom's figure appeared beside me. "Maybe you're coming down with something?"

The buzzing sound got clearer, and I picked up a few strange syllables. I combed my hair away from my face. "I don't think so." Viruses and bacteria rarely made you schizophrenic.

Thom placed a hand on my forehead. "You're burning up."

Bizarre words were recited like a soft prayer as a chorus of voices chanted. I checked the four corners of the room for the source of the sound. "Did you hear that?"

"What?" Thom's eyebrows creased in worry. "Lana, what's going on?"

The prayer stopped, and I questioned whether I'd heard it at all. Perhaps it had come from another room?

Flashes of four cloaked figures kneeling in a circle superimposed over my vision. In the middle of the circle, a fifth silhouette stood with his back to me, arms raised to the sky. A symbol marked the stony earth at his feet, the chiseled drawing of a snake made luminous by the light of the moon.

A snake? This was another test.

"Liam is testing my brain again." Ready to storm in the neighboring room, I beelined for the door. Thom and I were on a date, and I wasn't in the mood to train my mind against him.

But after a few dizzy steps, I paused, hands wobbly on my thighs.

Thom grabbed my shoulder with his good arm. "You're freaky pale. Sit on the bed. I'll get Liam."

"No, I—" The room spun into a kaleidoscope of colors. "I need to lie down."

The last thing I heard before crashing to the carpet was Thom shouting for Liam's help.

21

SOOTHE MY SOUL

Alana

The air entering my lungs tasted bitter as I regained consciousness. The scent of overcooked eggs was all I could process at first. *Ew.* Where did that stink come from?

Thom's voice came into focus. "I don't know. We were watching a movie, and she burned up. She said she could hear something then fainted next to the bed."

"I'm awake," I said, a ball of cotton in my mouth. I moved my fingers with incredible difficulty as if I was navigating in a tub of jelly.

A hand pressed against my forehead, and strong arms hoisted me up. I tried to hold my head up, but it was too heavy. *Way too heavy.*

"Alana, look at me," Liam said.

My face crunched as I peered through my eyelids. Why did the bedside lamp burn so bright?

The chant in my head resumed, and I tried to pick up the words but failed. *What language is that? Not Latin, not French, not Spanish...*

Liam looked worried, so he wasn't messing with me. Where did the voices come from if not from him?

His thumb grazed my cheek, and a sluggish smile tugged on my lips. His cold hand felt heavenly against my hot skin, and I swear vapors rose into the air. He carried me to the bed. I needed rest. So much rest. Darkness fell over my eyes.

A slap on my face forced them back opened. "Hey, none of that. Tell me what you heard, exactly."

Ow. He hadn't put much force into it, but still... My eyelids dropped, and he pinched my arm. "Alana."

He was so annoying. Didn't he see how exhausted I was? Maybe if I answered his question, he'd leave me alone. "Voices chanting in a bizarre language."

A litany of curses escaped his mouth. He rolled up his right sleeve and yanked the curtains away from the window. Red patterns glimmered under the ray of the moon, runic symbols running from his wrist to his elbows. That piqued my curiosity. Who knew Liam had tattoos?

"A blood moon," he said, the steel in his voice hardening.

A what? It seemed to work him up quite a bit.

"What's happening to her?" Thom asked.

Liam cradled my face in his hands, his voice was low, almost sweet. Deathbed sweet. "Alana, can you see anything?"

"A snake."

Liam's face paled, and he turned to Thom. "It's Frank. He's using the blood moon to claim her."

"Possession?" Thom asked as if he couldn't believe it.

"The oldest trick in the book."

What were they babbling about? *Possession? As in exorcism?*

I wanted to burst out in laughter, but it required too much energy. I felt incredibly weak but light as a feather, like a hot-air balloon threatening to rise into the air at any moment.

"How do we protect her?" Thom asked.

"We can't. We must beat him to the punch. Get my sacrificial knife from the car, the gold, waved-bladed one. And get my bag."

Oh God! Here we go!

Liam rearranged the pillows so I was almost sitting up. He yanked the bedside lamp in the air and snatched the electrical cord from it. I knew what he would do before he tied my wrists together above my head.

The real-life production of my nightmare was about to take place, and I had VIP seats. I felt strangely disconnected from my body, a part of me watching overhead, saying I told you so. I wanted to protest, but a vivid hallucination prevented me from breathing. There was a specter in the room, its dark form undulating against the oily surface of the ceiling. Even in my altered state, I knew that wasn't good.

Thom returned with the oh-so familiar blade. "What now?"

"Strip her."

Excuse me?

"What?" Thom echoed my alarmed thought.

"There's no time to be a gentleman. Strip her to her underwear."

Thom hesitated and tugged gently on the pajama bottoms. I congratulated myself on wearing no-frill, classic, black underwear and keeping my bra on. Thom considered my camisole, his face scrunched like it was the hardest puzzle in the world, and ultimately cut it. My bound hands prevented him from passing it over my head.

The soft brush of his fingers on my ribcage as he pried it away made me chuckle, "It tickles."

The boys looked at me as if I had lost my mind, which I had.

Thom winced. "Why is she like that?"

"The ritual starts with a serious high."

A+ for the Shadow Walker. I had never done drugs in my life, but, at that moment, I wondered why. I didn't even care that I was going to die.

Liam held the golden blade between his palm and muttered under his breath. A stony bowl set in front of him, he sliced his right wrist open, and dark blood poured. He filled the bowl to the brim and tied a makeshift tourniquet around his forearm with a leather rope. I guessed special dagger wounds didn't heal as quickly. He fumbled through his bag and got out a bone similar to the one in my vision, also wrapped in leather.

I giggled. "You carry the funniest stuff around."

Liam dipped the point of the blade in his blood and brushed my hair away from my face. "Alana, I'm not going to lie. It will hurt like hell."

He didn't have to explain. I had known this would happen. He'd carve me and kiss me and—oh! He'd kiss me. A flush rushed to my chest, and I heated in anticipation. That part of the dream had always been weirdly pleasant.

My voice was childlike when I said, "You'll draw pretty tattoos on me."

Liam frowned. "You know about the tattoos?"

"I dreamed a little dream—" I paused, bile rising in my mouth.

My balloon burst. A sickness had taken hold of my stomach, and my high was crashing down. Liam took extreme care not to draw more than a faint line of blood as he drew a first rune on my clavicle. He'd lied. It didn't hurt at all.

The dark ink bubbled against my fevered skin and sank inside my pores. A quake rocked my body from the tip of my head to my curled toes. I shrieked. The blood pierced and burned like pure acid, and I writhed against the bed.

Liam started a second rune. "Hold her down."

Thom pressed on my shoulders.

"Stop, stop, STOP!" I begged. Both their jaws clenched in such perfect sync that they could've been twins.

A waterfall streamed over my cheeks, but all the tears in the whole wide world wouldn't be enough to extinguish the fire raging inside of me. "Stop! Why are you doing this?" My vision jumped from one place to the next like a drunken bee. I wailed and tried to kick Liam's face, but he gripped both my ankles and tied them down to the foot of the bed with a leather thread. His touch helped with the pain, but he quickly let go and resumed the carving. "I hate you!"

I tugged and contorted, but I couldn't break free. Thom and Liam spun, stretched and doubled in my blurry vision. The smoke rising from the runes disintegrated the bonds between my cells, and I was left in shambles.

Breathing heavily, I drifted in and out of consciousness.

The moon rose in the sky until almost every inch of my skin was covered. All the layers of my dermis itched, set ablaze by a million flames. The charring licks made me want to die. I wanted the fire to consume me and free me from the scarring pain.

The dark mass above, quiet since earlier, stretched and swirled before it descended over me. An icy storm wrapped a leash around my senses as if my entire body had been plunged into a tub of ice, and the fire flickered. A nefarious essence slithered its way into my mind, each neuron whimpering in misery. An unimaginable migraine split my head as I tried in vain to keep the dark frosty tendrils at bay.

Ice burns, too.

"Hello, Alana," a hollow voice whispered. *"I'm Francis William Hale. How do you do?"* A cruel laugh resonated in my mind.

Liam leaned over me. "Frank is ahead. Talk to her."

Thom cradled my face. "ALANA. Look at me. Look into my eyes. That's right."

He danced in front of my woozy vision. I was tired, so tired... I wanted it to end. If I could only rest my eyes for a minute, everything would be better.

Liam sat close, the heat of his body softening the ice. "Ok, I'm ready."

He raised his ring pendant to his mouth and kissed it. "Ek Heita Loki. Blakkr konungr, heyra ek hugr."

The symbols scorched my skin, the dark markings turning bright orange, the pain excruciating. Liam chanted, eyes black, and the surrounding darkness thickened.

"Fight him," the specter whispered. I arched my back against the mattress, hips gyrating in the air as I tried to twist out of reach. Liam grabbed my hipbones and pinned me down.

There are no words to explain the emptiness that gripped me. Anger, fear, disgust, lust, want, love, hate. All the human emotions had condensed into this incomparable *need* for Liam to stop whatever he was doing. Despite the fever, I could feel the ritual was changing me on a molecular level.

Living shadows spilled from Liam's fingers onto my stomach. Serpentine, they crawled and hissed, eager to swallow me. "Hǫfuð,"

Liam grazed my ear and goosebumps rose all over my body. "Hjarta," he pressed his palm against my heart. "Hǫnd," he entwined his fingers with mine. "Eða andi," he leaned over and kissed my forehead. "Ek eignask ykkarr sál."

The malevolent spirit inside me snickered, *"The coward can't kiss you properly. I will kiss you, girl. I'll kiss you good..."*

My body thrashed beyond my control, and my eyes rolled inward.

The locks of my consciousness gave in, and I could see myself lying in the middle of a hexagonal room filled with doors, all of them hanging wide open. I ran to close the doors to keep the malevolent spirit out, but each time I smashed one shut another re-opened. I was blind and powerless to resist the corruption creeping inside. *"Tell Walker you belong to me."*

"What's happening?" Thom yelled.

Liam growled. "It's not working."

My eyes blinked of their own accord. A cruel, deformed voice rose from my throat, "You call that a kiss?"

Thom cringed and jolted backwards.

A look of pure hatred passed on Liam's already serious face, and he lunged himself at me. Thighs on both side of my chest, he flattened me to the mattress and closed his hand around my throat. "Get. out."

But I could already feel the tainted thing inside me taking root. I tried to rip it out of my skull, but, like a weed, it grew and grew as far as the eyes could see.

"Your precious little witch is mine, Walker," the wraith said using my lips.

"Like hell!" Liam sliced the leather tourniquet around his arm.

Blood splattered everywhere. On my chest, in my hair. A shower of red. He crushed the gash to my mouth.

The rot hissed, urging me not to swallow. Liam grabbed the nape of my neck, brushing away the hair drenched by blood and sweat. "Alana, it's not too late. We can still do this. Tell him to fuck off," he said sweetly. He was in full demon-mode, yet I wasn't afraid. We were so close our noses were touching. "Give in, Alana."

I anchored my gaze in his and took a big gulp of blood, the

wretched fire traveling down my throat. The corrupted pressure inside my skull lessened, so I drank more. I felt different. Powerful. Alive. I dug my nail into his skin, thirsty for more.

Liam trembled as his shadows slammed into me, and I welcomed them. They set ablaze the infested neurons, and an immense blast wave fragmented the weeds. Fire and ice battled for control while I huddled against the broken glass of the walls of my mind.

I felt pulverized.

After a moment of peace, the alien presence crept back inside, and weeds pervaded the ground again. I wasn't alone in my head.

The glacial cold gave way to smoldering embers, the voice in my head no longer vicious, but caring. *"Don't worry, princess. I got you."*

The pain, the ice, everything burned to ashes. It was over.

As if all the puppet strings had been loosened, I relaxed against the mattress. Liam's weight vanished.

"Now what?" Thom asked.

"We wait to see if it sticks."

"What if it doesn't?"

Liam's voice hardened. "We kill her."

I blacked out.

22

WALK ON

Alana

I conquered Mount Wake-Up that day like an explorer planting his flag on top of Everest. Cold, lightheaded, exhausted, but without the pride of accomplishment, I forced my languid body to carry on the downward trek. The real struggle had only just begun.

I snuggled close to the volcano of heat lying next to me and hung on to oblivion a minute longer, sad to let go of its comfort.

Thom's voice came into focus. "Do we have to hurry home?"

The sound came from the other side of the room which meant the warm body next to me had to be Liam.

"No. Frank used all his juice. He'll need time to recharge," Liam answered, his voice but a whisper as his arm grazed mine.

Thom's voice got louder as he said, "Get rest. I'll stay with her."

"I can't. I'm drained, and her flare is acting out. I have to stay close and conscious."

That explained the unusual sleeping arrangements. As the shroud of sleep diluted, my mind screamed at the weight of all the memories from the previous night.

"How did Frank do it?" Thom asked as if a piece of the puzzle eluded him.

"He needed a drop of her blood and a lock of hair."

"Where the hell did he find that?"

"Must have been closer than we thought and approached her while I was distracted. My fault."

"Why hasn't Frank tried this before? With the others?" Thom asked.

"It's different. I tasted her. It's a demon thing. It's more... personal." The uncertainty in the word floated in the air. Either Liam didn't know exactly why, or he was uncomfortable talking about it.

"This is fucked up. Are there any side effects?"

Side effects? My ears perked up.

"I'm not sure. I've never marked anyone. I'll probably be able to track her over great distances, but other than that I don't know."

"That's good, right?"

The exhausted tone turned bitter as Liam said, "Good? No, believe me, nothing is *good. My* mark is tattooed forever into her skin. She'll throw a hissy fit."

A hissy fit? Why? I wasn't an idiot. I knew what would have happened if he hadn't torn Frank out of my head. True, I wasn't too thrilled about the tattoos, but if I was mad at anyone, it was myself. My reluctance to speak about the dream had sealed my faith.

My ability to predict the future merited a big five out of ten. Yes, my dream had mostly come to pass, but the details had been horribly wrong. I was alive, and Liam hadn't kissed me.

There was a long pregnant pause before Thom whispered, "Do we need to talk?"

"Talk about what?"

I blinked.

"Nothing. I think she's waking up."

I might be a little vain because my first instinct as I opened my eyes was to check for the tattoos. I was covered in dried blood and struggled to distinguish between permanent marks and blood stains. At least, I hoped it wasn't all permanent.

Liam stiffened, waiting for my *hissy fit* to take place.

Our shoulders brushed, and I searched his gaze. "Thank you." I turned to Thom. "Thank you both very much." My voice was one hundred percent steady, despite my dry mouth, and I pressed on my eyes to ease the itching. I patted my hair down, the sticky curls a whole new world of mess. "Need to shower. Badly."

I wrapped a sheet over myself and stood. The room blurred. *Whoa, I need to take it easy.* Dizziness threatened to send me flying to the ground. Thom acted as a crutch, and Liam placed a hand on the small of my back, steadying me upwards.

I took a minute, making sure I had my bearings, and inched towards the bathroom. Liam followed, never more than a step behind me, and I remembered the part about my flare acting up, and him needing to stay super close. *Well, this will be awkward as hell.*

Liam sat on the closed toilet seat while I considered the bathtub-shower combo with embarrassment. This was so… bizarre. I set a towel and my bag right next to the bath, let the bed sheet fall to the floor, and stepped in the tub. Dried blood cracked on my arms as I moved, and Liam's distinctive citrus scent made my mouth water. It was like I'd been dowsed with lemonade. Surprised that the blood smelled so sweet, I sniffed my skin, and a tinge of incense and musk tugged and twisted my guts.

Cheeks burning, I yanked the curtain closed behind me. It looked awfully sheer. "Your eyes are closed?" I asked, my voice too unsteady for my taste.

"Yes."

"Promise?"

"Yes."

"Swear on Thom?"

A soft chuckle echoed around the room. "Cross my heart and hope to die."

I unhooked my bra, stepped out of my underwear and tucked them below the towels behind the shower curtain.

"Besides, I spent all night drawing on every inch of your skin. I've already seen all there is to see, anyway," Liam said in jest.

Without thought, I grabbed the shower head, opened the cold water and splashed him with it. I peeked to check if he'd opened his eyes, but no.

He passed a hand over his face to wipe the water away. "You're not playing fair."

I giggled. I felt closer to him somehow, which made sense. He'd been inside me. *Oh no*. Bad choice of words.

I scrubbed myself clean in a hurry, the water at my feet turning brownish red because of the blood and inspected my tattoos. Snake-shaped, the one over my breast had a swirly line acting as a tail with a wider part for a head, maybe four inches in diameter. *Not bad.* Butterflies are cuter, but it wasn't a foot-long snake or a scary skull.

I couldn't hear anything but the water running. A voice kept chanting in my head that I was buck naked with Liam less than a foot away. Maybe talking would uncoil the knot in my stomach. "What language was that, earlier?"

"Old Norse."

I paused, a goop of shampoo in my palm. "You speak Old Norse?"

"Yes."

"How?"

"Learned in demon school."

Was he messing with me? I peered behind the curtain again.

He looked serious enough.

When I pictured his life after the demons had taken him, I imagined violence and brutal killings, not classes and essays. Thom had given me a good picture of their lives before and after, but the blank in the middle, the five years Liam had spent away from his family, were a complete mystery. This Old Norse matter was the first hint, the first piece of the puzzle.

"You hoped it would enhance your curriculum?" I asked.

He cracked up. "Required credits."

I massaged my scalp. "Along with maim and kill?" No answer. The mood was right. If only I could get him to keep talking, I might satisfy my curiosity. "Let me guess. Frank was the jock who bullied you?"

"Something like that." The timbre of his voice had switched from relaxed to withdrawn.

Why? I shut the water off, patted one towel down my body and wrapped one around my head. I bent down to reach in my bag and selected clean clothes, getting dressed before stepping out of the tub. I crammed the tainted underwear into my bag and headed to the exit.

Liam didn't follow. "Wait."

"Wait what?"

"My turn."

I'd forgotten he was covered in blood too. He started to unbutton his shirt before disappearing into thin air. Nice trick. He wouldn't have to wonder if *my* eyes were closed.

I didn't dare move, afraid I might bump into him. I stayed in front of the mirror until the water was turned on and only then sat in his place by the tub.

Thom entered the bathroom and put Liam's bag on the sink. "Here. Fresh clothes. I'll take care of the van."

"Thanks," Liam answered.

As weird as it had been to shower next to Liam, this was weirder. Flustered, I nibbled on my fingernails, crossed and uncrossed my legs, and scratched a pimple on my neck until it was raw.

"Stop doing that," Liam said.

"Doing what?"

"Fidgeting. Your flare is extra slippery today, and it makes it hard to control. If it gets any harder, I'll have to lay over you."

God, has he heard what he just said? Could someone help me dig my mind out of the gutter? I sat straight, hands on my thighs. "Sorry."

Pull yourself together. You must be all red. What if he notices? Take a deep breath. You're shaken up, and God knows what this ritual entails. You heard him: there might be side effects. Concentrate on that.

Especially when he's naked and all you can think about is how fine he looked in that black button-down shirt of his when he hovered above you. Do not think about how his skin felt against yours or how you thought you saw desire in his eyes.

Do not think about how fierce he looked when he cut himself to protect you or how he made you his in a way you can't even comprehend. And most important of all, do not think about the damn kiss he was supposed to give you. Don't think about how much you wish he'd—

The water turned off, and I sat still, small droplets of water misting over my knees. A puddle of water appeared next to the tub, and a towel vanished from the rack.

The bag Thom had brought in moved on the vanity, and I turned away. The rustling of fabric tickled my ears, a furious blush on my cheeks.

With a sigh, Liam appeared. The electric blue dress shirt with white buttons and turned-down collar looked familiar. One of Thom's.

"No more clean shirts," he explained.

His shoulders shrugged and wiggled beneath the fabric, Mr. *Black-Is-Easier-To-Clean* was uncomfortable to be wearing such a bright shirt, but the splash of color suited him.

Along with the wet hair that had grown in the past few weeks, his features looked softer, boyish. Though he was 29, Liam hadn't aged like a human and didn't look a day older than Thom wearing blue.

While we walked to the car, his shoulders wiggled again.

I gave his arm a soft squeeze. "Stop worrying. You look great."

I didn't know who was most surprised to hear the words, him or me, and I quickly stopped touching him as Thom waved us over from the back of the parking lot.

The huge vehicle was gone, replaced by a blue Toyota. Thom had abandoned the van in plain sight and had called in an anonymous tip. The owner would be reunited with it, and my conscience was appeased.

The boys argued about who should drive. Thom wanted Liam to rest, but Liam insisted he'd rather drive since he couldn't sleep anyway. In the end, Thom slept in the back while Liam drove.

Sundown re-energized me. My thoughts cleared, but I felt restless, different. More attune to the universe... or something less cheesy but to that effect. I looked at myself in the passenger-side mirror and clicked my tongue at the sight. My hair was all frizzy again. Comb in hand, I tamed the bulk of it and passed the time braiding it into a cute fishtail.

The memories from the ritual where still a tangled mess, and I attempted to iron them out one by one, not willing to miss or overlook any details in case they turned out to be important.

I was at the part when Liam had chanted in Old Norse, and asked, "Why Old Norse? Were your ancestors Vikings or something?"

"In a way."

"What way?"

He shot me a glance. "You know Loki?"

My mouth curled up. "I know Tom Hiddleston."

Liam rolled his eyes. "Loki is a Norse God. Our legends say he came to Earth in human form, impregnated a beautiful woman, corrupted her blood, and, voilà, my kind was born."

Liam descended for a Norse God... Well, that explained his weird charisma, at least. "Can I see your ring?"

He looked taken aback. "My ring?"

"Yes, it looked pretty old. I'm curious." I leaned towards him. Not to spook him, I gently hooked my fingers beneath the leather thread around his neck. The era when he struggled with my touch seemed like a million light years ago, but I'd learned my lesson. The pendants appeared. The silver key was shiny while the ring had a dark stony finish. Iron, I realized.

An iron ring, iron prison, iron in blood, iron had a love/hate relationship with Liam. "Why does everything have to do with iron? I thought it hurt your powers, not the other way around?"

"Iron is like most potent substances. In small doses, it's beneficial. Too much, and it's poison." His gaze fell on my hand holding the ring. Under the rays of the moon, the tattoo snaking around my fingers fluoresced.

"Will they ever fade?" I asked. I already knew the answer, but I didn't want Liam to know I'd spied on his conversation with Thom.

"Yes."

My eyebrows crunched. I was positive he had said forever. "When?"

His hot breath caressed my cheek, and our eyes met. "They'll disappear when I'm dead."

Possession. *Demons are known to mark lesser species. The rituals vary among breeds, and the effects differ. Can be avoided by consuming a specially brewed tea, though the recipe is unknown.*

THE HOUSE TOWERED against the stormy sky as we pulled into the driveway. I'd texted Lilah four hours ago with Thom's phone, to give her our ETA, and she was waiting for us outside, sitting in a wicker chair.

I stretched as I got out the car. Lilah skipped towards Liam and laced her arms around his neck. He hoisted her up in a bone-crushing hug.

Thom put a hand on the small of my back, "You okay? You look sad."

I nodded. The safety of the house didn't appeal to me. I saw it as a prison still, and my mood darkened. Bag propped over my shoulder, I walked to Lilah.

She let go of Liam to hug me. "I was so afraid for you guys."

Liam had called her after Vicky's warning, asking Lilah to stay at the house until we knew what Frank was planning. The guys hoped he wasn't aware of Lilah's whereabouts, but they didn't want to risk it. While we were on the road, she'd been cooped up at home, worrying about us. Alone.

We gave her the cliff notes version of our troubles as we moved inside, and she listened, her eyes often flying to Liam's as if they were having a silent conversation.

Liam moaned when he closed the door behind us. My demon beacon had been all over the place since the ritual, and he hadn't slept in about 50 hours. "Do not wake me unless the house is on fire," he said before he disappeared.

We all deserved a good rest. Lilah followed me into my room and sat on the bed, her legs dangling, and I unpacked my bag.

"Was the ritual as painful as Thom said?" she asked.

"Worse."

A grimace deformed her calm features. "I can't believe this Frank was in your head."

"The guys didn't want to talk about it. Do you know who he is?"

"Liam told me once that Frank was his biggest mistake, but no more than that."

Biggest mistake? "Maybe he killed their parents?"

"I'm pretty sure a demon named Marcus killed them, but I could be wrong. They never speak of it—" She stopped as her eyes fell to my tattoo, the serpent's tail visible at the edge of my shirt.

I inched the fabric down my breast to show her the whole thing.

"Oh, it's a tiny version of Liam's."

I wet my lips. "Liam has one?"

She nodded. "Big one on his upper back. You never saw it?"

"No."

I'd never seen Liam without a shirt. Was he ashamed of his tattoos? Not with Lilah, apparently. I inspected the marks again. Away from the light of the moon, they were not phosphorescent, and the tan ring around my index and middle finger was discrete. The one behind my ear was barely noticeable, moon or no moon. The one licking my left breast would be the hardest to conceal if I ever needed to. The dark burgundy snake was staring back at me in the mirror.

A devil's mark.

In my history class, we'd studied how 16th-century Ecclesiastes put women on trial for being aligned with Satan because of similar marks on their bodies. They were believed to be permanent markings of the Devil on his initiates to seal their obedience and service. Maybe they'd been onto something real.

Nowadays, I wouldn't get burned at the stake for my tattoos. All I had to worry about was the obedience and service part.

23

PRECIOUS

Alana

"What the hell is wrong with the world?" I pointed to the newspaper lying on the table. They had found the bodies of a dozen girls my age dismembered, and the article pushed the envelope far enough as to put a descriptive picture next to the headline. Media, these days! Delivering morning papers would soon be an R-rated job.

Liam ignored my question, engrossed in a book at the other end of the table.

Thom peered over my shoulders. "Yeah. It's horrible."

I dropped my bagel to the floor, and its buttered part kissed the ground. A rag in hand, I cleaned up and threw the ruined bread away. "Why aren't we doing anything about it?"

"Well..." Thom paused. I knew that *well* of his. It was the *well, I'm about to say something you won't like*. "We don't meddle in human investigations. Could get messy."

I crossed my arms over my chest. "What if it's not? What if a demon did this?"

Liam's eyes shot up from his book to Thom. "Always blaming demons. You see what I was saying?"

Thom grabbed the paper from my hand and read the article. "Wait a minute. She might be right about this." I shot Liam a victorious grin. "Twelve women found in a dumpster, dismembered, hearts are missing."

Liam rubbed his jaw. "What are you thinking? A ghoul?"

"Or several." Thom disappeared for a moment and returned with the bestiary in hand, the huge book I'd fretted over during my first week at the house. "Yeah, fits the profile,"

That freaky book was written in Old Norse. "You can read this?" I asked.

He shrugged. "Yeah."

Was everyone around here fluent in Old Norse? It was a dead language. And did they have to act like it was the most natural thing in the world?

Liam scratched his neck. "It looks ghoulish, but so what? Can't go around hunting every low-grade demon on the East Coast."

My temper flared. "Why not?"

Our eyes locked. "None of our concern."

"It doesn't concern you that a monster is killing innocent girls?"

"Absolutely not." The disdain rolling off his tongue sparked a rebellion in my heart.

Why did he always act like he didn't give a damn about anybody? "Then why *on earth* would you bother to save me?"

"Maybe I shouldn't have."

"You're full of shit."

Thom slammed the newspaper in the middle of the table. "Stop. You guys have been good since Montana. Please don't start again."

He was right. We had been so good since the possession incident. No quarrels. We'd talked like normal people, and the four of us had gone to the movies the night before, without incident.

Why ruin it now?

It killed me to say the words, but I apologized. "I'm sorry."

Liam's arms fell at his sides. "We can't turn into demon hunters.

We're lucky enough my kind mostly keep to themselves, but if we cut the head off pure breeds for no reason, we'll be safe nowhere."

Thom's head tilted to the side. "I hear you, but this is a ghoul. You know they don't register on any other species radar."

"Ok, let's kill this ghoul." Liam gave in without sounding bitter, and it was my turn to be taken aback. Since when did Liam compromise?

Thom's brow furrowed.

I bit down on my thumb. "Can I go with you?"

Two pairs of eyes zeroed in on me as the guys said in unison, "No."

GHOULS. Lower cast of flesh-eating demons. They stink and pose a minimal threat except for their poison. Their fingernails hold a powerful venom that can paralyze for hours.

THOM AND LIAM came home from their ghoul hunt late that night, and I got up from my comfortable position on the couch to greet them. I could hear voices, but they stayed outside. I motioned to Thom from the window to crack open the door, so I could ask them what was going on.

The stench that immediately attacked my nose was so wretched that bile rose to my mouth, and I pressed my lips together hard not to vomit. Thom and Liam looked horrible, a black goo dripping off them as they kicked their running shoes off.

"Agh, what is that?" I asked.

Liam smirked, closing the distance between us.

I backed away, using the door as a shield. "Stop!"

"It was your idea to send us after a nest of ghouls. You owe us a hug."

"I'd rather hug you later if that's okay."

He retreated, and I reopened the door.

Thom grabbed my arm and pulled. "What if I want mine right now?"

I shrieked in surprise, not moving quickly enough, and ended up in his arms and soiled by the disgusting liquid.

"Thom!" I protested.

He gave me a sheepish grin.

"Careful with your arm," I said.

"My arm's fine." He grabbed a smudge of goo in his hair and splattered it on my face.

I groaned. The stuff was repulsive. I escaped his grasp, but he ran after me, and I cried out. We danced around each other for a minute, his body blocking my way back to the house. I ran for it, but he tackled me to the grass. Laughter quaked our bodies, and our gaze met, my pulse very aware of his strong body pressed against mine. He grew serious too, and his gaze dropped to my lips.

A torrent of icy water hit me, and I yelped.

"Let's keep it G-rated people. I'm still here," Liam said. He'd gotten a hose from the backyard and showered Thom and me with it. From his wet hair, dripping shirt and goo-less appearance, he'd already cleansed himself.

Thom rolled off me and stood. He threw his shirt on the ground and welcomed the purifying water. When he was almost free of goo, Liam splashed me again.

Giggles bubbled up my throat as I tried to steal the spray gun nozzle from his hands. He sidestepped, but I grabbed the bulk of the hose and pulled real hard. The nozzle flew from his grip and fell halfway between us. I jumped but slipped on the wet grass and ended up sprawled on my back at Liam's feet. He bent down to grab the sprayer, and the forceful jet hit me square in the chest. A real smile broke out on his face as he soaked me in icy waters.

I held my hands up in surrender.

Liam's relaxed features darkened, and he was suddenly very interested in the bushes on my right. "All clean." He let the hose fall to the ground.

I stood, picked it up and aimed at Liam's face. "I think you missed a spot."

He shot me a dark look. "Leave it alone, will you?"

My eyes narrowed, and I turned to Thom for an explanation to Liam's mood swing, but he was squeezing water out of his clothes.

Glancing down to my own shirt, I noticed my white top had become almost translucent and crossed my arms over my chest. A wince of disgust shot up my spine when my fingers dug into a forgotten spot of mucus. The black muck was easily the most disgusting thing I'd ever smelled. I couldn't believe they'd made their way back in Liam's precious car, so I checked the driveway. An old truck was parked there instead of the Vanquish.

"You stole another car?" I asked.

He followed my gaze. "Obviously. You think I would ruin mine? We'll have to burn the thing down to get the smell out."

It made sense. I didn't feel as queasy about stealing anymore, especially if it means killing a bunch of heart-eating monsters. "Good idea."

The praise coaxed a low whistle out of him. "I'll be damned. We might make a grown up out of you yet."

I stuck my tongue out.

Thom put both hands on my shoulders and pushed me inside. "Now, I need a cold beer and a bowl of popcorn."

THE NEXT DAY, I walked in on a gruesome combat between Thom and Liam. They expected Frank to cause trouble again, so Thom had doubled his hours in the gym. The wrestling match was brutal. Liam was using his powers. No human speed for Thom; he was a pro.

But even with his immense and impressive skills, it was too much like watching a lion battle a house cat. And I could tell the lion was holding back. Thom took a mean punch straight in the face, and I winced.

Liam winced, too, his last punch already turning blue on Thom's face. "Enough."

"No, I'm fine," Thom said.

Frank brought out a side of Thom I'd never seen. A broody, secretive man. I still hadn't a clue what Frank Hale had done.

Liam pointed to me. "Alana's here."

The mood shifted. Thom scurried over to the front of the room to retrieve a little blue box with a matching bow. "Here, for you, from the both of us."

A gift? I opened the present. It was an iPhone. I'd thought about getting one in California, but I didn't have anyone to call. Plus, I feared the temptation to call home would be too great. Taped behind the phone was a leather thread with a small silvery pendant. "A key?"

"A key." Thom said, grinning from ear to ear.

"But I can't go outside by myself?"

"You can now."

My eyes widened. "What?"

"Don't get too excited... just in the backyard."

"What about my demon beacon?"

"Over the last few days, Liam noticed your beacon has changed, probably because of the ritual. We checked in the books and found a precedent. It's safe now."

"It is?" I looked at Liam who hadn't said a word, and he nodded. It seemed too good to be true. Just like that, I didn't have to worry about the demon beacon?

Liam scratched his head. "You're claimed. It changes everything."

I didn't know if I liked the word *claimed,* but if it meant I could go outside on the terrace without having to berate Liam, I was all for it. Yay for the tattoos!

The guys were a foot apart, standing in front of me, and I was so pleased I leaped forward and threw an arm around each of them. Joy radiated through my entire body. I was being promoted from prisoner to sidekick. *At last.* Yes, it would have been cooler to control my beacon myself, but I sucked, so who cared?

The group hug seemed to make Liam uneasy, so I stepped back. "I can't believe I don't have to worry about this beacon thing anymore. Soon, everyone will want tattoos, even Lilah."

Liam chuckled. "Don't spread the word too wide. I can't go around carving a piece of my soul in just anybody."

Wait.

"By the way, the guy from California, Duncan, he didn't turn. We'll look for the next one," Thom said, unaffected by Liam's declaration.

Liam grabbed his water bottle and passed a towel over his face. A piece of his soul... Was he being poetic, or literal? He walked out before I had the guts to ask, but it had felt literal to me.

"Do you want to train?" Thom asked.

My hand raised to his bruised cheek. "Looks nasty. You should be more careful."

"I don't want Liam to go easy on me. Frank won't." The grim curve of his mouth returned, and I was seized with the sudden need to erase it.

I grazed his face and stepped closer. "Still, I hate to see you hurt."

My move was unequivocal. I might as well have said, *time to kiss me now*. I felt it was important we kissed. Right this minute. As if our future hinged on this breath, on this moment. Soft and hesitant, his lips brushed against mine...

Lilah opened the door and said, "Have you guys seen my phone?" She froze, taking in the scene. "Whoops. Sorry." She doubled back, but once again, the moment had passed.

My hand flew to my mouth to stifle a laugh. The interruptions had been so many that I felt we had to discuss it. Douse this almost-kiss routine with honesty. "Is it me, or do we have the worst timing?"

Thom chuckled. "We do." He scratched his neck and shot me a serious look. "Lana, I like you. I think it's pretty obvious."

Blood rushed to my cheeks. "I like you, too, but I'd kind of promised myself not to kiss you."

"Funny. Me too."

"You did?" I was confused. Why would he promise himself not to kiss me?

"Not like *not kiss you ever*, but wait until things are different. Until you're free to be wherever you want to be with whoever you want."

God, he'd read my mind. To me, it was about being in control of my life. To him, it was about choice. He didn't want a love-the-one-you're-with girlfriend, and I understood.

His thumb grazed my cheek. "I can wait if it means doing it right."

I nodded in agreement, secretly disappointed. Waiting was another word for rut.

THAT NIGHT while laying in bed, I downloaded music on my new present and set up my contacts which only included Thom, Lilah and Liam. I sent out a few funny GIFs to Lilah, but, like an invisible force pulling me in, I kept opening the contact app. Three times I put in my parent's number and deleted it.

Their number at my fingertips, my throat constricted, and my hands started shaking. What wrong would it do to dial? I didn't have to speak. Just hearing Mom's voice on the other side of the line would be heaven. I pressed the dial button. The icon for an outbound call appeared, but I hung up a second later and took a deep breath. *Be strong. If you call, it'll be too tempting to speak. If you speak, you'll put them in danger.*

But I wanted to call. I wanted to call so much that resisting the pull was agonizing, and I choked on a strangled sob. I thought about them every day but forced the pain and uncertainty to the edges of my mind. I had to believe I'd made the right decision, but, sometimes, I doubted. What if they were in danger anyway? What if my silence hurt them more?

I wiped my tears with a tissue and blew my nose. My heart skipped a beat when my phone buzzed. Maybe I hadn't hung up in time and they were calling back?

But it wasn't them. It was a text from Liam.

Don't call.

How in the world did he know? I looked around, expecting him to pop out of the shadows.

Are you sure you can't read my thoughts?

I can hear you crying.

Oh...

Don't call. I'll check on them.

Okay. Good night.

Three little dots at the bottom of the conversation signaled he was typing a response, so I waited. After a minute, they disappeared, and I stowed the phone away in my bedside table.

THE FOLLOWING MORNING WAS STRANGE. I misplaced my cup of coffee twice, sat down so far on the edge of a chair I fell to the ground, walked straight into a closed door, and got entangled in every piece of fabric I brushed. Thom and Liam were nowhere to be found.

A string of curses escaped my lips when I poured four cups of water half an inch to the right of the coffee machine. As I was about to write it off as one of those days, I realized what was happening. I couldn't be such a klutz. Liam was messing with me, following me around and moving things. It had to be.

With an evil plan in mind, I zoomed to the cupboard and got Liam's favorite mug. It said, "Best Brother Ever," but the "best" had been stricken out and had the word "only" written over it in red. Liam loved it because he always made a point to drink his morning coffee in it. I held it over the open space in front of me and let it go.

It immobilized in midair as Liam appeared in front of me. "Why are you trying to kill my mug?"

I laughed. "Busted."

His lips stretched into an almost grin. "The coffee machine gave me away? What if you'd been wrong?"

Faking a solemn seriousness, I said, "Your precious mug would have been collateral damage."

He considered my answer before his half-grin stretched all the way into a smile. "Ruthless, I like it."

A giddy smile stuck on my lips, and I bit the inside of my cheeks to make it fade. *Why am I so... thrilled? It was funny but not that funny.*

Liam cleaned up the rest of the spill. For a second, we stood facing the counter in silence.

"Want to try something new today?" He asked, one eyebrow raised in question.

For the first time ever, he didn't look at me, at our time together, as a chore. He looked pleased, on the verge of excitement, but tame. Like he was trying to reign in the happiness threatening to show. Like it was his job to be gloomy all the time and that morning he hadn't felt like going to work. I didn't know what I'd done to deserve that look, but I wanted to do it again.

I followed him to the gym. He grabbed a long wooden thing in the weapon's closet and threw it.

My hand rose just in time to catch it. "What's this?"

"It's a katana. A wooden one called a Bokken, for practice. It's long, so it allows you to stay farther away from the fight. Daggers are up close and personal. You don't want to get up close and personal with everything that's out there."

I didn't doubt that statement one bit. "Did Lilah learn all this weapon stuff?"

Liam's lips twitched. "Lilah doesn't harbor a secret obsession for slaying demons."

Hands clenched around the wooden sword, I raised it into the air. "Not secret."

"First, stop holding it like a baseball bat." Liam gently pried my fingers from the handle and placed them in the proper position. "Hold it with your hands as far apart as possible. A firm grip with your pinkie and ring finger, and more loosely with the middle and index fingers." As he talked, he moved closer and placed my arms at the right angle. "Now, strike horizontally."

I gave the space in front of me a nice slice.

"And vertically... That's good, but you should really use your shoulders more." The heat of his body distracted me as he molded his arms to mine to show what a proper thrust looked like. "And spread your legs." Goosebumps rose on my neck, and my mouth dried up. "You should center your weight in the back until you're ready to attack."

My hearing got fuzzy. Flustered, I angled my neck to the side, tilted my head up to meet his gaze, and my hair grazed his chin.

As if he was only just noticing how our bodies pressed against one another, he sidestepped and rasped his throat. "You got it."

He explained the difference between the directional cuts, demonstrated how to do maximum damage and got another Bokken from the closet. When his hand closed around the hilt, the world shifted.

We were no longer in the gym. Instead, we stood outside an impressive Asian temple. Five square-arched roofs were stacked over one another and towered above us. The doors of the temple were open to the nice weather. Colorful flowers bloomed on each side of a stony path. Cherry trees surrendered their flowers one by one to the gentle breeze, and a greenish lake scintillated in the back of the courtyard. *Wow.*

"It's breathtaking. Are you making it up?" If he was, he had a delightful imagination.

"No, I've been there. I know you're getting stir crazy, and we can't exactly travel right now."

The thoughtful words were a diversion to catch me off-guard, but I blocked the sneaky attack at the last second.

My tongue pressed against my front teeth. "Trying to sweet talk me into letting my guard down?"

"Me? Never."

I put the theory to practice. Downward strike, parry around, and try to get your opponent off balance.

Liam pointed out I would most likely fight weapon to claws, not sword to sword, but it was fun and a good work out, so we practiced for a while. It was surreal to spar in such an exotic location, even if it was an illusion. It felt real enough, and I swallowed a tinge of disappointment when it faded away. Liam stowed both Bokken back into the closet and retrieved a real katana. I listened closely as he gave me instructions on how to draw it without hurting myself. The drawing part was easy, but as I sheathed it without enough respect for the sharp edge, I cut my thumb. Droplets of blood fell to the ground. I cried out in pain and brought the small, superficial wound to my mouth. *Ow. Worse than a paper cut.*

Liam drew a sharp intake of breath and took a few steps back. "Don't worry. I won't go crazy again."

"I'm not worried." The words flew out of my mouth without thought.

The way his eyes softened, I knew I'd said something right... for once.

I went to bed that night no closer to figuring out my powers, but my martial arts were on point. What good would it do me if I couldn't walk out of here? Also, there was a hint of elation keeping me awake. I didn't dwell on why, but I no longer felt in a rut. I was on the verge of... something.

24

TOXIC

Alana

A few days after my first katana training, Thom went to Washington to help Lilah with a new closet door in her apartment. I was antsy to go out and do something. Blow off steam. When I heard Liam talking on the phone about a ghoul they'd missed during their last hunt, a dangerous idea struck me.

Tired of sitting on my ass practicing skills I never got to use, I begged Liam to let me tag along and fight my first demon. He'd said himself that ghouls were stupid, and we'd practiced every day.

We left the car behind and made our way closer to the monster's territory on foot.

A thick fog made the urban neighborhood look unpredictable and dangerous. In the air, the eerie smell of gingerbread contrasted with the acrid smell of urine. A bakery must have been baking cookies nearby.

Nervous, I tucked back a strand of hair that was coming loose from one of two folded Dutch braids securing my thick mane on top of my head. I didn't want to give myself an accidental haircut with the razor-sharp samurai sword.

Liam had mocked me, saying he didn't expect this hunt to be so fancy, and I'd retorted that he was such a girl for noticing my hair.

We explored the sketchy neighborhood for signs of ghoulish activity for more than half an hour until Liam asked, "what's with your obsession with learning how to kill demons anyway?"

I cocked my head to the side. "Demons are bad."

"Demons are people, too."

I grinned. "You should make that into a T-shirt."

He bit back a smile and tilted his head to the side. "Walked right into that one, didn't I?"

"Sure did."

We walked around a pile of junk.

A soft squeaky sound was audible before a big, wet, hairy thing zoomed in between my legs. I jumped about a foot into the air and let out a high-pitched girlish scream.

Liam's hand muffled it in an instant, his right palm pressed against my lips. "It's just a rat."

Just a rat? That thing must have been at least three feet long, not counting the tail. I'd probably alerted everyone and *everything* of our presence within a two-mile radius.

Liam's hand fell at his side, and I gritted my teeth together. "It was huge."

"A rodent of unusual size," he said with a quick nod.

A gush of wind blew past us, and the wretched smell of decay hit my nose, making me hate my big mouth. Why had I insisted on coming? "I think I'm going to be sick."

"Let's turn back," Liam offered.

"No. I can do this."

"If you vomit and get eaten, it'll be on you."

The comment grated at my temper, his effaced tone bordering on condescension. It reminded me of the old Liam. The one I couldn't stand. "Thanks for the vote of confidence."

Liam stopped and pointed to the middle of the alley where a creature hunched over something I couldn't distinguish from a distance.

"Remember, decapitation works best. Few things regenerate without their heads."

I stared deep into his eyes. "Do you?"

He clicked his tongue and disappeared into the fog.

Serves him right.

Step by step, I approached the demon. A noisy chewing sound rose from its position over a half-eaten human torso. It raised its head at the sound of my footsteps, a weird purple tubular chunk hanging from the corner of its mouth. My lips quivered as I recognized the purplish tubes as guts. Hearts were the meal, guts the appetizers, and I didn't want to find out what the dessert might be.

Isn't there a golden rule that you shouldn't disturb an animal as it eats?

About four feet tall, the ghoul's six pairs of eyes flashed as they spotted me. Its bald, over-sized scalp had deep and raw sores that oozed black goo. *I can do this.* I would succeed if only to wipe Liam's smirk off his face.

The thing snarled and bared two rows of deadly teeth. Its grotesque legs crouched towards me as the poisonous nails sliced the air. My pulse quickened, and my hand trembled. *God, what the hell am I doing? I'm not Buffy.*

Ghouls were slow, so I had to stay away from the paralyzing claws and wait for an opening to chop off its long neck. I moved in slow circles around the monster, keeping a few feet between us at all times in case it tried to pounce. I switched directions often and analyzed its movements patterns. Impatient, it hissed, and I caught a glimpse of a rotted, bicuspid tongue. The sight was so jarring that I pursed my lips in disgust and froze.

Concentrate. My palms were sweaty, and I had to wipe one hand at a time against my pants, my control over the long blade faltering. The anxiety fuzzed my vision, and I felt both extremely hot and numbingly cold. Dark spots danced in front of my eyes. *Am I about to pass out?*

"You can do this, remember your training." Liam's calm voice echoed through my mind, reminding me that I wasn't alone. No matter how

dangerous this big bad demon was, I had bigger and badder on my side.

The veil lifted, and I could no longer hear my blood whooshing at my temples. Both hands around the katana's handle, I gripped it tighter and resumed circling the beast. I kept the distance between us the same, stepping back when it inched forward. Ghouls sneaked up on their prey, but this one didn't have the element of surprise, and I had studied its speed for a few long minutes.

Botching this was not an option.

Finally, it balled its crooked fists and pranced forward like a disarticulated monkey. The faster it moved, the clumsier it looked.

Moving as fast as I could, I feigned to rotate clockwise but leaped forward instead, the blade raised in the air. It reacted quicker than I expected, and I zoomed out of the way. Its talons grazed my side. *That was close.*

I turned back to face the enemy and held the blade high to keep it at bay while I regained my composure.

"You're doing great," Liam said through the mental tether.

The kind words gave me confidence, and I did a variant of my earlier trick, this time keeping less space between the beast and me. Its eyes followed me to the left, but at the last second, I veered right and sliced the air with all my might, blade angled to slash its neck.

My stupid eyes closed at the moment of truth.

I blinked.

My katana was stuck halfway through the neck. The strike lacked strength and hadn't severed the head. I panicked and jumped backwards, freeing the edge of my sword from the putrescent flesh. The big head tilted towards the sound side of the neck, and the ghoul gurgled angrily at me, alive despite the huge gash.

Half-mad, I roared and swung at the neck leftover, over and over again until the head tumbled at my feet. *Yes!* Mom would have been appalled by the sight, her little girl dancing over the corpse of a stinking beast, but I didn't care. I'd done something tangible, something good. I'd helped make the world a better place.

Liam appeared right beside me and clapped. "Well done. You've got guts if not brains." That was as close to a compliment as I'd ever gotten, so I brushed aside the jab. He met my high five in mid-air. "Lesson number two. You can't leave demon corpses lying around, so you got to fillet this one *good*."

My eyes opened like saucers. "You're kidding?"

He tapped his index against his month. "Or I can finish the job, and you retire from your career as a demon hunter."

I huffed and turned back to the mangled body at my feet. Half the job was already done. Black goo splashed on me as I chopped the demon in small pieces. I glared at Liam, but the situation was so absurd that I had to bite my cheeks not to laugh. Liam's lips quirked in a genuine smile, a gentle playfulness replacing his usual sarcasm. Shoulders braced over the shredded prey, I couldn't take it anymore and laughed until tears prickled my eyes.

I could get used to this.

Liam's smile vanished as his gaze fell on something behind me. I glanced over my shoulder. *Shit.* A demon three times the size of the dead one towered above us. Queen ghoul, I guessed, grimacing at the thought. These monsters had mothers, too.

Gravity shouldn't have allowed for such a big head on such an emaciated body. It bared its gray teeth. There were three rows of them, each five to six inches long like a shark on steroids. Nuggets of its previous meals were wedged between the pointy mini-swords. Monsters didn't floss.

Goosebumps branded my skin as I took a few careful steps backwards and retreated a foot behind Liam. I tossed him the katana. "I got the last one..."

Focused on the twelve-foot-tall threat, he caught the weapon with one hand, and a deep chuckle shook his throat despite the seriousness of the moment. The blade looked like an extension of his arm as he drew a few practice circles in the air, and I envied his skills.

I thought my *bigger and badder* demon would slice this new menace up in no time.

I was wrong.

The tall buildings around us crept closer and closer as the beast corralled us deeper and deeper into the labyrinth of back alleys. After many failed attempts, it cornered us next to one another, our backs against a tall dumpster. The end of the line.

I was exhausted. My lungs burned, and my legs cramped as I battled to keep my wits about me despite a strong urge to drop to my knees. Liam's earlier chuckle at my cheekiness was long forgotten, his face deep in concentration. This new beast was trouble, no doubt about it.

"On the count of three, you're going to run as fast as you can on the left. Do not stop. You understand?" He said mentally.

I nodded.

"One, two, three." Liam leaped, and I made a run for it.

But not only was this ghoul model much faster than its progeny, it was much, much smarter. A vicious backhand punch had me flying, and I landed on my ass, dazed.

Liam managed to cleave an arm but missed the neck. The thing dashed and took a bite off his side, its teeth digging deep. A powerful roar barreled my eardrums. Liam balled his hands together and hurled them at the ghoul's cranium to free himself. The beast staggered, and Liam squatted in front of me, feral, his stare never leaving the monster that had just tasted him.

I propped my legs under me as he motioned for me to be quiet. *"Don't move. Ghouls stench too much to smell us, so they rely entirely on vision. We might get lucky."*

Might? I prayed Liam's powers would work because, otherwise, we would not get out of this situation unscathed.

Twelve eyes blinked in all directions as they searched for us. From this angle, my face was inches away from the bite in Liam's left side. Clots of blood stuck to his shirt, a huge chunk of flesh missing.

The gash ran deep into the muscles, the deep fascia torn. It was a miracle he could even move. More blood poured out of the capillaries like foam, a shade darker than it ought to be. The bubbles intensified as if the blood's temperature was rising to its boiling point. The wound swelled, pulsated and shrunk under my gaze. New skin grew over the lump of fresh cells, blended at the edges, and formed a smooth surface.

Barely a minute after the bite, the wound was only recognizable by its lighter shade and because it stood in the center of the shirt's hole. Fascinated by the phenomenon, I brushed the patch of fresh skin. Liam laid his hand over mine to stop my movements.

The beast turned all its eyes towards us. Palm flat against Liam's side, sandwiched there by his hand, I stayed very still and hoped to God the ghoul would turn away. It didn't.

It took a few gooey steps forward until it was above us. Up close, I noticed its serpentine leg hair squirm against the decayed edges as if a million angry worms had been stitched to its skin. Liam dove for the discarded blade, and the monster's talons gripped his back.

With a growl, Liam shot upwards and sliced the demon open from its groin to its mouth. As relief flooded over me, he stood with the blade angled downward before crashing to the ground face first. *Shit! The venom!*

I hurried to his side. "I'm here."

His entire body was flaccid, and two long nails were embedded in his back. I removed them, tore the small holes in his shirt into bigger ones, and looked at the wounds. They did as the bite had done and shriveled in a matter of seconds.

As my fingers let the fabric go, I noticed a silver glow emanating from Liam's back. Curious, I widened the holes again. The serpent between his shoulder blades glowed under the moonlight, identical to mine, but bigger. *Nice tattoo.*

I focused back on my task, grabbed the side of his shirt, and struggled to roll him on his back. "How much do you weigh, God damn it?" Muscles screaming in pain, I succeeded.

Seeing Liam so vulnerable and unable to move creeped me out. A hint of consciousness behind the silver of his eyes told me he saw me. I stripped from my hoodie and wiped the goo and dirt from the street off his face.

After I was done, I balled the ruined fabric, placed it in under his head to act as a pillow, and inspected the street, making sure we were alone. When I was confident no threat was about to jump from the dark, I sat crossed legged beside him. "Let's hope Daddy ghoul doesn't show up."

My shoulders hitched when he answered, "Ghouls are hermaphrodites. They have both male and female reproductive organs."

I glanced back at the creature. Liam was right. *Yuck.* "You can talk?"

"Larynx, lips and tongue are the first muscles to recover. Ghouls like to hear you scream as they eat you." He didn't look as angry as I thought he'd be to be stuck in this position.

"Yikes." I bit my lips. "Never bring me ghoul hunting again, whatever I say."

"Amen."

I drummed my fingers on my thighs, thinking this was the perfect chance to ask questions. Might as well take advantage of the fact that he couldn't walk away from me. "I saw your tattoo. Why a snake?"

"It's my mark."

"You chose it?"

"I always loved the Garden of Eden stories. Especially the serpent."

I hugged my knees and angled my face to him. "Who knew we'd get matching tattoos..."

He laughed, and I mean an actual, gentle laugh.

I grabbed his cold, lifeless hand. "Thanks again for saving me that night. And tonight."

His fingers twitched against mine, but he stayed silent.

My nose wrinkled. "I wish I could heal you. Repay the favor."

"I'm pretty sure your powers wouldn't work on this."

"Still. It doesn't look comfortable."

"It won't be long now."

"I thought the venom worked for hours?" I said with a frown.

"Not on demons."

Too bad, I was almost looking forward to an hour or two of questioning.

Loud clanks reverberated through the creepy backstreet. A truck was unloading merchandise close by, and the whines and screeches of metal grating against metal scraped at my eardrums. This place reminded me too much of that first alley and of the horrible henchmen. My heart accelerated. "I can't wait to get out of here."

"I thought we were having a heart to heart, but okay." Liam whooshed to a standing position and extended a hand in my direction. An unusual glint in his eyes turned my insides to jelly. I placed my small hand in his, and he pulled me up. Cramps stiffened my bruised muscles, and a pained groan escaped me.

The heat of Liam's body enveloped me. His legs were shaking, and even though he acted as if he was the one steadying me, I knew better. I snared my arm around his midriff.

"Let's go home," he whispered into my ear, his breath hot on my neck. The way he'd said the word *home* made my heart squirm in a very unfamiliar way.

25

WHERE IS MY MIND?

Alana

I knocked on Liam's door at nine the next morning. Something I had never done, whatever the hour. Ever.

Was he still there? Had he gone for a run in the woods? Without me? I gnawed on my thumb, hoping I hadn't missed him. At least, he didn't disappear for days at a time as much as he used to.

A strange agitation plagued me. I'd changed twice before settling on my yoga pants. I didn't want to appear as if I was trying. *Trying what? I don't know what I'm doing. I should go back to bed.*

Eyes thick with sleep, Liam interrupted my inward rambles. He opened the door wearing only jeans, and I lost my train of thought. Silence stretched on.

"You wanted something?" Liam asked.

I'd knocked. *Right.* "I thought... I wanted to see if you were willing to train again today? Now? Maybe?"

"You want to train? What time is it?"

"Nine." I deserved his dumbfounded look. We'd gone to bed at two in the morning, and nine was early for me on a normal day. I shrugged. "Can't sleep."

The *nightmare* had recurred last night. For the first time since the ritual. In a loop. A vivid, Technicolor, multi-sensory, and deeply disturbing loop.

His eyes zeroed-in on my hands, and my eyes flew to the cup of coffee I was holding. Liam's mug. He passed a hand over his sleepy features. "You made me coffee." It wasn't a question. "Yeah, sure. Let's train. Let me get my shirt."

He walked away from the door, offering me a full view of his snake tattoo. I glimpsed around the room. The drapes were shut and plunged it in complete darkness. Bummer. I was dying to know if the bed with the big posters and the black sheets from the dream matched his. The one at the motel didn't have posters, and it bugged me. Why would I make up such a weird detail?

Liam took the mug from my hand as he closed the door behind him and walked to my room.

My mouth was dry. "What are we doing?"

"It's a bit early for sword lessons, maybe later. Now, we meditate. I'll push you into a trance, and you'll try to respond to my questions telepathically."

We sat crossed-legged facing each other, like I had done a few times with Lilah. I dried my palms on my pants before he grabbed my hands. I hated mediation. I felt silly and nervous and embarrassed, and my palms were getting sweaty again.

Liam's eyes were closed. "Don't think about how silly this is. Concentrate."

I copied his stance. The warmth of his hands was the only thing registering. I didn't feel any different and couldn't hear anything. And then I did.

"Don't fight it. Relax." As it had the night before, his voice echoed in my mind, so clear it had a flavor. It tasted sweet. *"What's two plus two?"*

A clichéd math problem. But the words stagnated, not projected as they should.

"Breathe deep. Try to think loudly."

An itch tapped at the base of my skull. *Can you hear me?* I tried. But no.

Frustrated by my failure, I stiffened and squeezed his hand tighter. The darkness transformed into a spider web like the one I'd found in my mind when Liam had helped me heal my hand. It stretched for miles in front of me, but instead of being made of a yarn-like material, the threads were hard as steel. I traced my index over one.

She's too tense. She won't succeed. Her hands are cold, and her aura's darker today. I should let her rest. She sucks at using her powers but is a natural with a sword. Figures.

I grabbed a smaller, darker thread. Images pounded into my brain like a jack-drill on a rebellious piece of concrete. The current swept me away into a downward spiral of foamy, treacherous waters.

A blonde man gave Liam a thumb's up and slumped a corpse in a hole in the ground.

A young Thom, fear in his eyes.

A beautiful woman sobbing.

Myself, crying with my face in my thighs against the gym's wall.

Before I could make sense of it all, I crashed back into my body violently.

Liam ripped his hands away. "You read my mind."

"I didn't mean to, I—"

"What did you see?" He shook my shoulders a little. "Alana, tell me what you saw." He sounded downright panicked. What was he afraid I might have seen?

"You thought my aura was darker today." I winced at the pain of his fingers digging into my skin, and he relaxed his hold. "I heard you think I suck at magic but was a natural with a sword. That's all." It wasn't entirely a lie; I didn't know what to make of the other stuff.

"Jesus!" He shot upwards and grabbed a fist of hair. "Never do that again." Storming out of the room, he slammed the door shut with a loud bang.

What the hell had just happened?

AROUND NOON, I fell asleep reading against the kitchen window. As I came to, I heard Thom and Liam talking. They were in the living room, and I could hear every word from my cozy nest in the breakfast nook.

"Did you check for the next potential?" Thom asked.

"Not yet."

"Why not?"

"Never got around to it."

Thom cleared his throat. "Are you okay?"

"Yes, why?"

"Do you want to talk about... things?"

Liam's tone hardened. "What things?"

"Personal things."

There was a long pause.

"What's on your mind, Junior?"

"I hate it when you call me that," Thom said warmly.

I could hear the matching smile in Liam's voice when he answered, "I know."

"I read all about possession rituals, and I'm pretty sure you were supposed to kiss her. Kiss her, not peck her on the forehead. In fact, I'm pretty sure most demons go beyond that..." Thom trailed off, his voice so low I barely heard it.

My brows pulled together. I'd been asking myself the same question. My dream had been wrong about a lot of stuff, but Frank had made it clear Liam was supposed to kiss me during the ritual.

Thom continued, "I know you, man. You don't care about this stuff. You'd kiss anyone—err, not anyone, but you know what I mean. That got me thinking. Maybe you didn't kiss her because you wanted to kiss her for real. Does that make sense?"

I held my breath, and my heart stopped beating. Liam couldn't have noticed my eavesdropping yet, and I had to know the honest answer to that question. Thom had to be wrong.

"Let me get this straight, you're grilling me with questions because *I didn't* kiss your girlfriend on the mouth? Or *beyond*?"

"Well, yeah."

A few seconds passed before they both erupted into a fit of laughter. "And she's not my girlfriend."

"Yeah, sure, whatever you say."

"But seriously?"

"Thom, I promise you. I'd *never* want to kiss your girlfriend. I can't stand her half the time. She had blood in her mouth, probably bit her tongue while thrashing around. I couldn't do it."

The words reverberated in my head. NEVER. WANT. TO. KISS. They dripped with such contempt that they echoed deep in my chest like a magpie's laughing crow. The sheer idea of kissing me was not only a bad meal to chew, but a bad meal sprinkled with dust and left in the sun to rot.

Sourness rose to my mouth, and my cheeks got hot. The acid in my stomach agglutinated in a hard mass. Of course, I knew Liam wasn't into me. Thom must have banged his head this morning to come up with such a ludicrous question.

But I remembered with vivid preciseness everything that had happened during the ritual. You'd expect the contrary since I was out of it part of the time, but the feelings, sounds and tastes had been carved deep, way beyond a normal memory. They were branded into my soul instead of my brain. I could re-live it at will when I closed my eyes.

And I knew for a fact I didn't have blood in my mouth that night. Liam was lying.

THE VENOM in Liam's words kept on stinging, and I retreated to my room to finish my nap. Drowsiness fell over me like soft snow, my mind wandered, and right before I lost consciousness, I saw something. It wasn't real, not a vision, rather a long-forgotten memory.

I was in bed with someone. I felt different; stronger, sharper. Every muscle in my body was ready to spring into action.
The person I was lying next to was me, Alana. Waves of copper hair framed my peaceful face, my heartbeat quiet but steady. A powerful smell tickled my nostrils with every breath and drove me crazy. A halo glowed around that Alana, drawing me closer and closer. I raised my hand to touch her neck, to feel her pulse, but fisted my fingers and resisted the urge.
I hid my face in her hair to inhale the sweet tantalizing scent before exiting the room without a sound. I walked to the basement, to the bathroom in the corner of the cell, and thought I belonged in it still. My hands grabbed the sink and fragmented the porcelain as if it was dry sand.
"Fuck." My voice was hoarse. I met my gaze in the mirror. My eyes were dark and dangerous, and I could hear them, the demons, hissing at me to take what I wanted.
I was Liam.

I awoke with a start and suffered from a serious whiplash, a weird tingling sensation behind my eyes. Stumbling to the bathroom to splash water on my face, I fought to catch my breath. Adrenaline chased away the lull of sleep. I rested my hands on the sink and pressed on the porcelain. I remembered crushing one with barely any force at all.

It had to be a side effect of the meditation. My brain was processing the string of images I'd seen in Liam's mind. His shame tasted like rotten spices in my mouth.

When was this? I closed my eyes to concentrate despite the numbing headache. It was his first night out. The night I'd run to Thom's room. *How dare he invade my privacy like that?*

Fear. Confusion. Anger. My mind was reeling, and my blood boiled. *Here I was thinking he was nervous to touch me when we were actually sleeping buddies? What other secrets does he keep?*

Liam Walker had sins to confess.

I knocked on his door with the verve of someone ready to trample it down.

As I waited for it to open, Thom's voice rose from downstairs. "Hey. What are you doing?"

"I need to talk to Liam." I tried to hide the edge in my voice. Thom would arbitrate our conversation if he thought we'd fight, and I didn't want that.

"He's in the kitchen. Are you okay?"

"Bad dream again," I lied.

"Want to talk about it?"

I bit my lower lip and shook my head. "No. Thank you, though."

Disappointment flickered in Thom's eyes. I'd brushed him off, but I didn't care.

Somewhere along the way, I'd gotten distracted. I'd tried to kiss Thom, been rejected by an illusion, and had obsessed way too much over the damn dream and on why Liam hadn't kissed me. I needed to refocus my efforts.

This wasn't my life. This was purgatory. I had to find my way out and start over. I needed a new life filled with new people, where I could build myself a new set of hopes and dreams. None of which would involve demons and supernatural powers that were not my cup of tea anyway.

The more I repeated the words in my head, the more I believed them. This wasn't the new normal. This was still a prison, and I'd gotten too comfortable in my metaphorical orange inmate jacket. And too close to the guards. This was a new me, and the new me wanted answers. No half-truths and sideways glances, but real answers. Was Liam manipulating me? Would he sabotage my training on purpose? Despite all his speeches and all his warnings, did he enjoy playing with me?

I found the devil in the kitchen, his head in the refrigerator. Maybe if he'd looked at me, I wouldn't have said what I said.

I growled, "Why are you such a bad teacher? Do you want me to fail?"

He let go of his snack and straightened up. "You woke up on the wrong side of the bed?" His gentle tone almost unraveled me.

I had rehearsed this interrogation. How could I be inclined to let it all go so quickly? "Are you controlling me?" I asked point-blank.

"Controlling you?" he repeated like he didn't understand my question, but Liam Walker was anything but innocent.

I had to be right, then. The ritual had other side-effects. The visions, my ability to read his thoughts, it had all started after the ritual. What if its influence went beyond that? I couldn't stand Liam before, but now I had all these *feelings*.

"That piece of your soul bit. Is it controlling me?"

Liam's eyes narrowed. "Are you accusing me of something?"

"Are you confessing to something?"

He rubbed the arch of his brow. "Alana, believe me. If I had any control over you, we would not be having this conversation."

I bounced from one foot to the other. "Is it possible? Could you be doing it without realizing it?"

"No!" He looked revolted by the idea, and I was tempted to believe him. His tone softened, "Listen, I know I almost ate your head off this morning, and I'm sorry."

The last ember of anger flickered, and I came close to letting it go. *No! Guard up, remember? Real answers!* "It's not about that. I don't care about that." I clicked my tongue and blew air out of my mouth to buy time. "You sabotaged my first success this morning. You're supposed to teach me witchcraft, but you dick around instead. I'm tired of it."

He froze. "I dick around?"

I played with the hem of my shirt, averting his gaze. "Yes. I want you to be professional."

The silence thickened.

Why wasn't he calling me out on being a total bitch? How could he be so calm? I wanted him to crack, to confess. He had secrets, and I wanted to rip them out of him one by one until he was in pieces. I had to know if I could trust him or if I'd been a fool.

But I didn't say that. Instead, I gritted my teeth together and said, "Teach me to control my powers, so I can leave this place. FOREVER."

Liam towered to his full height, his spine rigid, and his eyes dark. He sounded ferocious and gruff when he said, "You want to learn. Fine."

26

DEAD INSIDE

Alana

Liam kept an unforgiving hold on my shoulders as he guided/dragged me outside. The heat of his hands escalated my heartbeat.

"Where are we going?" I asked.

"You want to use your powers. Let's use them."

"How?"

He didn't say, and it didn't surprise me. I went along with what he was doing despite the dangerous look on his face. The blame lay on me. I'd asked for this, had invited the devil out to play. Might as well see what would happen. We sprinted through the woods, and I wondered if his plan was to exhaust me, or if he even had a plan. Finally, he came to a stop.

The path was narrow and the earth wet and slippery. A rustling in the branches alerted me to an outsider's presence, and a hiker came into view, but Liam's intense stare was all I could see.

He gripped my shoulders. "You haven't accepted what you are or what I am. I'm not your babysitter, not your guardian. I'm the thing that hunts for you, hungers for you." His nails dug into my neck. "You've forgotten... We've both forgotten. It's time we remember."

The word *hunger* formed a ripple of need in my stomach.

A hiker closed in, but he couldn't see us. In his mid-30s, he was a spandex fashion victim. I didn't know what the hell was going on. Did Liam know this man? Unlikely.

He'd said, *let's use your powers*. My eyes jumped up to meet his. To use my powers, I needed someone to heal. The stormy silver eyes betrayed Liam's intentions, confirming my hunch, and I shouted, "No!"

Too late. In a single string of motion, Liam smashed the hiker's face open, broke his leg, and punched him in the stomach hard enough to cause considerable damage. Nausea slithered its icy tails around my stomach, and I rushed to the man's side. He was in bad shape, and I didn't dwell too long on the white area I was positive was his bared tibia. I screamed over my shoulder to the very unstable demon behind me, "Why would you do that?"

Liam appeared calmer, arms limp at his sides. "Heal him."

"God, that's the master plan? I can't." I felt it in every bone of my body. Whatever I needed to find was beyond me. Liam had said it best: I wasn't ready. And it might cost this stranger his life.

"Try."

"I'm too angry to concentrate right now."

"Maybe it's exactly what you need."

"I can't heal him anymore than I can kill you with my thoughts, no matter how much *I try*." Fury threatened to overwhelm me. An emotional chasm opened inside my heart, and I was afraid of what lay deep in the precipice. Cold sweat stuck to the nape of my neck, and the heaviness in my ribcage twisted into a painful knot.

Liam grabbed my arm. "Try. You want to learn magic for the wrong reasons. You want normal. News flash, princess, you'll always be a freak. You'll always be broken."

I shrugged his hand off me. "Are you speaking to me or to yourself?"

The spark in his eyes dimmed, and he stepped back.

My eyes about burst out of their sockets when he turned to walk away. "ARE YOU LEAVING?"

"Heal him if you can. Or don't. I don't give a fuck."

How could he act this way? How could this be the same man that had hunted ghouls with me? "Please. Do what you did to heal my hand."

A wry laugh passed through his lips. "That was different. It was barely a graze. And you've been out of my system for weeks."

"Give me your phone." I'd left mine at home. I wasn't used to carrying it around.

"Jesus, you're blocking yourself. You're not even trying to understand your powers."

"Liam, whatever brought this on... it's wrong. It's not you." I squeezed his arm and searched for his eyes.

He motioned to the man. "This is what you asked for. I'm not *dicking around* anymore."

A thought dawned on me. Maybe this was all an illusion. *Yes!* Liam wouldn't kill to teach me a lesson. I fisted the front of his shirt. "Is this real? You love freaking me out... Liam, is it real?"

Our gaze locked. "I wouldn't think twice about killing this man. He's nothing to me. He's as real as you and me."

My eyes fogged. "How could you?"

A hot hand traced the slope of my neck. "There is darkness in our world, Alana, and our powers come from that darkness. Embrace it."

I gritted my teeth together. "It's your world, not mine."

"If you believe that, you need more help than I thought."

Anger and disappointment tightened my guts. "I don't need your help."

"Matter of fact you do."

"Then, I don't want it."

"Okay." The sense of abdication in his voice was absolute.

Our chests heaved with every breath. I stood in front of the precipice again and gulped. His hands cupped my face. The touch was in deep contrast with our words. It was soft, distracting.

My next witty repartee got caught in my throat. I needed to get away from him and gather my thoughts, so I pushed him hard in the chest. "Stop touching me. Leave me alone. I need a break from you and your condescending bullshit."

A dark glint flashed in his eyes as he disappeared.

I lost my balance and slumped to the ground. "Jerk." He had to be close enough to hear me. He wouldn't risk leaving me and my blazing aura alone, especially since I was about to call other people here. He had to be sulking in the shadows.

I found a phone in the hiker's pockets, called 911, used the GPS to give them our location and told them to hurry. I tried to stop the bleeding as best as I could. What if he died? What if he suffered permanent damage? I'd unleashed my personal psychopath on this man and felt responsible.

The first responders came in with a stretcher and pulled the man from the ground. "What happened?" They asked.

"I found him like this," I lied.

"You okay, miss?"

No, I'm definitely not okay. I held in the tears knowing Liam was nearby. "Yes."

The paramedics offered me a ride to the hospital, but I refused and lied about my address and name. Feeling numb, I started to make my way back. My mind hazy, I didn't see the small hole in time and plunged face first into the dirt. *As if I needed this today.*

I shifted to my ass and grabbed my swollen ankle. It throbbed, and I whimpered. Unshed tears from before spilled over my lids, but I wiped them away with the back of my hand. I stood up, put a little weight on the swollen left ankle and winced at the fresh wave of pain. *No. Not going to work.*

Sprained ankles were an annual occurrence. If I walked home and hung to my stubbornness, I'd be limping for weeks.

My skin crawled as I shouted, "Liam!"

No answer.

"Liam stop being a jerk. I need help." The word *help* tickled my ears. "I know I said I don't need your help, but now I do." Pride hurt my throat on its way down. "I'm sorry."

The words sounded fake. "Sorry," I repeated, this time managing a dash of honesty.

God, he left me for real. I grabbed a sizable branch on the ground and used it as a crutch. On flat terrain, it would have been fine, but the hill was steep. I climbed one painful step at a time, a metallic taste in my mouth, and my teeth cut through my bottom lip to keep the whimpers in. Blood flooded my mouth.

The autumn sun fell too fast in the sky. By my calculations, I'd still be at least half a mile from the house at sunset. In my white tank and shorts, I wasn't dressed for an evening hike and shivers shook my body.

After another twenty minutes, I had to make a stop. I inspected the blisters on my palm, a testament to how tight I held the makeshift crutch and groaned. As I was about to resume my painful trek, I felt him. I felt him before I saw him and turned to where he would appear.

Liam's eyes roved over my body from head to toe.

Great. Stuck in the role of the damsel in distress again. I frowned when he didn't move. Was he waiting for an apology? For me to admit I needed him? Was he considering leaving me here in this state after my vehement speech about not wanting his help? Was he that callous?

"Well, did you come to gloat?" I said, shattering the silence. My right leg screamed in pain from holding my entire weight for too long.

A low grunt escaped his tight lips, and he whisked me up in his arms. I wiped the relief off my face. The heat of his body felt amazing, and I begrudgingly snuggled into him, my cold hand against his sweater. My ankle pulsated in gratitude, swollen from the abuse. "If this man dies, I'll never forgive you."

Why wasn't he saying I told you so? Where were the "you made me do it" and the "it's your fault"? "Don't you have any wise-ass remarks to say?"

Jaw clenched, he stared dead ahead. Silent.

"You're a piece of work. You hurt that man for no good reason. Too bad there are no prisons for your lot. I'd get a much-needed vacation." Angry babbles should be outlawed. My pulse was erratic, his mutism more unnerving than our fight from before. "Wipe that frown off your face, I know you're bursting with glee. Want me to say it? You were right. I need you. It's what you want, no? To hear me say it? You must be feeling so smug right now—"

"Never pretend to know what I'm feeling."

The silence following his quiet words was suffocating.

27

GONE

Alana

My reflection struck me from the standing mirror in the corner. No older than sixteen years old, jet black hair cascaded in big curls around my face. My beauty had once been my number one asset, but my skin was chalky, unhealthy, like I'd been sick for months.

There was an insatiable ache inside my bones, pervading my blood, my entire body wasting away while I waited for him. I heard his voice in my head all the time, telling me he missed me, promising to visit soon, very soon.

"I'm here," a whisper came from the dark corner of the room. My heart fluttered in my chest and exhilaration coursed through my veins.

The boy was handsome. A cry of joy popped out of my lungs, and I hugged him hard.

He hushed me, reminding me we had to be very quiet. Nobody else could know he was here.

I giggled, giddy to have him in my arms at last. It had been too long. His black hair was identical to mine, but his eyes glowed silver and it upset me, for some reason. A pout on my lips, I said, "You changed." He was taller. I noticed his muscles were fuller and harder as I ran my hand over his torso and shoulders. The ache in my bones tightened.

"You changed, too." His hand gently explored the new, supple flesh of my chest, and I moaned at the touch, the ache now smoldering embers deep in my belly.

I undressed him, and he undressed me, both of us eager to commit to memory the new us. He pushed me towards my bed.

Sleeping without him had been hard. Before the men had taken him away, he'd sneak in most nights. I was cold without him.

"God, you are so beautiful," he said.

I blushed. "Don't talk about God like that." I was so perfectly happy, lying beneath him.

He looked down at me like I was his whole world, and he was mine. He leaned to kiss me, and I chuckled when his tongue rubbed against mine. It tickled. I caught a glimpse of us in the mirror. I no longer looked sick, my cheeks rosy and my skin glowing like it used to before his departure. Everything was better when he was around.

"Is everybody nice to you?" He asked.

I told him all about Matthew being a jerk to me. He got angry, and I didn't want him to be, so I rolled him over and climbed unto him. He got quiet and wet his lips. I kissed him, using my tongue too, and he relaxed. The ache was now between my thighs, and it burned. I shifted to alleviate the pain and rubbed against his leg. The ache pulsed, and I exhaled loudly. I tried it again and smiled at the feeling. I wanted more. I wanted so much, but I didn't know what or how.

We switched places again as he tried to keep me still. "What's happening?" he asked.

"I don't know. It tickles there too."

"Where?" He asked, and I grabbed his hand to show him. He never liked that part of me because it was different. "Here?"

I nodded, a sharp pleasure erupting as he touched it.

"What does it feel like?"

"Good," I breathed.

Something hard pressed into my thigh as he shifted above me.

His eyes widened when he realized he was inside of me. I purred. Why hadn't we tried this before? We were so close this way. "Good?" I asked, and he bit his lips nodding solemnly. He moved inside me. I smiled.

I stared deep into his eyes as my body tingled in pleasure. The ache was gone.

My love, my missing half, my twin.

I WOKE up in a cold sweat, shaken to the core, and crawled to the edge of the bed, the need to retch imperious. Bile burned my stomach and throat. I'd been Emily Walker. Shared her body as she made love to her twin for the first time. And I'd had an orgasm. *Yuk.*

Thom's hand stroked my back. "Hey, are you okay?"

I'd reverted to my old habit of sleeping in Thom's bed. The last few days, I'd barely gotten a whiff of sleep. *The nightmare* had looped again, flanked by various memories of Liam's past. They all revolved around his hunger for witch's blood and showcased the many imaginative ways he might devour and kill me.

This was my first Emily dream, and I prayed it'd be the last.

Thom's eyes flicked over to the splatter of vomit on the carpet, and I explained the dream, skipping the gruesome details.

"It's impossible," he said as he stroked my back.

"I'm telling you what I saw."

"Is it possible it was just a dream?"

Ugh. No. "Incest happens. I'm telling you she got pregnant from her brother. I don't dream about twisted things like that."

Thom ran a hand over his face and sighed. "I'm not saying you made it up, but there must be another explanation. Shadow Walkers can't have kids. Ever."

I gritted my teeth together. Whatever Thom had read in a book or been told, it was wrong. Clara Walker had been James' child. "James Walker can."

Careful to spare my ankle, I stumbled into the library and ripped the diary off the shelf. "Thomas Walker thought his sister had been raped by this Matthew kid, but he was wrong. Emily and James were lovers." I took a deep breath. "Why in the world would I dream about that? Does Liam even know?"

Thom's lips pressed together. "I don't think so."

Too bad I couldn't ask. Liam hadn't returned home since he'd dumped me and my throbbing ankle on the couch three weeks ago. I'd called the hospital a few days after, and the man from the woods had barely survived.

Thom interrupted my turmoil by wrapping me up in a hug. "It must suck to dream about this stuff."

Understatement of the year. I didn't want to admit how real these visions felt, and how confusing they were. There was something wrong with me. Why else would I get these weird visions?

Oblivious to my inner doubts, Thom served me a glass of milk and coaxed me back to bed.

Later in the night, a weight on my chest forced me to open my eyes. Emily Walker stood next to the bed, looking as she had in my dream. Her dark curls bounced as she grabbed my hand in hers and pulled for me to get up. "Come, Alana."

Come? Come where?

"You need to know. You need to understand. Come."

I followed her outside the house, our bodies light as feathers as if gravity had released its hold on us.

The sun blazed over the trees and sweat flowed down my back in a matter of seconds. The white plantation house on my right contrasted against the deep blue sky, and the humid air surrendered whiffs of fresh paint and wood chips. A man was rocking a small baby in his arms. I approached him, and Emily put a hand on my shoulder. She looked at the small girl with tears in her eyes. "My Clara."

A cloaked figure walked across the grass and removed his hood. He gazed at the baby with love then straight at me. *James Walker.* He put a finger over his lips and waived me over to another woman holding another baby. Long red waves flew down her shoulders, identical to mine.

As I was about to gaze upon her face, the world bled into darkness.

Emily grabbed my face. "You have to know who you are, prevent what's coming. You have to understand." She dug her fingernails into my neck. "Alana, you have to *remember.*" As if she was being sucked into a black hole, Emily shrunk and disappeared. Her scream of terror was like liquid ice being poured down my ears.

WHEN I OPENED MY EYES, my hands were smeared with mud. Vapor rose as I exhaled. I wasn't in bed anymore. I was standing outside the Walker's mansion, ankle-deep in a rain puddle.

What the fuck? I wiped the rain away from my eyes. I was soaked to the core. And cold. The droplets turned to ice spikes across my wet skin, biting down on my flesh.

Thom's voice reached my ears. "Lana!"

I ran across the lawn.

The flashlight in his hands created streaks of light through the rain. "What happened? Are you okay? I woke up and couldn't find you." He wrapped his arm around me.

I cowered into his warm embrace, his raincoat smooth against my skin. "I woke up outside."

His brows creased at the sight of my bare feet. "You woke up outside?"

"I sleepwalked, I think."

A groan grated his throat, and he closed his eyes before passing a hand over his face. "Jesus! What's going on?"

"No idea."

No idea at all.

28

JUST LIKE FIRE

Alana

Thom's arms were tucked around my midriff, and his regular breaths tickled my neck. Between the heat of his body, the soft comforter, and the silky sheets, I'd achieved perfect physical comfort, but I couldn't let myself sleep, terrified of losing myself in the mayhem of vivid dreams. Terrified of whatever revelations awaited in the rich darkness.

Last night's sleepwalking incident fresh on my mind, I pulled the house key from my necklace and let it fall to the floor. This way, I wouldn't leave the house under anyone's influence but mine. I screwed my eyes shut, and a powerful, full-bodied shiver descended from the base of my neck to my toes. Something was off. The air hanged on a breath that reeked of wilted flowers and disappointment.

A gentle breeze flirted with the curtains, and the light of the moon seeped through the crack. I disentangled my limbs from Thom's and stood to close the blinds. As I stepped forward, goosebumps branded my arms, and the cold air wasn't to blame. I hurried to the window and peered outside. My heart leaped and cringed at the same time, leaving me breathless.

Liam was digging in the garden with a big shovel. His leather jacket smeared with powdery dirt, he executed the task as an automaton, the strokes regular and without thought. He stepped away from view, and I gasped as he reappeared, my knuckles gripping the windowsill. A young woman hung from his grasp, dead and badly beaten. No, more like tortured.

Liam dumped the body into the hole and started filling it, one scoop of earth at a time. One detail jumped at me, leaving a sour taste in my mouth. She had my hair and shared my general shape. My fingers grazed the glass, and Liam eye's darted up to meet mine.

The robotic movements stopped, and the shovel hung in mid-air. A dark frown crunched his features. Why did he look so displeased? The total absence of a smile on his face made me feel like a fool for the excitement rushing through my blood, and I stepped back. "Thom." I made my way back to the bed and patted his arm. "Liam's here."

That got Thom's attention, and he sat up. "Where?"

"Outside."

He shot out of bed, and I rushed after him after securing one of his sweaters around my shoulders.

By the time we thundered outside, Liam was done with grave digging, the shovel planted on top of the brand-new tomb. Fog licked the soil, and I wondered how many bodies were buried in the backyard. I'd suntanned next to a cemetery. Very macabre.

Liam's eyes traveled between Thom and I, and heat radiated on my cheeks. He'd caught me staring out of Thom's bedroom window, and our disheveled appearances were giving him the wrong idea.

"Where were you?" Thom nailed the annoyed-father impression. Liam was way past curfew.

Liam sighed, "With Vicky."

About a dozen unwanted mental images assaulted me. That woman was sex incarnated and thinking about her always made me feel super embarrassed. Through no fault of my own—I blamed her powers—I'd dreamed about her. Fantasies are harmless, but she always popped into my brain uninvited.

To hear, even loosely, about someone else's sex life was a pet peeve of mine. It had been a long while since my last dance in the sheets and picturing Liam having sex with Vicky... well... it was icky. *You fuck her until you pass out,* Liam had said. Would I ever be able to erase those words from my brain? Maybe it explained my discomfort with her guest appearances in my daydreams. Vicky-related thoughts led to Liam-related thoughts. Allowing Liam into my sexual realm was not an option.

Lips pressed into a thin line, Liam straightened his jacket, "Something happened." His hand hopped from his brow to his mouth before landing on the back of his neck, and he met my gaze head-on. "Your parents are missing."

My heart skipped a beat. "Missing?"

"Don't worry. I don't think they were taken."

Don't worry? Was he fucking kidding me? I felt like putting my hands around his throat and squeezing. Hard.

"I swung by your house yesterday, but they weren't there. I checked, and they both left their jobs without a word a few days after you disappeared," he explained with a soothing tone.

My brain struggled to digest the news. "I want to go home."

"It's too dangerous," Liam said.

Thom stroke my arms and angled me to him. "We'll go." He gave Liam a pointed glare.

Liam shook his head. "It might be a trap to lure her there."

"What if it's not?" The anger in Thom's voice as he addressed his brother was sharp and out of character. "I was worried sick. Thought something happened to you. You disappeared with no word, nothing."

Liam arched an eyebrow. "Alana didn't tell you?"

Fuck me! Why was he bringing me into this? I'd postured about having a vacation from him, but I'd been talking out of anger and frustration. He couldn't blame me for icing Thom out. I hadn't asked for that.

"Tell me what?" Thom jerked a glance in my direction and waited for an answer.

My cheeks burned. "I might have asked Liam to give me a little space."

Thom let go of me. "What? Why didn't you say so?"

I wished I had a pillow to scream into. "I, well…" I had nothing of substance to say, so I shrugged. I didn't care about the fight with Liam anymore. My parents were missing. Where were they? Were they still alive?

Not inclined to argue over a dead girl's grave, I walked into the house, changed, grabbed the keys to Liam's car, and refused to budge until the brothers agreed to take me to my parent's house. Not the most grown-up way to win an argument, but they caved. A win is a win in my book.

SOMEHOW, we made it to my hometown without killing each other.

We argued about whether we should barge in or case the place first. Thom and Liam stalled by forcing me into a motel room on the outskirts of town so we could figure things out.

The stucco walls were yellowed by age and cigarette smoke, and the carpet was peppered with suspicious stains. I sat on a shitty bed in front of the boys, no closer to agreeing on a plan of attack since all their plans required my absence.

"I couldn't care less if a thousand of them are waiting for us with pitchforks instead of arms, I'm going." I said, arms crossed.

"If it's a trap from my kind, they'll be ready to snatch you," Liam said.

I shrugged. "You'll be close."

"Can't keep tabs on you while I fight."

"You did at the warehouse."

He snorted. "I almost ripped you open that night."

The honesty in his words made me pause, but my resolve was stronger than any residual fear for Liam's bloodlust. "I don't care. I'm going."

Three things happened at once.

Liam pushed me down against the king-sized bed, a loud clunky metal sound reached my ears, and a cold metallic device snared around my wrist. Our eyes met briefly as he straightened back up. Liam had used his lightning reflexes to cuff me to the headboard. The string of actions had taken less than a second.

I turned to my ally for help. "Thom?"

He averted my gaze, "Sorry, Lana. I agree with Liam."

He agreed with Liam? Agreed to leave me behind, cuffed to this stupid bed? No way!

"Come on, Thom. It's my house. How will you know if something is out of place? If they left a message, it must be subdued, so only I will see it. I have to come."

Thom hesitated, his blue eyes rising to Liam. The cold logic was hard to overlook.

Liam huffed. "No, we talked about this. She stays here, or we don't go at all."

They *talked?* Why would they talk about this without me when I was the most concerned? It was my parents, for God's sake, not theirs.

"I know, but she's making a good point. Maybe we should bring the camera?" Thom offered as a compromise.

"No need. I'll recreate the scene when we come back. It'll be as if she came along."

Why did they always ignore my presence? "I'M RIGHT HERE."

"Yes, and here you'll stay," Liam said.

Red-faced, I pointed to the cuffs. "Untie me. I'm serious. It's *my* house. *My* parents. I *need* to go."

"See you in an hour." Thom walked out. He was still angry at me for not mentioning my fight with Liam.

Liam hovered in the doorway and held my glare. A bitterness at the back of my throat stung. I had this eerie feeling I would never see him again. What if it was an ambush, and I could have helped? Why did they regard me as an obvious liability instead of a possible asset?

"Wait! You can't do this! It's my life!" I growled. "What if I have to pee?" I called out moments before the door shut behind Liam.

"Hold it."

I growled to an empty room. The headboard groaned as I pushed, pulled and kicked, but it held its ground. Liquid anger scorched my bones. Standing next to the bed, I failed to contort my hand through the hole of the cuff for a few minutes before I gave up and tried to pick the lock with a bobby pin from my hair. They always made it look so easy on TV, and I spent at least 20 minutes jabbing the pin against the metal even if I knew I was making no progress.

All of the sudden, the air sizzled. Every hair on my body raised, and I froze, trying to pinpoint the source of my malaise.

The entrance door exploded, bashed in by an incredible force, and my heart did a triple somersault. A man stood in the rubbles. With his checkered unbuttoned shirt showing a white tank top, he looked more like a cowboy than a demon, but I wasn't fooled, no stranger to his shimmer. Bulging biceps threatened to burst out of sleeves rolled up to his elbows. Sandy blond hair cut short, his lips stretched into a flashy smile that was all viciousness and teeth.

Frank Hale. No question.

29

DEMONS

Alana

"Ain't you a pretty thing." A thick southern drawl colored his words. Malicious eyes dragged from me to the cuffs. "Liam, you dog," he snickered as if Liam could hear him.

Left wrist tied to the bedpost, I couldn't do much beside stand there, helpless and wide-eyed. If I survived the night, I would kill Liam for leaving me this way, ripe for the picking.

The Shadow Walker sprawled on the bed beside me and nonchalantly crossed his arms behind his head. "You know, Liam thinks the sun comes up just to hear him crow, but he's a stupid fuck."

Oh, agreed.

A dry chuckle died in Frank's throat, and he shifted towards me, propped up on one elbow. "This feud ain't about you. It never has been," he lowered his voice in a conspiratorial manner. "Me and him, there's a history. Ya' know?"

With a leer directed at my cleavage, his hand reached up to run through my hair. I flinched away. Quick as lightning, he got up and flattened me against the wall, my free arm twisted behind my back. A whimper of surprise fell through my lips as he caressed my curls and pushed them behind my ears. I tried to wiggle out the crushing hold but ended up pressing my hips into his. Wrong move.

A metallic glint reflected off his left hand. A stony finger-claw ring elongated his index finger, the tip razor-sharp, and he trailed it along my jaw to my neck. A swift motion sent the buttons of my blouse flying, my lace bra now exposed.

My throat bobbed. This guy was not messing around. Fear sank its nasty teeth into my indignant heart. Frank scratched a bloody line along the dip between my breasts, and I swallowed back a sob as his tongue licked it, not wanting to give him the satisfaction.

A second, younger demon appeared at the door. From the tip of his cowboy hat to the heel of his boots, he was the cartoon version of Frank. "What's the hold-up?"

"Getting a taste."

"Will you hurry the fuck up?"

A regretful look on his face, Frank released me. The other demon walked out, and the vicious smile reappeared. He leaned over to my ear. "The half-wit thinks we'll deliver you to the stupid clan, but I won't. You're mine." A depraved tongue dipped into my ear.

I fought against him and tried to kick him in the groin.

"If you don't want to play nice, I'll be rough." He punched the headboard hard, blasting the wood into a million shards and freeing my hand.

Frank dragged me outside and packed me as luggage in the trunk of a car. Same model as Liam's but stark red. Darkness blinded me. Thom and Liam had to be at my house by now. They would never make it in time to save me.

Fuck! I should have talked and stalled Frank. I'd never been afraid of enclosed spaces, but I sensed a panic attack spreading fast. Screaming, I punched and kicked at the matted inside trunk until my hands where raw. It's never too late in life to develop a stinging case of claustrophobia.

In the pitch black cramped space, I contemplated death. And spit in its face.

This was my second abduction; I hadn't fared well the first time.

Losing my shit wasn't an option. I forced deep breaths down my lungs, crawled and aligned my ass with the trunk's end, thighs against my chest, ready to kick the hell out of whatever waited on the other side when the lid would open.

After about an hour, the rumble of the motor decreased. We took a few tight turns.

The car came to a stop. A door slammed shut. Keys jiggled. I flattened my legs against my torso.

The trunk opened, and I sprang into action. The younger demon cursed as my sneakers crashed in his face. He staggered backwards, and I rushed to my feet. My heart sank at the sight of the closed indoor garage. No escape.

Frank laughed as he slammed the driver-side door closed. "You're feisty. I like it."

Frustrated, the mini-Frank forced both my hands behind my back. Despite my struggles, he pushed me to the second floor of the house without much trouble. Huge brass bolts adorned the doorway of the room he guided me to. I dug my heels in front of me, but he was strong and flung me inside as if I was nothing more than a paperweight.

The click of the bolt behind me sent a shiver up my spine. I glanced around. No windows. The room was sterile with only a bed, a night stand, and a locked cabinet. An old-fashioned chandelier was the only source of light, and the smell of burnt incense spiced up the air, barely covering an aftertaste of desperation. The set-up evoked either a torture chamber or a sex den, and both options curdled my blood. The black silk pillows matched the sheets, and the four bed posters looked darn familiar.

Frank materialized and catapulted me onto the bed. A wire in his hands, he tied my wrists to the headboard. The metal line dug into my skin, and blood trickled down my arms as I struggled against the restraints.

I'd been a fool.

Frank had been the one killing me in my dreams all along.

Here.
Tonight.
Naked on black sheets.

30

HEATHENS

Alana

Frank took his sweet time perusing the contents of the oak cabinet as he hummed a soft tune. He wanted to signal he wasn't in a hurry. There was no escape, no hope.

Nobody was coming.

His hungry gaze roamed over me, and I felt dirty. This man corrupted everything in his path. "You're beautiful." He looked at me expectantly as if he was waiting for a thank you. A hollow glare was all he got.

He clicked his tongue in anger, smoothed down my hair, spread my ruined button-down shirt on both sides of my bra and went back to the cabinet. What the hell was he doing? With an expensive-looking camera in hand, he snapped pictures of me. After a few shots, he set the camera up on a tripod, and a red light opened.

Horror chafed my heart. This monster was going to rape and kill me... And he was going to film it.

Pleased, he kicked his shoes off and snaked his body on top of mine, pinning me to the mattress. As his face came level with mine, I spat at him, and he grabbed a fist of my hair. "Why are you so worked up?" He chuckled.

I'd die before I let this psychopath make me cry. I swallowed my fears and hopelessness and summoned all the anger I could muster.

He seemed to read my thoughts. "Oh, dear Alana, I will not rape you."

Frank's bulky hand brushed the swell of my left breast, his demeanor transforming, his touch hesitant, almost shy. He traced my snake tattoo from the tail to the head with muted reverence. "I thought there'd be nothing sexier than to mark Liam's thing. I was wrong. Seeing his mark on you, knowing he'll tear the earth apart looking for you and fail, is even sweeter."

A shudder of revulsion sliced through my stomach as his hand cupped my breast over my bra.

He stopped. "I can do a spell, and you'll consent. No rape needed." He was delusional. "But I don't think I need to. I think I can do better." He dipped his head and licked the tattoo as his body blurred and reshaped itself into one I knew well. Blond hair turned black, and his frame got taller and leaner. The silver orbs even lost their wickedness. The low baritone of Liam's voice sent goosebumps up my spine as Frank said, "I wonder if he'll feel it when I enter you, wonder if he'll feel your walls clench around me as you come."

My body's reaction was disturbing, even if my mind knew it was a lie. Liam. What I wouldn't give for him to be here for real.

Liam's form trailed kisses from my collar bone to my stomach, and his tongue dipped into my belly button. I closed my eyes, not wanting to see any more.

A hand grabbed my jaw. "Hey! Eyes open at all times."

Why? Is he hoping I'll forget who I'm in bed with and get turned on? No chance in hell.

"The camera is for Thom. I'll broadcast live to Liam through the mental link, but I wanted a little something for Junior. The images of his brother between his girlfriend's legs will be branded into his mind forever. Fun."

The weight over me disappeared, and I opened my eyes. "You're sick."

"Oh, I'm sick? What about you, Lana?" The pet name sounded sinful on his lips. "Do you get off on flirting with two brothers at the same time? You have them eating out of the palm of your hand. Maybe you want them both? I don't judge you. I get off on twisted things too, but I'm *evil*." He mimed air quotes with his fingers at the word *evil*.

"Whatever you think you know about me, you're dead wrong."

"Do you want to know how I realized you were important? I wanted to brand you to piss Liam off. I mean, he was obsessing over your blood so much that I asked myself: who's this girl? What does she taste like? But it wasn't serious. No, I realized your importance when Walker spent three weeks tracking me for my failed attempt. Almost got me, too. He doesn't give a damn about anyone but Thom. Tell me, Lana, what makes you so special?"

Liam had spent the last three weeks hunting down Frank? Why hadn't he said anything? Why had he lied and said he was with Vicky? Why was I glad to hear it?

Frank grabbed a minuscule vial from the closet and dangled it in front of me. Looked like blood. "Consent is rhetorical, but pleasure… pleasure is a thing of beauty. You'll moan my name as I fuck you, and Liam will always remember the pleasure on your face, but never experience it for himself. It's poetic." Frank smiled using Liam's lips. A hollow smile all shades of wrong.

"Stop," I said through my teeth. "Stop being him."

"Why? Don't you get it? We're the same he and I. Both sides of a coin."

"You're *nothing* like him."

"He must have filled your head with fairy-tales. Don't lie to yourself, girl. I'm no Saint, but Liam… " his tone softened, "Liam's a particularly vicious beast." The genuine fondness in his voice clashed with the rest of his fake, sugary demeanor. "He's muzzled now, but I never met a more passionate killer."

A smile played with the corner of his mouth. "Once, he went so far off the deep end three of us had to hunt and sequester him. The carnage in his wake was attracting too much attention, but his blood lust gave us all goosebumps. He was ravenous. Magnificent."

I loathed this distorted image of Liam that Frank was trying to imprint on my brain, and the urge to defend him surpassed the fear gathering in my stomach. "He wasn't himself."

"Wasn't he? He likes to think of himself as two separate entities. The demon versus the man, but they're indistinguishable. Liam is the beast and always will be. I'm surprised you don't see that, considering how he almost devoured you." One minute, Frank's voice dripped with hatred, and the next it bordered on infatuation. What had Liam done to spark this weirdly intimate vendetta?

A part of me was dying to know. "Why do you care?"

A bittersweet sadness transformed the fake Liam to such a degree that I could almost see beyond the illusion. He met my gaze head-on. "I only ever loved two people. I lost them both. Isn't that how every story ends? Death. Loss. Emptiness. Every other ending is a reprieve."

The quiet desperation in his voice wasn't fabricated. I pressed on. "And Liam killed them?"

Frank arched an eyebrow at me. "You're a smart girl. Don't play dumb."

"Liam was one of them."

A waved blade identical to Liam's in his hand, Frank approached the bed. "I like you, I must admit. It's a shame your story ends here, but it'll be quick for you. If you're waiting for Liam to break through the door, don't. You'll be disappointed." He was talking from experience. "He can't track you here. My advice is: don't fight it. Pretend I'm him; you'll go in peace."

The tip of the blade danced against my collarbone, the metal cold on my skin. My chest constricted. The sad broken man disappeared, and the vicious monster ready to play with its food returned.

He carved the flesh with enthusiasm and licked the blood as it rose from the rune-shaped wounds. "You're really something. I'm happy he didn't kill you."

I aimed to kick his face, but he grabbed my ankle and dragged his blade from my heel to my knee, slicing my skinny jeans. "The more you fight, the deeper I cut. Deal?"

I stopped wiggling.

"Better." He tilted the minuscule vial and poured one drop over the scrapes. Smoke rose, and a sickeningly sweet scent pervaded the air. "Look at me."

The command was supreme, absolute, incontestable, and I obeyed.

"Smile."

My muscles relaxed, and a bright smile stretched my lips. For a second, I not only smiled but felt actual happiness. The manipulation eroded, and tears rolled down my cheeks. The fake feelings were hollow and dissolved quickly, but I got the general idea. This potion would turn me into a willing slave.

Liam's eyebrows raised as Frank said, "Do you know how beautiful you are when you smile?" He didn't wait for an answer before he kissed the hollow of my neck.

How long would it take for the potion to override me completely?

Before I got my answer, but after I said things that would hunt me until the end of time, a loud commotion rose from the hallway. Frank disappeared in a whoosh.

Hope inflated my chest as the door hung open. Frank hadn't ordered me not to move, so I twisted on the bed to grab the zigzagged blade left unattended on the nightstand with my feet. Sweat gathered of my forehead as I inched it towards my hands, careful not to drop it. Blood rushed to my temples and made the room spin.

My fingers shook as they curled around the handle of the weapon. *Just an inch closer.* Groans and growls erupted from the hallway, and my heart sank when I heard a sharp cry of pain.

God. Liam.

By the sound of it, he wasn't winning. But was it real? How could I tell? Maybe Frank was the one in pain and hadn't dropped his glamor, yet.

The young voice of Frank's acolyte thundered, "If you weren't a Walker, we would have killed you long ago."

"I'd like to see you try, nitwit," Liam said.

My heart wanted to believe Liam was really here. Adrenaline pumping through my body, I sliced the wire and leaped to my feet. I pulled on my blouse and fastened the only button that had survived.

"Liam, I've missed you, brother," Frank said using Liam's voice.

This was utterly confusing.

"Frank. Missed you in Illinois."

"You're off your game, comrade. Did you get my gift? She looked freakishly like your girl, no?"

His gift? Was he talking about the dead girl?

"I'll tear you apart." The hushed tone was lethal.

The distinctive sound of breaking glass reached my ears, and the walls shook as if elephants were playing squash against the gypsum. Then silence.

My entire body was numb. Who'd won? I peeked into the hallway. Frank was impaled to the wall, unconscious or dead while the younger Shadow Walker laid on the floor. Liam was standing in the middle of the hallway, bloody and out of breath.

Relief washed through me and made my whole body weightless. Without thought, I ran to him. His arms closed around me and pushed me flush against him. "Hey, you're fine."

I buried my face in his chest.

"I'm here for you," he said as he stroked my hair.

Here for me?

I stepped back from the embrace and looked up at his face. A whimper escaped my lips. I was being duped. The real Liam was to thank for this moment of clarity and not for both his training and his constant warnings. The thing that betrayed Frank as he tried to pass as Liam was the way he looked at me... like he worshiped the ground I walked on.

"Are you okay?" Even the voice was off, too caring.

"Yeah," I lied.

It was incredibly cocky of Frank to remind me he could look like

Liam before trying to hoodwink me. He assumed too much, assumed Liam smiled, assumed we were close. Assumed Liam would choose to touch me. It made me curious about the Liam he'd known, but this certainly wasn't mine.

"Are you sure?" He was onto me.

I needed to sell that I believed him until I could think of a plan. A few tears rolled on my cheeks. "Is it over?"

He pulled me into another hug. "Don't worry. He's dead."

My cells screamed in disgust, but I hugged him back. "Thank God."

Liam was never here. Frank wanted me to think he was. I had to go along with whatever script Frank had in mind. With some luck, I'd see an opening. The dagger lay on the floor. I'd let it fall before running to Liam. *Stupid girl.*

Frank entwined our fingers, and I bent down to grab the weapon. A fake smile plastered on my face, I squeezed his hand. "In case we get into trouble again."

Would he buy it?

"Let's get out of here."

I nodded. I wasn't going down without a fight, even if I was bound to lose. Frank thought he had me fooled, but how long would he keep up the charade? It would be too dangerous for him to bring me outside, where Liam might get a whiff of me with his tracking powers. Wherever this was headed, it was nowhere good. The earlier I acted, the better my chances.

We reached the top of the stairs, and I pulled gently on his arm. "Liam? Thank you." I stood on my tip-toes and pecked him on the lips.

As Frank turned away to hide a wide grin, I saw my opening. As fast as I could, I raised the blade and aimed for the eyes. Blood gushed everywhere, and a litany of curses thundered.

I ran.

I flew down the stairway, taking three steps at a time. If I could make it beyond the door, maybe I could buy some time. Frank was fast and strong, but he couldn't walk through solid walls.

A hand latched onto my hair, and I came to an abrupt stop. My cries of pain echoed in the stairwell. Frank's other hand closed around my wrist and crushed it until I let the dagger fall.

"Aren't you clever?" He gripped my throat and pushed me against the wall. I saw stars. With his sleeve, he wiped the blood from his face. The cut oozed dark burgundy, and he melted back into himself. I'd missed his eye by half an inch.

Frank pressed and pressed on my neck until my eyes threatened to burst out of their sockets. The lack of oxygen made me lightheaded, and he lessened his hold, but barely.

The other demon leaned against the wall, laughing. "She got you good."

Frank tossed me into his sidekick's arms. "Let's take care of Walker. Wouldn't want him to bleed to death before the show."

Wait. Liam was actually here? Bleeding out? My insides turned to stone. *No.*

Frank's little helper grabbed me by the arm and forced me back up the stairs. My eyes searched the empty corridor in vain.

Frank snickered and pointed to an empty wall. "So close and yet so far. Your knight in shining armor is dying inches away, but you can't see him," his voice hardened, and he turned to the other demon. "Take her inside and tie her up real tight."

Obedient, the demon dragged me into the torture room and pushed me down against the wretched bed. *Helpless yet again.*

I was damn tired of being helpless. I was no longer afraid, but royally pissed. Why were demons so strong? I clawed the arm pinning me down and dug my fingernails as deep as I could. I drew blood, and a fire raged inside as I growled. Something in me clicked into place. A long-lost piece of the puzzle was finally found.

A wicked piece.

The demon's mouth twisted into a silent scream, and I gaped as his arm pruned and shrivelled. The arm evaporated as if all the water in the cells had been sucked dry. I staggered backwards. The rest of his body followed until all that was left of him was a thin film of dust on my arms. My entire being hummed with power.

My eyes locked with the silvers orbs of Frank's, who was standing in the doorway. Disbelief written across his face, genuine fear visible, he said, "What are you?"

"I'm the witch who's going to kill you." I didn't know where all that guile came from, but Frank vanished into thin air, so he must have bought my bluff. Shocked, I scampered into the hallway. Liam was really the one impaled to the wall, and a two-foot-long spear poked out of his chest. Frank hadn't fabricated that part of the story.

His head was bent forward, his neck slack, and his eyes were closed.

31

STARVING

Alana

"Liam!"

Silver eyes snapped open at the shrill edge of my voice. I took one good look at the scowl he gave me and was reassured that it was actually him.

"What happened? Where's Frank?" He said, his voice shaky as hell.

"I don't know." Beyond freaked out, my feet were itching to run out of that wretched house. What if Frank came back? I'd threatened him, but I had no idea if I could do *that* again. I didn't even know for sure if I'd done it at all. "Let's go!"

Liam didn't budge. "I'm a bit busy." His fingers closed around the spear's wooden lance, and he winced. His back slumped against the spackled wall behind him, and my eyes widened. *He's hurt.*

Liam was never hurt. He'd been shot at, his arm had been mutilated by a dog-man, he'd sliced open his wrists, and a ghoul had taken a bite out of his chest, but never had any of that stuff actually *hurt* him.

He studied the spear embedded in his chest with a mix of annoyance and amazement and cursed to hide a whimper as he pulled the thing out of his chest. Dark red blood gushed out, making my heart rate go wild, and his bothered expression switched to apparent awe.

"Liam?" I squeaked.

His eyes flew to mine in the first vulnerable look he'd ever directed towards me. A hint of fear mingled with plain surprise as he breathed, "I'm not going anywhere."

My mind refused to process his words, and adrenaline rushed to my temples. I gripped his arm and leaned to look at the wound.

He shielded it with his hand. "Thom's in the garage. Go get him." Even near death, his commanding tone grated at my temper like nothing else.

"Hell! I'm not leaving you here." The puddle of blood was pretty big now. Too big. The weapon must have severed something important in there for it to bleed so damn much. "Why isn't it healing?"

"Alana—" The rest of the sentence died on his lips as he choked, his voice crushed by pain.

I shouted his name again, but his eyes hardly opened. His face turned white, and his body slipped to the floor. "Find Thom."

Sobs rocked my chest as I shook my head. "I'm not leaving you." Nausea fisted my guts. I needed to save him, and I had the power to do it. I just didn't feel capable. Liam was going to die because I was too dense to know how to use my own powers. Crappiest witch ever.

Tears rolled down my cheeks, and I closed my eyes, trying to pull myself together. I had done this before. I could do it again. But what if I messed up and killed him instead?

God, I had to try. It wasn't a small injury or a stranger. It was a dying Liam. The life drained from his face, and ice gripped my heart. Blood dripped on the floor like a watch ticking, urging me to act. I pressed my fingers into the wound. Deep. Hot blood and soft flesh competed for my attention.

Everything around me faded away, the sky crumbled, and the earth swallowed me whole. A strike of pain brought me to my knees. A human would have been dead on the spot, but he could feel the agony of every passing seconds as the hole the bony spear had made into his heart killed him.

Images whirled around me. Unintelligible at first, flashes of his life appeared.

A woman was crying. "Liam, honey, it's me. It's mom." We growled at her, trying to reach her through the bars of our cell. We needed to kill something, anything. Everything.

Strawberry-blond hair fanned against the pillow next to us as we jolted awake. We were lying next to Alana, we realized. Fuck, *we thought,* she could've woken up and found us there. *We needed to get our shit together and fast.*

We were in the gym with Thom. He was all sweaty from his workout.
"You're sure, man?" Thom asked.
Why did Junior insist on having this conversation again? It was awkward as hell. "Absolutely," we lied.
"Cause I'm falling for her."
We'd noticed.

The memories were flanked by something else. Not dreams, but lifelike pictures the other demons shared with him. The past and present of every Shadow Walker bled together and created a complicated web entangled with his neurons. It cursed him with detailed visions of things happening miles away or centuries back. A vortex threatening to pull him in at every turn. The Collective.

Liam didn't show pain because he was always in pain. The process allowing him to keep the others from reading his mind was complex and exhausting, and it didn't prevent them from broadcasting. Forced to watch his parents' murder happen live, a void had carved into his soul. He truly believed most people couldn't be saved. Not even himself as he was linked to them forever.

I wanted to scream, but my/our lips wouldn't budge. I saw his childhood, his bond with Thom. How it was between them before he was taken compared to after. Liam was broken, even considered himself a monster. Thom hadn't changed. He was warm, open, and happy most of the time. He was proud to fight the good fight while Liam considered it payback to the ones that had stolen his life away.

The demons had taught him how to be the fastest, the brightest, and the most efficient killer he could be.

And he'd liked it. It was simpler, easier not to battle with the demon every day. To give in. A vivid memory washed out all the others.

Frank grinned at us with a genuine, boyish smile. His body was lean, his bright features trustful and open, and we reflected his excitement as we hugged him hard. "Good to see you man." He was our best friend.

"Things were boring without you. Good thing you passed."

"Ever doubt I would?" We asked, but Frank hadn't doubted. It was easy to pass when the alternative was death.

"Did you stick to the plan?"

We dragged our shirt over our head and turned, so Frank could see our back.

"Sick. Check out mine."

We raised the shirt on his back. The mirror image of our snake was tattooed into Frank's skin, and we grinned.

Marcus appeared at the corner. With sharp facial bones and an aquiline nose, he looked more like a raptor than a man. A click of his tongue killed the laughter in our throat. This man was the bane of our existence. He motioned for us and Frank to follow, and we did.

"Now for the reward. Believe me, it'll blow your mind," Frank whispered.

Marcus handed us a syringe filled with a burgundy liquid. It looked like blood, and we recoiled. Drugs had never appealed to us. It seemed like a hollow, fabricated pleasure. Not like running at full speed through the woods, the wind at our back.

Frank tied a tourniquet around our forearm and sensed our hesitation.

"Trust me, man."

We nodded and took the small, inconsequential syringe from Marcus's hand. How bad could it be? We pressed the plunger, not expecting anything in particular.

The rush was overwhelming. A few drops, and we flew to heaven.

"So?" Frank asked.

"It's surreal. I feel powerful... I feel like I'm THE shit..." There were no words strong enough to describe the rush.
"I know, right?"
We already wanted more.

Liam had been undone by three tiny drops of witch's blood. Months had bled together. The need, the hunger had swallowed every bit of his humanity. The only truth he'd known was the one brought on by the next fix, the next high. The next kill.

I couldn't have imagined a life so empty. So... cold.

A tied-up man begged for mercy before we inserted the needle into his arm. Blood dripped into the pouch. He was a big man, so there would be lots of it. We looked at the other pouches at our feet and calculated how much we could steal without Marcus noticing some of it was missing.
Probably a quarter of a liter.
We couldn't wait. The first pouch full, we plugged the thing straight into our arm. God, we'd been running on stale blood for too long. Ecstasy slammed through our flesh, and we rolled to our back next to our prey, ragged breaths heaving our chest.
The warlock died as we came alive.

The flow stopped. Liam's mind rivaled with my own to chase me out of his brain. The web of steely strings came into focus. I tugged on a string and concentrated on myself. I'd never get another chance to know what Liam Walker really thought of me.

Flashes from the night my life changed for good appeared. I relived it through his eyes. I saw how he'd caught up to me, how he'd killed them without blinking, not only doing it because he had to but because he wanted to. It turned from bad to worse when the more powerful demon arrived, and I witnessed Liam's hesitation as he considered using my blood. He risked losing himself, so the sane thing to do was to let me die. He almost did.

But he craved my blood and talked himself into saving me for

Thom. Thom was his only real tie to humanity, and he loved him beyond reason.

His mind tried to corner and eject me from the memories. I held my breath, but his defenses faltered. There was something he desperately didn't want me to see, and I pressed on. Going back to the night I cut myself, his potent desire for my blood, my powers, engulfed me, and I gagged.

He craved it every second we were together and got frustrated about having to teach me. He hated himself for thinking about it, and he hated me for reminding him of his own weakness.

At first, the demons would send visions of him killing me. The high it brought him was maddening. The voices tried to sway him. I saw glimpses of our first arguments and how he'd provoked them to keep me away from him.

The voices failed at getting me killed, but he wasn't always strong enough. Sometimes, the urge would get too strong. Sometimes, he would use his powers to get close and observe me without my knowing.

Don't touch Alana. Stay away from Alana. Drive her away from you, he kept thinking, and the voices dulled for a while. Without their constant influence, he finally stopped thinking about my blood so much. For a while things were good.

But he could feel something else rising, and he was disgusted by it. His demons spoke to him again and preyed on feelings he didn't know he had. *"You want her,"* they said. *"Take her."* He tried to shut them up, but they knew they had something. *"What harm would it do? Maybe she wants you too."*

In the midst of our most heated fights, when he felt like giving in, the voices taunted him. *"Thom always got everything he wanted. Now, he has her and you still get nothing."*

A dark part of him agreed.

He needed to get away from me, but he had to stay as close as possible, and his feelings were choking him. My name was engraved on his bones, filled his guts, floated in his chest, wrapped around his brain, and danced in his blood. He wanted me gone, but I was crawling under his skin, day after day, putting his sanity in jeopardy and ruining his life. That's how he saw it. And he kept repeating to himself that he wasn't attracted to me for real. He thought the demons had planted the idea to manipulate him.

I arrived at a brick wall in his mind and pushed through.

"Alana, I swear if you don't get out of my brain right this second, I'll kill you," Liam threatened as he expelled me from his memories violently.

I re-entered my consciousness, enthralled by the bittersweet taste of Liam's soul. The connection had been raw. The confusion, the frustration... It was overwhelming.

My heart bled at the intensity of his hunger for me.

Shaken and out of breath, I blinked. We were standing face to face, unwittingly holding unto each other for dear life, my fingers buried in his sides and his on either side of my face. His wound was gone. My vision danced before my woozy eyes.

A vengeful snarl bared his teeth, his face livid. The intrusion had wrecked him. For a second, I thought I'd pushed him too far, and that he was going to kill me. Thought he'd snap my neck with a swift twist of hands, so he could be free of me.

The enormity of what I'd just done sunk in. I'd snooped into his most private memories, into his spirit. On purpose. I held my breath, my heart pulsing in my throat.

Liam let out a desperate growl. Pain dropped its tight leash as he gave in. When he gripped my neck and crashed his lips on mine, I died.

A kiss heavier than the sun.

His tongue begged entry into my mouth, and I welcomed it in an instant, thrilled and scared of my reaction. The limits between our minds were blurry, and his genuine surprise as I melted against him tore down both our defenses.

My heart falling out of my chest, I kissed him back.

A husky pant reverberated deep in my belly as I threw my arms around his neck and clawed him closer. He spun us around and pressed me up against the wall, the strong but gentle hold sending shivers down my spine. His demanding lips brought my senses to their knees.

A soft brush on the nape of my neck.

A sharp nip on my bottom lip.

A playful bite on my earlobe.

His beating heart pressed against mine...

I mirrored his lust drop for drop, my greedy fingers gripping his hair, my famished lips diving for another bruising struggle. I couldn't get enough. *We* couldn't get enough and got lost in this kiss shattering our souls. Liam was the epitome of wrong for me, but I didn't care. All I needed was him, all he wanted was me, and for the first time, we agreed on something.

Without warning, Liam let go of me and almost flew in the opposite direction. No longer pinned against the wall, I fell a couple inches and whimpered, cold now that the heat of his body had deserted me.

The connection between our minds snapped like a spider web breaking after being stretched too far. The recoil sent me to the ground, and the world spun so fast I emptied my stomach on the carpet. *Whoa.* Over the ringing in my ears, I heard loud footsteps approaching and turned towards the noise to see a blurry Thom coming up the stairs. The sight of him was an icy shower pouring down on me, and I gagged again.

Thom ran at full speed towards us. "Are you okay? The damn minion locked me in a fucking closet, and it took forever to break down the door." He was moving too fast. I could see two of him hovering above me.

Bringing my hand to my lips in disbelief, my mind dropped back into place. "I'm alive."

Thom wrapped his jacket around me.

Liam got up, dusted off his clothes, and picked up the weapon that had almost killed him off the floor. I already knew how his face would look: like nothing happened. The mask was back on.

"I'm so relieved you guys are all right. I was scared out of my mind." Thom squeezed my hand.

Terrified my face gave me away, I squeezed his hand back but didn't dare speak. I needed a moment to collect my thoughts. Guilt scorched my heart. If Thom knew, he would hate me. Hell, I hated myself. It wasn't like my run-in with Vicky. I was painfully aware I had kissed Liam of my own free will.

Tears pooled in my eyes, and I wiped them away discreetly. Thom had been right all along, Frank too. Liam Walker was a liar. A liar who did want to kiss me.

I was a liar, too.

And a killer.

32

SHARP EDGES

Alana

The air was charged with guilt and secrets, and goosebumps branded my entire body as Liam drove us back to Virginia.

My thoughts were all over the place. The muscles in my legs, back, and arms were sore like I'd been thrown into the washing machine. As my nerves settled down, flashes of Frank lying over me constricted my throat, and I exploded into tears. I hid my face in Thom's chest and sobbed, all the terrible things that had almost happened swirling around in my brain.

I'd almost been raped. Liam had almost died. My hands shook at the thought, and a fresh batch of tear rolled down my puffy face. The adrenaline had taken over during the actual events, but exhaustion, sadness, and this overwhelming fear that Frank was following us home flooded in now.

The more I hid inside Thom's embrace, the more Liam's hands tensed around the wheel, and I cried until I didn't even know what I was crying for. Frank's words echoed endlessly inside my skull. "Do you get off on flirting with two brothers at the same time?"

Had I flirted with Liam? Yes.

The admission cost me, but it was the truth. And he had flirted back in his own intense-sexy-demon way. How had I cultivated such a state of denial? He might as well have pulled my pigtails and called me, "Carrots."

"Are you sure you're okay?" Thom asked as he ran a gentle hand through my hair.

My heart throbbed at his kindness. I needed a distraction, fast, before I burst into tears again. "How did you guys know where to find me?"

"Liam tracked you."

My eyebrows crunched. "But Frank said he wouldn't be able to. Doesn't he know his stuff?"

Thom shifted in his seat. "He assumed the protective wards around his house would cut off the link. He was wrong."

It seemed too good to be true. Frank wasn't an amateur. "Why didn't they work?"

"I don't know," Thom said.

Liam shot us a glance via the rear-view mirror. As soon as we made eye contact, his sight jerked back to the road, and I got a sense he knew exactly why.

"Here, I got this for you." Thom reached for the front seat and handed me a big family album. "I found it on your bed."

I opened it to the middle. On one picture, my dad was holding me in his arms. I wasn't older than four or five years old. On the other, I was waiting for the school bus to pick me up. Hugging the album to my chest, I whispered a strangled "thank you."

Unable to carry on a conversation, I faked sleep. The boys spoke in hushed voices. They were at a loss as to why Frank had taken off. Liam didn't talk about his injury or the healing, and I wondered how he managed to sound so calm. He had to be at least half as rattled as me, and I couldn't utter a single word without feeling breathless.

Hours passed, and I dozed off.

I woke up to the sound of the car door being closed. Thom traced lazy patterns on my back and gently coaxed me back to reality. "How are you feeling?"

I tucked my messy hair behind my ears and stretched out my numb arms. "Better." I was surprised, but it was the truth. My eyes itched, and my throat burned, but my stomach had settled back into place, and my heart rate had returned to normal. The front seat was empty.

Thom followed my gaze. "Liam's acting weird."

I shrugged and played dumb, not knowing what to say, not wanting to disrespect him further by lying to his face. It wasn't like Thom expected me to have incredible insight into his brother's behavior.

Thom cleared his throat. "Where did Frank go? Why did he vanish? Did Liam do or say something you didn't understand?"

I should have told him about liquefying the second demon. It was the proper time. My skeptic side kept arguing that it might have been an illusion, but I knew I'd done it. I expected to feel ashamed, anguished, and overall disgusted with myself. I didn't.

The rush of power that had buzzed through my fingers was fresh in my memory along with the short-lived but powerful elation it had brought. No matter how much I tried to rationalize it, I had taken pleasure in extinguishing a life, and I couldn't talk about it for fear that the flush of exhilaration would return to my cheeks. Sure, it'd been a clear-cut case of self-defense, but I shouldn't have enjoyed it. I shouldn't be *proud* of it. I shouldn't wonder if I could do it *again*.

I bit my bottom lip and said the first thing that came to mind, "I don't know what happened to Frank. I hope he rots in hell."

Thom nodded in solemn agreement. I decided to tell him later when I didn't feel so on edge. When I no longer had the taste of Liam's kiss on my lips.

We walked back into the house and closed the door behind us. For the first time, I didn't think of it as a prison. Familiar and safe was all I needed. Thom offered to stay with me, but I needed to sort through my emotions alone.

I took a long, steamy shower to wash—or rather burn—the events of the day off me. It was no use. The kiss was an apocalyptic mistake, but I still wasn't thinking clearly.

Electricity ran through my body at the mere thought of Liam as if it'd been plugged directly into a power line and dowsed with water. Despite all the other gruesome stuff that had happened, the kiss remained the clearest memory of all. A polished pearl in a stack of dusty pebbles.

As I closed my eyes, I relived it. Both our heartbeats ringing in my ears, the rough wall grating against my back, Liam's strong, solid frame holding me there. His tongue dancing against mine, his breath on my neck, the gentle nibble he gave my skin, and the contrasting fire in his eyes as he'd pushed away from me.

To make things worse, I could also remember it from his point of view. I remembered kissing myself, how soft my lips were, how sweet I tasted. How delectable it felt to give in, to get a bite out of something so forbidden.

The mouth-watering scents haunted my nostrils. Lemons and coconuts. I remembered the desire coursing through his veins, and how hard he was...

Shoulders hunched against the ceramic, a sigh parted my lips. Soaked, and not just because of the water, I snaked my hand down my body and whimpered when I brushed the sensitive skin between my legs. *God, yes.*

Flustered, I hesitated, peering around the room. Could Liam be here? Watching me? I knew he'd done it before. Maybe not while I was in the shower, but so many lines had already been blurred, and I'd felt his hunger...

Soon I was panting and didn't care if Liam saw me or not. Or maybe I cared.

Half-mad, my knees buckled, and I moaned his name. If he was there, there would be no question as to whom I was thinking about. No question if he should appear. No question if I wanted him to step inside this tub and take me against the cold tiles. *No question.*

I came hard. Icy water soothed my fevered skin, and I vowed never to think of this moment, this faux-pas, ever again.

I was kidding myself. I'd had a blinding orgasm thinking of Liam Walker. There was no going back from that. How was I supposed to act around him from now on? I wanted nothing else to happen, did I? Of course not, he was insensitive, manipulative, and, most importantly, not human. After invading his mind, I'd never forget that.

On the other hand, I understood him more than ever before, probably more than anyone ever could. He hated me, but he wanted me. Or, better yet, he hated me because he wanted me.

"What I saw, it wasn't half of it," I said out loud. I knew for each moment I'd seen, he'd kept thousands from me. Thousands of horrible things he'd done. He pushed down his own nature as he fought the constant urges to control, to cheat, to kill. He was a demon, so he had an excuse for his crimes, but what was mine?

No, I had no excuse for the way I'd acted besides the intensity of the moment. And fantasizing about hot shower sex was no way to atone for my sins. I'd betrayed Thom, betrayed myself. How could I choose darkness instead of light? I didn't want pain. I didn't want to be the shadow's lover. Liam wanted me. He didn't love me. A world of difference. In fact, he was utterly convinced that he was too broken to love anyone but his family. Thom was the sound choice, but I'd wrecked it all with one bad call. One moment of weakness.

One moment of passion.

I HID in my room for hours, my brain caught in a maze, until Lilah cracked my door open. "I just got in. Are you okay?"

"I don't know," I answered honestly.

She walked to the bed and sat next to me. "Thom told me what happened. Did Frank hurt you?"

I knew what she meant and shook my head.

"Thank God," she grabbed my hand in hers but frowned. She crossed and uncrossed her legs, averting my gaze. "Alana?"

"Yeah?"

"What did you do?" At first, I thought she was talking about the disintegration thing, but she added, "You feel ashamed." She met my gaze. There was no judgment in her big blue eyes, but I had the distinct impression she already knew.

But how could she know? The idea of Liam whispering his secrets to anyone was laughable. He was a very private person. Even Thom didn't have that kind of relationship with his brother, though he tried.

Lilah was the perfect confidante, always discreet. *Maybe I should confess. Maybe it would help me deal.*

"When I healed Liam," I started, ready to fess up, but somehow, I couldn't. "When I healed him, I invaded his memories. I could have stopped, but I was curious, and I pried into private stuff. Very private stuff." It wasn't strictly a lie, except I didn't feel bad about it, not really. I waited to see if she'd buy it.

"Oh. I thought—I thought it was something else." She patted my hand. "Never mind."

I didn't feel as bad as I should have for lying.

AT DINNER TIME, I knew I had to go down or Thom would be worried and ask more questions, but I couldn't face Liam, so I hoped he'd skip it. No such luck.

As I entered the kitchen, Liam served himself a beer, and his tense grip broke the bottle he was holding into a million pieces.

Thom frowned from his seat. "Ok, will someone tell me what I'm missing?" He turned to his brother, his jaw set in an angry grimace. "You're hiding something. I know it. What did Frank do to put you in this state?"

Of course, Thom assumed Liam's behavior had to do with Frank.

"Frank staked me with a demon spear, and I bled to death. " Liam paused and pinched his lips together. He swallowed hard, and his speech sounded less rehearsed as he added, "Alana managed to heal me but invaded my brain in the process."

The contempt rolling off his tongue irked me. "Gee, Liam, how about thanking me for saving your life?" I said, borrowing from one of his previous lectures.

Thom's face brightened. "You used your powers? Why didn't you say so? It's amazing news."

I played nervously with my fingers. "Liam didn't think so."

"You drilled into my brain." The undiluted anger in Liam's words resonated deep in my belly. Kiss or no kiss, he loathed me for what I'd done, and a bitter taste invaded my mouth.

Thom chuckled. "Congrats, Lana. You're officially a witch." He raised his glass, but I didn't feel like celebrating.

I stared obstinately in front of me and didn't let my sight wander for a second in Liam's direction. Even though he was trying to act as normal as possible, I could feel his stare latch on to me when he knew Thom wasn't looking. In Liam's mind, Thom and I were a couple, and he thought we'd had sex like bunnies while he was gone. He clearly judged me for kissing him since I was involved with Thom, yet I was terrified he would find out the truth.

At least this way, the guilt would prevent him from telling Thom about what had happened. Or rather prevent him from kissing me again.

Lilah tried to defuse the tension with her powers. I actually felt the push of her energy against mine, pressuring me to relax. When Liam excused himself, Lilah followed him.

I breathed a little easier with him gone, but Thom's enthusiasm annoyed me, and I acted a bit cold until he gave up on cheering me up. I felt terrible. It wasn't his fault that I'd made a crucial mistake that was eating away at me.

"Want to talk about whatever is going on?" Thom asked as we cleared the dishes.

"Don't worry about it. I'm just frazzled," I lied.

His shoulders sagged. "I don't believe that."

I had to stop lying to him, or I would ruin our friendship, too. "I can't talk about it yet."

His eyes softened, and he nodded. "Okay, just know I'm here for you."

I closed the dishwasher and walked to my room. On the stairs, goosebumps ran up my arms, and I squinted at the empty mezzanine.

There was something off. I sensed a presence, and I could see a shadow. A trail of hair at the back of my neck itched, and my eyes watered. The empty space thinned and melted away like wax, slowly allowing me to see beyond the illusion of nothing.

Liam's bedroom door hung open, and Lilah was facing Liam in the hallway, clearly upset and out of breath.

"I can't believe you just did that!" She gestured as she screamed, and a midnight blue aura thrashed around her.

"I'm so sorry, Lilah."

"It's twisted!"

Liam closed his eyes and pursed his lips, fists balled at his sides. "I know." The words pained him.

The tension in her body dialed down a notch. "You're a jerk."

"A big jerk. Please forgive me."

She put her hands on her hips and took a deep breath. Her eyes flicked over to me, and she whispered something for Liam's benefit.

"You see us." He sounded both surprised and displeased.

For the first time, I had been able to see through his deception without any help. At last, I'd achieved the impossible. I'd been in Liam's mind and seen how he used his powers. I understood well how he worked them to manipulate people.

This was the breakthrough I'd been waiting for, and yet, it felt hollow.

Lilah walked past Liam and managed a smile. "Congratulations, Lana. It's a huge step."

Does it mean it's over? I'm done? It was a bit anticlimactic. "Just like that?"

She wrapped her arm around my waist. "Not 'just like that.' You've worked hard. It happened this way for me too. One day you can't do it and the next you can. It's a yes or no skill."

Liam leaned against the wall, his back flat against the wall, his shoulders hunched. He wasn't inclined to celebrate, either.

"Did you feel an itch in your mind when you rejected the illusion?" Lilah asked.

Hearing her describe the sensation helped because it was exactly right. "It's like what I was seeing was too... spicy.

"Exactly!" She beamed. "Now, you get a crash course in masking your aura. It's pretty easy once you've learned how to dispel Liam's mind tricks."

Liam's gaze met mine, and we both looked away at once.

I forced my concentration back on Lilah and clasped her hand. "Teach me?"

The only thing worse than failing at this new all-important skill would be to let Liam teach me. To sit in front of him and hold hands... it would be unbearable.

33

MESS IS MINE

Alana

Holding on to an aura is like carrying a big red button around in your purse, one finger pressing on it all the time. A button you can never let go of because it would kill you. An obnoxious will-loose-my-mind-if-I-need-to-hold-it-for-one-more-second button.

My mind chanted in pleasure whenever I got a break, and, after a day of practice, I joined Thom, Lilah and Liam in the living room. Lilah was stretching on the carpet, her head to her knee while Liam and Thom played some first-person shooter game.

"Am I doing it right?" I asked.

Liam nodded curtly, and Lilah applauded.

Thom paused the console and raised his water bottle in my direction. "Congratulations!"

My shoulders sagged. "It's exhausting." I had a better understanding of why Liam had been so adamant about me staying close to him. I couldn't imagine holding down someone else's button on top of my own. No wonder he was such a sourpuss.

But it meant I was free. After months of failure, I'd passed my

Witches 101 course. Cheated my way to success by peeking at the teacher's answer booklet.

Lilah smiled and folded her legs. "We should celebrate."

I looked down and pushed on the carpet with the tip of my toe. "To be honest, I don't feel like celebrating." I crashed next to Thom, and my hands trembled as I opened the family album he'd brought back from my house.

Most pictures were of me. As a baby, as a toddler, as a teenager. The end section contained more recent photos. One was of me embracing Mom and Dad at my high school graduation. I swallowed hard, the picture bringing back happy memories that were far out of reach. *Where are you?*

Thom squeezed my shoulders. I flipped the page of the album and wiped away the tears flooding my eyes before Thom reached down and tore it from my hands.

"Hey, careful!" I said, gripping the album's cover.

"Alana—" He pointed to a picture. "Where is this? Do you know?"

The photo was torn at the edges, older. My dad was a lanky teenager about fifteen or sixteen years old. Three boys had their arms around each other and grinned proudly at the camera. The house in the background rang no bell whatsoever. "No, I've never seen this before."

"This is my dad." He pointed to one of the friends.

"No way!" I pried the glossy paper from the transparent sheath and turned it over. Elegant handwriting said: Rob, Dan and John, Summer 1976.

"Dan as in Daniel Walker," Thom said.

I frowned. "It's impossible."

Liam glanced over our shoulders and froze. "Fuck."

I shook my head in denial. "You guys are mistaken."

"I can recognize my dad, Alana. I've seen pictures of him as a teenager before." Thom ran to his room and came back with an old photo. "Here. My dad and his brothers."

Seven boys dressed in tuxes stood in a line. The three on the left were men, and the three to the right kids. The teenage boy from the picture was in the middle. There was no doubt Thom was right.

My dad had known Thom's dad? "How? Why?"

"Hell if I know." Thom turned to Liam. "You, any idea?"

The demon's expression darkened. "None. I'd never seen her father before. Or heard his name."

"You'd remember if your Dad had mentioned my father?" I asked, unconvinced.

"I was nine when you were born. He never spoke of you, either." Liam's tone was unequivocal.

My chest deflated. "And your father didn't keep a journal or anything like that?"

"No," Thom said with a brisk shake of the head.

Jitters hovered in my chest. "I guess that's a dead end."

Lilah leaned back and grabbed my hand. "I don't know what to do about this new puzzle, but, in the meantime, you should come to my place. I'll be your Washington tour guide. You've never been, right?"

My mind was reeling from the knowledge that my dad might be involved in the supernatural world, so I wasn't in the mood for tourism, but I swallowed my apprehensions and put on a brave face. "No. Never been."

Lilah smiled. "It's settled, then."

"Liam can go with you for the weekend. Make sure there's no *danger*." Thom said danger, but he meant Frank. "I'm almost done packing." The next potential was in Mobile, and the brothers were moving to Alabama for a while. I wasn't the only one sick of the house.

"I guess I could stay with Lilah for a few weeks." I had to get my thoughts in order, untangle the threads of my heart, and decide what I wanted to do with the rest of my life.

"We're going to have so much fun. I'm sure I can persuade you to move to Washington." Lilah said with a wink.

"Yeah. Maybe I will." It was a sound plan, but disappointment reared its head that neither Thom or Liam seemed unhappy to hear the news. Unease tightened my chest. Moving out the house, fine, but the rest… There was a finality in it I didn't like. For months, Thom had been my main support system. And Liam, well my emotions were still in knots, but I remembered thinking a few weeks without seeing him had been enough.

THE NEXT MORNING, I trekked my luggage down the stairs, feeling nostalgic. Thom erupted from the kitchen, and his eyes flicked from my bags to my face. The atmosphere was heavy, and I sighed. Did he also feel this was an ominous end to the little world we'd created?

With three strides, he closed the distance between us, his hand framed my face, and he pressed his lips on mine. No hesitation, no uncertainty.

I'd had a lot of mental practice for this kiss. Thom's lips were soft and smooth and applied just the right pressure, but the nabbing guilt ruined it. I couldn't prevent my stupid brain from over-thinking everything. A shrill voice in my mind screamed that I'd kissed both brothers this week.

But I was sick of doom and gloom. I wanted rainbows and butterflies. I raised my hand up to Thom's neck and deepened the kiss, hoping to shut my thoughts down. It worked for about fifteen seconds. Fifteen seconds of bliss during which I forgot I had secrets.

My heart did a 360 when I heard the faintest intake of air. We'd already established that we had the worst timing ever. I broke the kiss, my hand pressing against my lips, and glimpsed behind Thom, the blush on my cheeks radiating.

The thunderstorm passing over Liam's features and rolling deep in his silver eyes betrayed a tempest of emotions. Surprise, anger, jealousy, disappointment, but layered into a shroud of resignation. It all melted away into a neutral, slightly-tired look, and the sight had been so fleeting, I wondered if I'd imagined it.

Perhaps I was projecting my own feelings. Perhaps our kiss haunted me enough to distort reality. Perhaps I needed to have a long, honest talk with myself.

Liam was the hallmark of poise when he said, "Sorry, I'll give you guys a minute."

God, he must think I'm a train wreck. I didn't want to be *that* girl, this had to stop.

Thom's fingers grazed the back of my ear. "I've been wanting to do that for a long time."

I played with the hem of his shirt. "Me too."

His brows pulled together. "But?"

How insightful of him. "So much stuff happened... I don't think I should start anything right now."

"Because you're leaving? Or—"

I interrupted his next thought, terrified of what he might say. "Because I'm not."

"You're not?"

"I'm not like Lilah and the others. I have weird dream-visions of your ancestors, and my parents are missing. I want to go with you."

I'd been a fool thinking this supernatural world was purgatory. It wasn't just Liam's world; it was mine. Normal wasn't in the cards for me, and denial wasn't my best color.

Other witches needed to be saved. Liam and Thom struggled for weeks to find seers. They had to investigate each suspect and orbit the witch's life at length.

I'd help them. It would make me a definite co-murderer, but my scruples about killing bad guys were winding down. Would Thom understand? Did he want me around if I put *us* off the table for a while?

"Can I go with you?" I asked.

His arms wrapped around my shoulders. "I'll miss you like hell if you don't, so you won't hear one complaint from me."

Why was he so damn perfect?

"I'll go and pack the rest of the stuff," he said, averting my gaze.

I nodded and watched his retreat, smacking myself for my confused state, but happy with my decision to go with them.

The downside of staying was the awkward conversation coming my way. I felt obligated to clear the air with Liam.

While Thom packed his things in the truck, I cornered my complication as he was about to step outside. "We should talk, you know."

"About what?"

Was he serious? "About the kiss."

A hot hand covered my mouth, his body suddenly too close to mine. My eyes widened, and our gaze met. It took every single ounce of pride I had not to melt against him. My cells were fucked up. They sang under his touch.

"Shh," he pointed to the open front door.

I held his reproving glare until his hand fell to his side, getting ready to say my rehearsed speech. The kiss was a mistake, we were both shaken up, hell, he was dying at the time, but the words got caught in my throat. Under his scrutiny, they didn't seem as comforting or as honest as they had in my room.

I opted for plan B. "Why didn't Frank know you would be able to track me?" I was sure he knew the answer.

He scratched the back of his neck. "Our link is different from the one he has with his *girls*. Stronger."

"Why?"

"Remember that bit of soul of mine I carved into you?"

I clicked my tongue. He knew damn well that I remembered.

"Well, it went both ways. You *marked* me back."

We weren't talking about the ritual anymore. He might as well have said *kissed* instead of *marked*. "Why? I mean—how?"

He titled his head to the side. "You tell me."

My body quivered under the intense stare. I should have kept my mouth shut, but, instead, I blurted, "You shouldn't have kissed me." Why did I always freeze in front of him?

His eyes flew to the floor, breaking the spell. "Agreed."

Agreed? I was being a total hypocrite. Wasn't he going to call me out on it?

He put his sunglasses on. To my stupefaction, he smiled. "Cheer up, princess. We both get our freedom back in 48 hours." He walked past me without a second glance.

How pleased he looked to be free of me. Thankfully, I wasn't staying for him or Thom. I was staying to save the next potential and find my parents, and I didn't care if it didn't suit Liam Walker because it suited me.

I ran after him. "I'm not leaving," I summoned my best aloof voice as I added, "I'm staying with Thom."

After a fraction of a second hesitation, Liam opened his car's trunk. "Right, yeah, sure. I know you guys are together. Whatever."

Whatever?

Whatever!

I helped Thom stow the bulk of my stuff in the pickup truck, my small overnight bag braced across my shoulder. Liam pissed me off. I didn't want him to crash our girly weekend in Washington, even if it was a sensible precaution.

Thom had both hands in his pockets. "I'll see you Sunday." He'd been super sweet, but I could tell my rejection had stung, and he wasn't going to hug me goodbye.

I picked at the ends of my hair. "Why is Liam coming? Lilah can tell me if I'm doing it right."

Thom hopped into the truck and slammed the door shut. "She can't. Witches can't see auras. Only demons and seers can. See you soon."

My mind tumbled as the words sunk in. I almost grabbed the opened window and asked him to repeat the sentence, but he had already put the car in gear. The comment had been inconsequential to him, but it stunned me.

I could see auras. I'd been seeing them all along. Thom was wrong. I wasn't a demon nor a seer. I was a witch.

Right?

34

TEAR IN MY HEART

Liam

Alana is asleep in the passenger seat, her light breathing the only sound audible as I drive from Washington to Mobile. Her aura is peaceful, not reigned in while she sleeps. Even the best-trained witches are vulnerable when they dream.

Lilah wasn't surprised by Alana's decision to go back to Thom. Next potential, here we come. Me, my brother whom I love, and his girl: the dream team.

Except I want her so much it hurts.

A video awaited Thom in one of our email accounts yesterday. Thank God, I intercepted it. The keepsake of Alana's evening with Frank wrecked my mind, but it would have done worse to Junior.

I cannot describe how I felt seeing my body in bed with her, kissing her. I should have felt anger, disgust, outrage... but it had left me hollow instead. How would you feel if you watched your most secret desires play out on tape?

Before we kissed, I was in denial about the whole thing. I thought the demons had crafted my lust for her. I even kissed Lilah to see if kissing another witch would give me the same high, but no. Forget witch blood. Alana's my kryptonite. I don't know which is worst, when she's mad or smiles, but these feelings are tearing me apart.

Junior kept saying she wasn't his girlfriend, that with her it was one step forward, two steps back, but I knew they'd get together. Watching them make googly eyes at each other was aggravating, but to actually see them kiss was way worse. Coming home to find them scurrying out of bed together royally sucked.

I've never been good at handling emotions, so I thrive when I have none at all. She's the tear in my armor, the one person able to get under my skin.

And I can't have her.

The slate must be wiped clean. Thom must never know. All for the best. Thom and Alana will be happy. They'll fall in love, marry, have kids… the American dream. A dream I do not share, nor deserve, or can even achieve.

I'll go with them for now and eclipse myself when the time is right. They'll be free of this life of hide and seek that's bound to end in pain and death. It's what I've always wanted, to get my brother out. Now, he has a reason.

All my guilt, frustration and disappointment are tied up in a neat bitter bow, except for one thing.

One tiny detail.

She kissed me back.

To be continued...

AUTHOR'S NOTE

Curious to know how Liam and Frank met? The **free** short-story prequel Lost Boys is available through my newsletter.

http://bit.ly/anyaslair

Wow, guys! Thank you for taking the time to read my debut novel. Did you know that reviews really help authors to promote their books? Please take the time to review on the Amazon page.

Behind the scenes:

This story took form almost ten years ago (Gosh!) because of a dream I had after I binged-watched Angel for the second time. Liam was Angel's name as a human, and I drooled to a few too many episodes of Supernatural that year, too.

Team Dean. Why isn't there more romance in that show? I kept hoping for a Ruby/Dean romance in Season 3, but then she chose Sam and turned evil... Ugh.

Since 2009, the character of Alana changed a lot and went through many phases. She's a mix of Buffy, Elena from TVD, and Lydia from Teen Wolf.

I hope you liked Book 1. Did you notice the chapter titles are song titles? All but a few. The story continues, though, and shit is about to hit the fan! See you in the next book. Sneak peek below!

Xoxo, Anya.

Facebook: **https://www.facebook.com/AnyaJCosgrove/**

Read book 2 now: **http://bit.ly/buywitchshonor**

Printed in Great Britain
by Amazon